Double Up

OHANA SURFING CLUB
Book Three

COURTNEY W. DIXON

This is a work of fiction. Names, characters, organizations, places, events, and incidents are either products of the author's imagination or are used fictitiously.

Copyright © 2023 by Courtney W. Dixon

All rights reserved

No part of this book may be reproduced, or stored in a retrieval system, or transmitted in any form or by any means, electronic, mechanical, photocopying, recording, or otherwise, without the express written permission of the writer, except for the use of brief quotations in a book review.

Published by Courtney W. Dixon: www.courtneywdixon.com

Beta Readers: Jeanette Lawson, Deb Richmond, Mary Ellen Dejmek, Kalie Marie, Nicole Arbuckle, Nikki Johnson, Jen Maryk, Martha Baker, Rachel Robinson

Cover Models by Xram Ragde (@xramragde) • Instagram photos and videos

Paperback Cover Art By: Tal Levin - https://www.instagram.com/caravaggia13

Editor: Anna Potter - https://pottersediting.wixsite.com/website

Formatting: Aubree Valentine - Beyond the Bookshelf Publishing Services | Facebook

TRIGGER WARNING

Trigger Warnings: Abandonment, alcoholism, underage drinking and pot smoking, homophobia, bullying, explicit language and sex. Not for readers under 18.

All mental health issues and sexual interactions were written with sensitivity and the utmost care.

ALSO BY COURTNEY W. DIXON

Kings of Boston

In Silence - Kings of Boston Book 1

In Retribution - Kings of Boston Book 2

In Strength - Kings of Boston Book 3

In Redemption - Kings of Boston Book 4

In Preservation - Kings of Boston Book 5

In Vindication - Kings of Boston Book 6

Ohana Surfing Club

Impact Zone - Ohana Surfing Club Book 1

Pura Vida - Ohana Surfing Club Book 2

Double Up - Ohana Surfing Club Book 3

Standalones

A Home in You - A M/M Stepbrother Romance

Trapped for the Holidays - A M/M Holiday Novella (Read for FREE!)

OHANA

Surfing Club

EST. 1983

DOUBLE-UP

Double-up (in surfing): When two waves combine, one large wave is closely followed by a smaller one. It is distinguished, as it breaks, by a midface step or terrace. A double-up wave is stronger and more dangerous than a regular wave and can be unrideable. But under the right circumstances, it might also provide the biggest, widest, and most spit-filled tube of a surfer's life.

DOUBLE UP SPOTIFY PLAYLIST

https://sptfy.com/DoubleUpPlaylist

CHAPTER ONE

Bayden

October 2015

I'D NEVER EXPERIENCED SPARKS BEHIND THE EYES AND A FLUTTERING stomach until I kissed Duncan Thomas in the ninth grade. I didn't even know what it meant to like boys until him. The lights danced behind my eyelids, and my stomach felt full yet hungry—hungry for him.

I'd read about feelings like these in young adult romances and watched them in movies, but to experience it first-hand blew my mind, and not only because he was my first kiss. His breath was wintergreen-sweet from the gum he had tucked away on the side of his mouth, and his lips were like little pillows that I could rest my mouth on forever.

Kissing him convinced me that I was bisexual, along with me saying yes when he asked me to be his boyfriend two weeks ago. I'd only been interested in girls before I met Duncan. I hadn't kissed a girl yet or dated one, but I liked them and thought they were pretty and smelled good. I'd often fantasize about having a girlfriend. Never a boyfriend, though.

Duncan had beautiful chocolate brown waves and matching eyes. That I found him hot, proved I liked boys, too. His brows and lashes were thick, and he had a really pretty smile, always wearing it crooked. Cocky yet confident. He cropped his brown hair short except on the top and the front where the thick waves fell into his face, making him look shy, but he was anything but. He had everything I didn't—boldness, confidence, and popularity.

The most amazing thing about this kiss—my first kiss—was that we did it by the school's lockers, in the hallway between Algebra and Spanish classes. In front of other kids. I recently learned I was bisexual, and now everyone probably thought I was gay. But if Duncan didn't care, why should I?

Duncan was the type of guy who got what he wanted, making him hard to resist. Not only did I want to give everything to him, but he also took what he wanted effortlessly. This boy was going places when he got older.

I had stood by the lockers after lunch when he just pushed me against them and pressed his lips to mine as if he had been kissing his whole life. When he pulled away, I chased his lips with closed eyes, feeling cold and empty without him. I wanted more.

So much more.

He ran his fingers through my hair toward the back of my head. I think I purred. "You're so cute, Zay. Fuck, you've got sexy eyes. Like amber stones that have those insects inside."

"So are you," I breathed, barely forming the words through my hazy and lustful mind.

Duncan gave me a beaming smile and pecked my lips. "I gotta go to algebra now. Let's meet up at Sunset Beach tomorrow after lunch. We can catch some waves."

Tomorrow was Friday, but we had a three-day weekend. "Sounds cool," I said, playing it off as no big deal despite my stomach flopping around with excitement. Would this be a date?

With one more peck to my mouth, he tossed his backpack over his shoulder and left.

My parents taught me a little bit about homosexuality and how it was a sin. Not that I paid much attention to it. Going to church and reading the bible was just another chore for me. Something I had to do because my parents told me to. They taught me sins, but it wasn't as if my parents ranted and raved against gay people.

Everything I read had been sort of an abstract concept, and if I ever saw two men kissing, I didn't really care one way or the other. But I knew my parents wouldn't like it.

I watched his retreating back as I also slung my backpack over my shoulder with a stupid grin and rushed off to American history class. When I walked into the room, it felt like all eyes fell on me. Shit, everyone saw me kiss a boy. Did it really matter? I really liked Duncan, and I wouldn't let anyone change that. I fed off of his confidence, making me brave.

At least no one said anything, probably because Duncan Thomas was my boyfriend and the most popular boy in school. I had no idea what he saw in me, but I didn't question it either. How did he figure out I'd like him because I didn't even know about my sexuality until then? Maybe it was a vibe I gave off. Did everyone know before I even said yes to him? Was I the last to know? Did it really matter in the end?

After school, I stepped outside, ready to take the bus, when Duncan waved me over from the parking lot. I jogged towards him, liking how my stomach always had butterflies in it whenever I saw him. When I stood in front of him, he wrapped his arms around my waist and pulled me close to give me a kiss on my cheek.

"My brother picked me up today. Wanna lift home?"

I looked at the Dodge Charger in royal blue and nodded. "Hell, yeah."

I climbed in the backseat covered in black leather, and Duncan rode shotgun, but he reached behind him to grab my hand. I really liked this boyfriend thing. He was fucking sweet.

"Zay, this is my older brother, Ewan. He goes to the University of Hawaii, but he's off tomorrow, too."

"'Sup," I said.

He smiled and nodded as he drove off. He and Duncan looked a lot alike.

"My bro said we can pick you up tomorrow."

"Cool, thanks."

I gave Ewan my address, and as we drove, Duncan kept playing with my fingers with his body turned, facing me.

He looked at me under thick eyelashes and with his usual smirk. "I thought you'd freak when I kissed you today."

My face turned beet red as I gave him a small smile and shook my head. "I... liked it."

"Cool."

Duncan leaned toward me, so I leaned into him, and he kissed me again. "I like kissing you, too."

I guess his brother didn't care. It was so cool to see that not all people freaked out about sexuality. That would probably help me with my new found sexual identity in the future. I didn't feel so weird about it or uncertain. Being with Duncan just felt right.

Ewan pulled up to my apartment complex, and I climbed out of the car. Before I walked off, Duncan rolled down his window. "One more kiss," he said.

I smiled, leaned in, and gave him a quick kiss. When they drove off, I scanned the area, making sure no one saw us. While kids might accept two boys together easier, adults seemed to have a harder time with it, especially my parents.

When I walked into my apartment, I tossed my backpack onto the floor and headed straight to the kitchen for a snack.

Mom was preparing dinner and looked at me as I walked in. "You look happy. Good day at school?"

I rummaged through the fridge, pulling out sandwich meat and mustard. "Yeah."

"What happened?"

"Nothing. Just a chill day."

I couldn't tell her the truth. Mom wouldn't like it if she found out I liked boys. Dad wouldn't either. My sexual orientation would go with me to my grave before I let my parents know. Honestly, it was a wonder I wasn't freaking out more after everything they had taught me. Probably because I didn't feel like I was sinning. I felt normal. I still felt like Zay. Just a boy who liked girls and boys. If they found out, they could just get over it.

Mom had her dark wavy hair pulled back into a ponytail as she rolled out dough on the counter. "Go eat your snack, and then work on your homework."

"Yes, ma'am."

I spread mustard on my bread and layered it with salami and cheese. "Uh, Mom?"

"Yes."

"Some guys at school want to know if I could go to the beach tomorrow since school's out. So, I'm going to head out in the morning. Can I do my chores when I get home?"

I went to the beach to surf all the time and had been in a couple of competitions, so it was no big deal as long as I got everything done, from schoolwork to helping Mom clean the apartment.

"If you promise to get it done when you get back. I don't want you complaining about how tired you are."

"I won't. Thanks, Mom."

I finished eating my sandwich and headed to my small bedroom, which was darkened out with black curtains. I flipped on my light to my room covered in surfing and band posters, a couple of trophies for surfing, and tons of books.

After pulling out my American History textbook, I fell into my bed, shoved my earbuds on, and studied for my quiz on Monday to get it out of the way.

Duncan texted me when he and his brother were in the parking lot. I grabbed my bag filled with a change of clothes, sunscreen, water, and a towel. Then I rushed to the balcony to grab my surfboard.

"Bye, Mom," I yelled on my way out the door.

"Wait! What beach are you going to so I know where to find you if something happens."

"Right... Sunset Beach."

"Okay. Be back no later than five!"

"Yes, ma'am."

When I got to the car, Ewan stepped out, grabbed my surfboard, and strapped it to the roof with the other boards.

Before I got in the back, Duncan got out and tried to kiss me, but I took a step back with a pounding heart. I couldn't risk getting caught by my mom. "Not here. Mom might be watching."

"So. My parents don't care."

"That's cool, but mine do. I'll get in a lot of trouble."

He looked disappointed, but nodded and got back into the car. When I climbed in, I touched his shoulder. "I'll make it up to you on the beach," I said, surprised at my boldness.

He smiled and nodded. "Deal."

When we got to the beach, we headed toward a group of kids from our school. They all waved and fist-bumped Duncan. I said hi to a couple of them I already knew, and he introduced me to the rest.

Duncan dropped his board and bag and slowly peeled off his shirt as if putting on a show for me. And what a show it was. We were both tall, about the same height, but he was broader with more defined muscles. I guess he had to be to play football. All his workouts showed on every little muscle that tightened with his movements. My eyes zeroed in on his happy trail, and my thoughts drifted downward, wondering if I'd get to see his dick one day.

After I removed my shirt, he looked up and down at my body, grinning. "So hot, Zay."

I smirked and hid my red face behind my long bangs, but I couldn't hide from him. I had muscles, too, from surfing all the time, but I wasn't broad.

He stood close, combed back my hair with his fingers, then pulled me into a kiss in front of everyone. I tried not to stiffen, but when he slid his tongue into my mouth, I melted into him, and my arms wrapped around his waist. The kids around us suddenly vanished. There was nothing to see and nothing to hear as I focused entirely on Duncan. I didn't know how he did that to me, but I liked it. Like we were the only two people in the world that mattered.

"Come on. Let's see what you got. I heard you've competed," he said, grabbing his board.

"I've done a little."

"So modest," he said, playfully punching my shoulder. "I heard you won some trophies."

"Yeah."

I grabbed my board, and he took my hand, pulling me toward the waves. This was my element. I breathed in the briny air and enjoyed the thundering sound of the crashing waves. They were big too. About five feet and pumpin'. Surfing would be awesome today.

"I'm probably not as good as you, Zay, but I love surfing, too."

"I'm sure you're great."

Duncan was probably good at everything he did. He even talked better than me. Though, I was more shy.

We dove into the water on top of our boards and paddled out toward calmer waters, where the waves started to swell. We had to dive under the biggest ones.

I saw the wave coming before I reached it and popped up as soon as the water curled. Then I was off, staying ahead of the curling lip, but it soon overtook me and created a barrel right over my head. I dragged my fingers along the smooth surface as I let it carry me away. It finally crashed, and I pumped my board with my back leg to pick up speed until I hit another wave. Before the lip curled, I took air, and when I landed, I wiped out.

When I reached the surface, I flipped my hair back, grabbed my board, still attached to my ankle, and hopped on to do it again.

I saw Duncan in the distance catching air several times before he fell. Yep, he looked cool as shit. And he was my actual boyfriend. It was hard getting used to that too, but I liked it a lot.

After about an hour of surfing, we pulled our limp muscles out of the water. I fell back on the communal blankets and dried off in the sun. Duncan fell next to me and pulled my face to him to kiss. His lips were salty and wet. God, I loved how he always wanted to kiss me. I felt wanted and needed. And the more he kissed me, the more I fell for him. With every kiss, he stole a little bit of my heart. It just grew smaller and smaller as he chipped away at it. Soon he'd own all of it.

The day wore on, and I lost track of time surfing, making friends, and making out with my boyfriend. I sat between his legs with my head resting on his shoulder, feeling like having a boyfriend was the most natural thing in the world. He had his arms wrapped around me and dragged fingers gently over my skin, sending waves of goosebumps across my skin. The other kids didn't care, and no one made fun of us at all. This was how it should always be. I couldn't have imagined a more perfect day.

I knew other kids had a hard time coming out. Hell, I didn't even come out. Duncan kind of forced it out of me by kissing me in school, not that I minded. It all worked out.

He played with my fingers and kissed my cheek, and I couldn't stop smiling like a nutjob. I wondered if it was too early to fall in love. Or if it was even love that I felt. Probably. Whatever it was, I never wanted it to end.

I sat up, turned to face him, grasped his face, and pulled him into a kiss. *Be bold like Duncan.* His hands fisted my hair when my tongue thrust into his mouth, and—

"Zayden?"

My heart stopped. I opened my eyes with my mouth hovering over his. Standing behind Duncan was my mom, wide-eyed, and her hand pressed to her mouth.

Fuck me.

I completely forgot to check the time, and I forgot to check my phone.

I scrambled off of Duncan and lost my ability to speak as my mind struggled to find an impossible lie. But I couldn't think of one because there was no way to explain what I had been doing other than kissing a boy.

Duncan stood with me and turned around. He gave my mom one of his charming smiles. "Hi, Mrs. Beckett. I'm Duncan—"

"I don't care who you are, Sinner!"

Her face morphed into anger, making me want to bury myself in the sand and hide forever. Then she rushed over to me, grabbed my arm, and yanked me away.

"Mom, wait—"

"No! We are going home now to pray. When your father gets home, we're going to talk about what to do with you. Get your things. We are going now."

I grabbed my bag and surfboard as I struggled to keep from crying, then I dared to look at Duncan. He looked fucking hurt. "I'm so sorry, Duncan. I'll—"

"Stop talking to that… that… boy!"

I ignored all the staring from the kids and ran off with my mom.

I shoved my board into the backseat, and as soon as we got in the car, she slapped my face. My mind went blank before I even felt the sting. My parents had never slapped or spanked me before, so I wasn't sure how to process this or what it meant. I knew I was in trouble, but Mom slapping me, it showed how much trouble I might be in for. The tears finally came as I cupped my cheek.

"How dare you! After everything we've taught you."

Her yelling made me shove my body against the car door, making itself as small as possible, unsure if she was going to hit me again. My cheek throbbed, burned, and stung. For the first time ever, I was afraid of her. I also realized right then that they hated queer people more than I thought they would.

Mom covered her angry face with her hands and started crying. "I've failed you. I did my best."

"You didn't… I…"

"No! You don't speak. As soon as we get home, you're going

straight to your room to pray while you wait for your father to get home."

I sank into my seat and stared out the window while she drove us home. The lush green valley in the distance was blurry through my tears. I was also terrified. What would my dad do? I rarely gave them a reason to be angry with me, always doing as I was told. But this was big.

No. There was nothing wrong with me. Why should this be a big deal? Kissing Duncan felt as natural as breathing. All the kids accepted us as boyfriends. No one thought we were sinners or gross. I just had to convince my parents of that. I knew they loved me. They would forgive me and see that it was okay. That I wasn't going to hell.

CHAPTER TWO

Zayden

THERE WAS NO DINNER FOR ME, AND I DEFINITELY DIDN'T PRAY AS I waited in my room for my dad to come home from work. Why should I beg for forgiveness if I did nothing wrong?

He didn't get home until after dinner most nights since he worked as a machinist, putting in extra hours to earn more since Mom didn't work.

When the front door slammed shut, my stomach bottomed out. He was home. I climbed out of bed and pressed my ear to my door as my heart thundered in my ears. The loud thrum was deafening. Mom and Dad were talking but kept their voices low, so I couldn't make out what they said, but I didn't have to because it was obviously about me and my 'sin.'

Dad's footsteps got louder as he headed toward me, and the closer he got, the more I shook. His steps sounded louder than my heart slamming in my chest. I took a step back when my door opened. Dad scanned me up and down, looking more pissed than I'd ever seen him. Red in the face, jaw clenched, and eyes narrowed as if he tried to control every fiber of his being to keep from lashing out. He grabbed my arm, dug his fingers into the muscle, and pulled me toward the kitchen, making my eyes water from pain and fear.

I tried to pry his fingers off, but he was too strong. "You're hurting me."

"Sit!" He said, practically tossing me into the chair.

I sat across from my mom, and my dad sat next to me as I rubbed my arm and kept my head down, afraid to make eye contact or to speak.

"Is it true? You kissed a boy?"

I nodded. "He's my boyfriend," I whispered, but they heard me anyway.

My mom gasped, and my dad fisted his hands on the table.

"Bullshit!" he yelled, slamming his fist, and making me jump. "My son is *not* a faggot! We have done everything possible to protect you from... that sin."

Mom mumbled prayers while my eyes watered more.

"I'm not gay," I said.

"What? Then why did you kiss that boy?" he asked. "Did he force you? Corrupt you?"

I shook my head. "No, sir. I'm... bisexual. I like girls, too."

"Unnatural. Liking boys is not normal, Zayden," Mom said. "God made us a man and a woman to be together. Biology says this, too.

I didn't understand why they hated this. Sure they told me tons of times what it said in the Bible, among other things, but no one cared at school. Not that I paid that much attention at church. And everyone accepted Duncan and me as boyfriends. If it was a sin, then why didn't it feel wrong? Why was he so nice and sweet to me? And why didn't the teachers discipline us?

"No. It's not unnatural. I like Duncan, and he likes me. He's nice to me."

"It's wrong, Zayden, and you damn well know it!" Dad hissed.

"Let's make him talk to Pastor Lowry. He'll set Zayden straight," Mom suggested. "He'll put him back on the right path."

Dad nodded. "Yes, and we can't let Zayden out of our sight anymore. He's not allowed to go to the beach without one of us. No more surfing competitions. No more riding the bus. He's to come home straight from school, do his homework, do chores, and nothing else. And no more boys!"

"What? No!" I panicked. I didn't want to be trapped for the rest of my life or until I moved out. And I didn't want to stop seeing Duncan. "Please, that's not fair! I did nothing wrong! I won't talk to the pastor because I didn't sin. No one else seems to care but you!"

Dad got really close to my face, making my heart beat faster, and my hands shake again. I could smell the sweat coming off of him from his long day at work. "Listen here. You will do as you're told. Your yelling at us proves you seriously need help. Lord help us if you're too far gone that you can't be redeemed and forgiven. Do *not* defy me, boy."

Frustration grew in me. Why couldn't they understand? There was nothing wrong with me. I wasn't evil or a sinner. I stood up and stared back and forth at my parents. "Or what?! I always do as I'm told! Always! I have never let you down before. Why are you doing this? Why can't you trust me and believe me? Why can't you love me as I am?"

"It's because we love you," Mom said, softening. "We worry about you and for your soul."

"No, you want to control me!"

Dad slammed his fist again on the table, making my heart stop for several seconds. "You will do as you are told, or you can get out."

My stomach lurched again, and the tears welled from fear and anger. "What?"

"If you won't confess your sins to Pastor Lowry and refuse to stop seeing that boy, we will have no choice."

"But... There's nothing wrong with me. Please. Trust me."

Mom looked away from me with tears in her eyes, but Dad was unrelenting.

"Get out," he hissed.

"What? No... Please!"

"You keep arguing with us, and you're not listening. If you refuse to change, then you cannot live here. We will not put up with it. You bring evil into this house."

"Dad? Mom? Please. I'm a good person."

"Please, son. Listen to us. We know what's right," Mom said, crying and refusing to look at me. "If you can't help yourself, then you need to go."

I wiped the tears and my running nose with the back of my hand, unable to process what was happening. I kept waiting to wake up from this nightmare. Were they really going to turn their backs on me? All for kissing a boy?

They cornered me, leaving me with no choices. "Fine. I'll... do it. I'll see the pastor." He wouldn't change me, but it would get my parents off my back. Could I live under lock and key until I moved out?

"It's too late. You showed your true nature. There is no help for you."

"But... please. Dad!"

"Get everything you can carry and leave."

Soon all my fear turned to a burning rage I'd never felt before. Rage at my parents. I was a good kid. I cleaned, helped cook, did all my homework, made good grades, and never talked back. I wasn't evil. They just proved that love had conditions. That I wasn't good enough for them and never would be. They would never accept me as bisexual. No matter what I did, they'd never trust me. Or love me. Not really. If they loved me, they wouldn't turn their backs.

I grabbed Mom's water glass and slammed it against cabinets, shattering glass and water everywhere.

"I hate you!"

Mom sobbed, and I ignored it.

"You're the ones who will burn in hell!"

I stormed out of the kitchen and to my room, grabbing all that I could carry, and shoving it into a duffel bag. I made sure I had toiletries, my cheap-ass phone and my charger, and two of my favorite books. I had to find a way to make money to get one of those pay-as-you-go phones. Once I had everything I needed, I pulled out my surfboard from the balcony and left without looking back or saying goodbye.

Fuck them.

I kept my phone as long as I could until my parents disconnected it two months ago. Duncan never called me once to check on me. I thought he liked me, but that was stupid. We were only fifteen. Plus, Mom called him a sinner. Why would he have called me after that? But it would've been nice if he had called to see how I was. But it had been three months with me not in school. He probably forgot about me, anyway. Found a better boyfriend.

Whatever.

I wanted to go to his house the day I got kicked out to see if his family would put me up for a while, but I had no idea where he lived, and I didn't have any other best friends. They'd probably say no, anyway.

The day was cold enough for a hoodie during the first week of January, and the drizzle soaked through my clothes, making me shiver. Winter had arrived, and the surf was rippin'. The season always brought out the big waves. While I should've been excited, all I felt was depression and anger these days.

I sat on the beach under a tree, hunched in my hoodie with the hood over my head, eating cold chicken noodle soup out of the can. I'd made a shelter for myself in a small abandoned building—more like a shack —squirreling away any money I earned in a hidden spot in the wall where I found a loose concrete block. It would've been warmer there, but I came to the beach daily to see if anyone wanted to learn to surf, giving them cheaper rates than the shops around here. It kept me fed enough.

Plus, I entered a couple of local surfing competitions that offered cash prizes. I won the second one for my age group, but not the first one. The money would tide me over for a while, at least. I could've eventually gone pro, but those days were over. Now everything was about survival as my future prospects diminished each day I was out here alone.

Whenever I could, I'd bathe in the local beach showers at night to wash my hair and body in my boardshorts and wash my clothes at the laundromat, then I'd head to the public library, charge my phone that I now paid for, and go online to check out the world I had missed, using their free Wi-Fi. Afterward, I'd read up on areas I felt I needed to study, but subjects like math were harder. As an added bonus, they had clean bathrooms. I hadn't been in school, and didn't know when I'd be back, if ever. But I didn't want to be stupid either or too behind.

I didn't plan to stay on the streets forever, but no one would hire me, especially a dropout. Maybe when I turned sixteen this September, but that was a long way off. Things didn't look too good for me after I did some online research. If I was truant or didn't have a home address, I probably wouldn't be able to find work unless they paid me under the table.

The worst part about my situation was the crippling loneliness. I'd always been introverted, but being alone out here with no real home was really scary sometimes, especially late at night. And some days, I'd suffocate from being so alone and afraid.

I only had to make plans, stay organized, and keep some money coming in so I wouldn't starve, then I'd find a job… hopefully. After that, I'd get my GED, and if I was really lucky, I'd go to college. But I doubt I'd make it that far. I was young, but I wasn't stupid. Getting off the streets wouldn't be easy. If it was, we wouldn't have such a homeless problem everywhere.

I quit crying a long time ago. The tears were wasted and changed nothing. All I could do was move forward as much as possible and deal with things that were in my control.

That didn't stop the anger, though. The longer I lived out here with my parents not giving a shit about what happened to me, the more I raged inside. It festered like an infection, spreading throughout my body. I used it to hide the grief and loss. I did everything right by them. Always doing what I was told and never talking back. But I wasn't good enough for them. They saw me as evil, so it was nothing for them to toss me away like garbage.

I finished my soup and tossed the can into the trash, and continued to sit in the cold, hoping someone wanted to surf. But only the die-hard surfers came out on cold, rainy days. Tourists usually drove around the island on days like this or hit the aquarium.

Since I wouldn't be making any money, I called it a day. I got tired of the drizzle soaking through my hoodie anyway, so I picked up my board and wetsuit and headed to my new home.

I walked through the streets of the North Shore, always keeping a lookout for cops, not wanting to get arrested for truancy. I perfectly timed everything from when I went to a coffee shop or library to study in the evenings and on the weekends to staying on the beach during the day, looking like I belonged there.

The tiny concrete building wasn't too far away. I double-checked to make sure no one saw me and pulled out my key to unlock the padlock I kept on the door. I had scoped the place out for a while to make sure no one came around here, but it seemed to be abandoned. Even better, it sat between trees, covered in overgrowth, keeping it hidden.

After quickly stepping inside, I locked the door behind me and turned on the camping lantern I had bought. It was one of the first things I splurged on when I found this place. The space wasn't any bigger than a small storage shed, but it was enough for me and dry. It had no windows, so at least no one could peek in.

I stripped out of my wet clothes and changed into new ones. I sniffed them to make sure they didn't smell too bad. The time on my phone said it was after school, so I pried loose the brick that held my money, and pulled out ten dollars, then put it back in place.

With a new hoodie on, I pulled the hood over my head to hide my face. I was tall, so I looked like an adult from a distance, but my face, not so much. After locking up again, I headed to the coffee shop close by with my phone, charger, pencil, and notebook, ready to get in more studying, which was mostly spent on YouTube. I could learn anything on there.

With a bottle of water and a warm sandwich, I sat down, plugged in my phone, and started working toward my future and getting off the fucking streets.

September 2016

I caught air off the lip of the wave, came down, and carved the water to do it again. My sixteenth birthday had just passed, and next month was October when the surfing competitions started. Which also meant I'd been on my own for almost a year. My money dwindled way too fast, and I hadn't been able to get a job. No one wanted to hire a high school dropout. At least no one turned me in to the cops yet. Somehow, I had to train. I needed to be sharp in order to win some cash I desperately needed.

I took the next massive wave, pumping my board fast through the barrel. I made it through right when the wave crashed over me, and I fell off my board. The wave and undertow were strong as I spun and spun, struggling to find the surface for air and careful not to get cut up by the lava rocks below. The area was risky to surf in, but I had to challenge myself. My lungs were about to burst when I reached the top, coughing out salt water. I flipped my long hair from my face and grabbed my board attached to my ankle. Except there was no board. It got ripped off from the leash.

Fuck.

I looked around desperately as another wave crashed over me. When I breached the surface, I swam toward the shallows, looking for any sign of my board.

When I saw it, the relief hit me fucking hard. I'd be screwed without it. When I reached my board, I pulled it onto the sand to strap it back onto my ankle, but there was only half of the board. I held the broken piece, looking, staring, as my mind tried to comprehend what I was looking at. It wanted to deny, scream, and fight what was clearly a destroyed board. I scanned for the other half, and when I found it, I knew then there was no fixing it. My chances of winning any sort of money to stay fed, clothed, and keep my phone going went out the window. The surfboard was my money maker. My only source of income. My luck had finally run out.

I grabbed all my shit and made it back to my little house. Inside had completely changed. I brought a chair in, an extra lantern, and a mattress with a blanket, and I hung up curtains someone threw away, pretending I had a window, and I had stacked some crates that held my clothes, necessities, and books that I bought for a dollar at the library. The place had been my home for almost a year now.

I tossed the broken surfboard on the ground in the corner and sat hard on my bed, running my hands through my damp hair. Then it all came crashing down. All that anger, frustration, loneliness, and desperation boiled over, and I broke down into tears for the first time in months and months. The helplessness surrounded me like a straight jacket, choking me, and making it hard to breathe.

I only had five hundred bucks left, which wouldn't last me if I wanted to fucking eat, especially if I needed to buy a new board.

Fuck it.

I needed to spend money to make money. I wiped my useless tears away and dug out all my cash from the wall, counted it, and shoved it in the pockets of my boardshorts. Then I tossed on a clean-ish hoodie.

The Ohana Surfing Club wasn't too far from me. About a fifteen-minute walk. They sold tons of boards, and I had bought a pair of boardshorts there once on clearance when I outgrew my old pair. But I usually headed over to Goodwill, where I bought T-shirts for a dollar.

When I got there, I walked in and looked around. The store was quiet for a Tuesday morning, and there was no one behind the register. Where was everyone?

I headed straight to the boards and tried to find any on sale. I couldn't buy a crappy one either if I wanted to compete and win. Shit. This was a massive risk. If I lost, I wouldn't have any money left for food. I had been doing so well up to now. I'd been surviving without my fucking parents.

The Lib Tech X Surfboard called to me. I lifted it off the wall and ran my hand across the smooth surface with tender and loving care. It was gorgeous and perfect for competing with. And fucking nine hundred bucks. Disappointment consumed me. The story of my fucking life lately. How stupid of me to assume a board like this would've been affordable. I was definitely good enough to win with this surfboard.

I looked around the shop again with no one still to be found. Where did everyone go? Maybe they'd make a deal if I won and repaid the rest for the board later.

Then a thought hit me. They'd never know, right? Well, eventually, they'd see their board missing, but it'd be too late because I'd be long gone before anyone caught me. I had always been a good kid and never stolen anything in my life, but I was desperate. And desperation made people stupid, but I had to take the risk.

I looked around once more, tucked the board under my arm, and took off before I could talk myself out of it. My heart pumped hard and at dangerous levels as I ran as fast as I could, and all the way back to my little home. I quickly unlocked it and went inside.

After propping the board up against the wall, I sat on the bed and laughed. Now I stood a chance of surviving again. If I kept competing and teaching, I could make enough to save for my own place one day. Maybe. But I didn't think anyone would rent to me until I was eighteen and had a job. No matter. I just had to last another two years.

I could do this.

CHAPTER THREE

Zayden

THE COP SHOVED MY CHEST AGAINST THE WALL OF MY HOME, YANKED my arm back, and cuffed my wrists together.

"You have the right to remain silent," he said. *Blah, blah, blah.*

How did they find me? I thought I was careful. I had been on my way home with the board after surfing most of the day to get my training in. The cop car slowed down on the road, following me. Then I fucking panicked and ran like a moron instead of pretending like it was perfectly legit for me to be there. If I had remained cool like it was normal for me to be walking on the sidewalk with an expensive stolen surfboard at sixteen years old on a school day.

Who was I kidding?

I made it home and tried to lock the door behind me, but they caught up with me and kicked it in with guns drawn. I dropped to my knees and placed my hands on my head as my heart leaped out of my chest. There was nowhere for me to go. It was over. No more being on my own. No more competitions. The only thing in my future was jail time and a record. The resignation was a cold and rough blanket, but it allowed me to give in without completely fucking losing it.

Once they looked around at where I lived and that I was homeless, they let me grab anything of value, so no one stole them. I guess they felt sorry for me or something because they didn't have to. Whatever. They bagged my shit up to give back to me when I got out of jail. We stepped outside, and the other cop locked up my shed.

The one cop who cuffed me placed his hand on my head and eased me into the back seat of the cruiser. Then we drove off to my new home for who knew how long. Life, as I had known it for the past year, was over.

"How long have you been living like that, son?" asked the older one of about fifty.

I shrugged.

"You taking drugs?"

I shook my head. "I'm clean."

He stared at my eyes for a while, then nodded and radioed in that he was bringing in the suspect of the stolen surfboard.

"Where are your parents?"

"Burning in hell, I hope."

He raised his brows. "You a runaway? We need to call them since you're a minor. They looking for you?"

"Don't even bother. They tossed me aside like garbage. They won't fucking care."

"Regardless, I need to get their names. If they kicked out a minor, they committed a crime. We need to bring them in for questioning."

Could I do that? Turn my parents in to be arrested for what they did to me? Fuck yeah, I could. Had I known that would've happened, I would've gone to the police a long time ago. They would've thrown me into the system, but at this point, the streets were worse… Probably.

"They're Janice and Stan Beckett." I recited their apartment address, and the cop jotted it down on his notepad.

"When did they kick you out, and why?"

I had seen enough cop shows to know I should've probably called a lawyer, but I also had nothing to lose now, but I couldn't tell them why. I stopped trusting people's reactions to my sexuality. "It's been about a year, and they kicked me out because I'm only garbage to them. I… was dating someone they didn't approve of. I did everything to be a good kid. But love was conditional to them."

"Who were you dating bad enough to have your parents turn on you?"

"You'll judge like they did."

His face softened. "Was it a boy?"

I looked up at him, jaw-dropped. "How'd…"

"It happens more than you think. Fucking assholes," he muttered when he and his partner looked at each other.

"You look pretty good, relatively speaking, for a homeless kid," the other cop said. "Some end up on drugs strung out and dying. Or barely hanging on to their skin, they're so hungry."

"I competed in a surfing competition and won last year. I also taught lessons whenever I could for cheap. I've been able to relatively feed myself and stay clean in the beach showers. Then I'd go to the library and read."

"Is that why you needed a board? To compete?"

"Yeah. My board broke while I was training on the Pipeline. I… hadn't intended to steal at first."

"Stealing is wrong no matter your circumstances. We still have to bring you in."

I sighed and nodded as my eyes watered. "I really tried to do the right thing."

"I'm sorry, kiddo." Then he turned around and didn't ask any more questions.

Once we got to the station, they interrogated me, and I told them again everything that happened but in more detail, from the day I kissed a boy to the day I stole the surfboard. They assigned me a lawyer, but I would've told them anyway. I had nowhere else to go now. I explained that my parents definitely wouldn't bail me out, preferring I rot and learn my moral lesson.

The only good news to come out of this was that because the surfboard was under a thousand dollars, they considered it to be third-degree theft. The police said I could end up in jail for up to a year with a two-thousand-dollar fine as if I had that much money lying around. Hey, at least I didn't commit grand larceny. Yay fucking me. Whatever. It was the end of me, anyway.

After they processed me, I sat in the jail cell with other losers to await my trial, whenever the fuck that would be. My eyes tried to tear up, but I hid it to not show any weakness in front of my cellmates. I was only a kid, but they had to put me in with adults because they had no other space to give me my own cell. One dude smelled like piss, making the peanut butter and jelly sandwich and coke a lady cop gave me earlier churn in my stomach.

Instead of giving in to my pain and fear, I let the anger surface. Anger was my friend. Anger at my parents for putting me in this position because they couldn't get past their beliefs and love me unconditionally. So they got a big *'fuck you'* from me. Everything was all their fault. All I could do was survive the best way I knew how. Now, hopefully, they'd be arrested for their abandonment. They fucking deserved it.

Two days later, I was going nowhere fast, still sitting in jail and pissing in front of creepy men who kept looking at me.

"Zayden Beckett," a cop called out to me.

I stood and approached the bars, seeing the police officer and another dude standing next to him.

"What?"

"You have a visitor."

"I don't know who that is. For all I know, he's some creepy pervert."

I went back to my bed and lay down with my back to them.

"I'll have someone take you to a private room, and I'll bring him," the cop said to the creep.

"Thank you, officer."

The cell door creaked open. "Do I need to handcuff you and drag you out, or are you going to behave and walk peacefully to the room to talk?"

"Fine. Fuck... whatever, brah."

I stood, and he led me to another room where the creepy dude waited for me. He actually didn't seem creepy at all, but what the hell did I know? He looked cute, actually. Handsome, but much older, like in his thirties or something, so I had absolutely no interest in him. He had dark hair like me but wavier, and he looked Hawaiian, but he had some white in him too. His eyes were a pale hazel brown that stood out against his dark skin.

He gave me a small smile, showing off some dimples, as I sat down.

"Need anything?" he asked. "Something to drink? Eat?"

I folded my arms, stretched out my legs, and shook my head. I tried to look tough, but on the inside, I trembled, and my hands were clammy as I bounced my knee.

"Who are you, and what do you want with me?" I asked.

"I'm Kel Quinn. My father, Jonathan Quinn, owns Ohana Surfing Club. You know, the shop you stole from?"

I looked down and swallowed hard as my heart raced. Fuck. He was probably here to guilt me about what I'd done. Fine, I hated the theft, but I was desperate. I felt guilty enough. I didn't need him rubbing salt in all my wounds.

"And? I've been arrested, and you got it back. Now, if we're done here, I have an important meeting with my gross cellmates."

"We are not done. I'm not here to tell you what you did was wrong. You and I both understand that already."

"So? Why are you here then?"

"Because I want you to tell me why you stole from us."

I scoffed. "Please. Why the fuck do you think, man. I'm a thief. A criminal. That's what we do."

"I don't think so."

"How the fuck would you know? You've only just met me."

"The Zayden sitting in front of me now is very different from the one I have on my cameras at the shop. You're trying to be defensive and act tough, but you were scared that day, and guilt was all over your face. I don't believe your original intention was to steal. I've watched that video over and over, and I don't see a criminal. Then when the police told me where you lived, I knew there was more to your story. So, here I am, wanting to hear it."

"Why? It doesn't matter. No one gives a fuck anyway. I can't take back what I did."

"I care."

"The fuck why, dude? You don't even know me."

"I'd like to help you," he said with this strange patience. He hadn't once gotten upset with me, no matter how many times I tried pushing his buttons so he'd finally leave.

"Why?" I asked again.

"Because it looks like you need it, Zayden."

"It's Zay."

He smiled and nodded, showing off dimples that lit up his entire face. "Zay. The police told me nothing because you're a minor other than where they found you. They mentioned you had no parents stepping in, so they've allowed me to speak with you. They understand my intention isn't to hurt you but to help. They're going to throw you into the system once you've served your time. First, you'll get tossed into juvie, surrounded by punks who won't hesitate to harm you, which will serve no purpose in helping you. Then, they'll toss you into foster care until you age out of the system in two years."

I sunk in my seat and let another piece of bad news hit me. I understood what would happen to me but coming from his mouth made it sound worse. But what fucking choice did I have?

"So?" I tried to sound defiant, but it came off as weak and uncertain.

"My dad and I had a long talk about you, and we'd like to see what we can do for you, but I need to know your story. We don't want to take you in if you have family out there looking for you. And legally, we can't until you're in the system."

Take me in?

I looked up at him, trying to squash the flickering hope. "What do you mean?"

"Dad and I want you to come to the shop to work and pay off that board that we'll let you keep instead of being sent into foster care. You will have a place to stay until you turn eighteen. You'll need to serve community service at the shop. My lawyer is certain he can convince the judge to allow us to foster you and keep you out of juvie. Especially since you have no other offenses."

I didn't even need to think about it. There were no other better options for me. I didn't survive alone for a year on stupidity. "Done."

Kel raised his brows. "No arguing or bad attitude? I honestly expected more of a fight."

"I'm not gonna turn away my only chance of staying out of jail and off the streets."

"Okay, then. Good. That went easier than I thought."

"This better not be a trick."

He blew out a laugh. "It's no trick, I assure you. We only want to help you, Zay. And we need help around the shop. Ready to tell me your story?"

I shook my head, not wanting to talk about it at all. I also didn't want to tell him I was bisexual and the reason my parents got rid of me, though I told the cops, but they weren't taking me in to care for. "It's not important. Let's just say my parents are dead to me as I am to them. I don't have any other family that I'm aware of. I've been on my own for a year. I've come to terms with my… loss and being on my own."

"How did you survive being so young?"

"I taught surfing lessons and did some surfing competitions. The last one I won, it let me save money for a while. No one would hire me, so I had to figure out shit on my own."

Kel's smile was broad and full of dimples. "I'm impressed. So, if you had money, why steal?"

I slumped in my chair again at my loss. It was only a stupid board, but it'd kept me going for a long time. "When my... board broke while training on the pipeline, I was desperate. I've also been running out of money. That's why I stole from you. I didn't have enough cash saved to buy a good board. I meant to buy it, but they were all so expensive. When no one was around your shop, I... just took it and ran."

"Well, the board you took is yours, and you can continue to compete if you wish. Hell, we can get you certified, and you can teach at the shop. I am also a surfing instructor."

That would be like a dream job. How did everything look so gloomy, and now suddenly bright? Maybe it wasn't as good as it sounded. "What's the catch?"

Kel laughed. "Smart kid. If you call going back to school, graduating, working hard, earning money, staying out of trouble, and off of drugs, then..." He spread his hands and smiled.

It took about a week to see a judge, make bail, and sign all the paperwork that would allow Jon and Kel Quinn to foster me. They did their best to get me out of jail as fast as they could. But the news wasn't all good. While I'd finally go back to school, I needed to repeat my freshman year. I studied, but it wasn't enough. Even worse, I had to go back to my old school. Maybe everyone forgot me by now, not that I had been Mr. Popular. Ugh, but I couldn't face Duncan.

When we pulled up to the surf shop, a pang of guilt hit me for what I'd done, hardly believing any of this was real until now. "I'm sorry," I said for the first time since meeting Kel.

"For what?"

"Stealing."

Kel gripped my shoulder to make me glance at him. "It's okay. You were in need. We've got everything all sorted out, and you have a safe place to live now."

"Thanks."

"Everything will work out. I promise."

While I felt better about everything now that I had help, the anger toward my parents never stopped. All of this was because of them. I should've been safe with them. I shouldn't have been a homeless thief.

When we went inside, an older man greeted us. He looked to be in his late fifties. He and Kel had the same eyes, but they didn't look much alike beyond that. Kel had much darker hair and skin, but they were the same build and height.

"Hello, Zay. I'm Jon."

"Hello, sir," I said, shaking his offered hand.

He smiled. "Just Jon. Let's show you around."

The two men led me upstairs first and opened a door to a room that they converted into a bedroom. Fuck, it even had a TV. But the windows looking out at the water were even better.

"You can decorate the room any way you want. Just let us know what you need. You have your own bathroom, and we have a little kitchenette. It's not much, but we put it in a few years ago so we could make our own lunch. Maybe we'll get it fixed up more now that you're here," Jon said.

"I'll take you over to the house I live in with my dad once a week so you can wash clothes, but while you work for us and live here, you're still cared for as one of our own. We'll keep you clothed, fed, and covered by healthcare. Once you've worked off the surfboard by judge's orders, we'll pay you hourly so you can start saving your money."

"I... don't know what to say," I said, looking down at my feet, completely mortified I stole from these kind people, and I wasn't sure I deserved it. Maybe my parents were right, and I was a bad person.

"Hey," Kel said, standing in front of me. "It's okay, Zay. You're forgiven."

"Yeah." My eyes watered, and I wiped my nose with the sleeve of my hoodie.

"It's going to be okay, kiddo."

"Yeah…"

CHAPTER FOUR

Noah

I HAD MY CHEAP EARBUDS IN, DANCING TO SOME TUNES ON MY CHEAP, used phone while Mom slept off her hangover. Or she was still drunk. I couldn't tell because she'd like been in there since last night. She had another date, and I knew because the dude left while I was eating cereal during breakfast. He gave me a grunt and walked out.

I rinsed all the dishes, loaded them in the ancient dishwasher, and turned it on. While that ran, I scrubbed the counters and swept the floor. Beer bottles and half-smoked cigarettes covered the living room, so I cleaned all those up, sprayed the room with air freshener, and vacuumed the stained carpet. When that was finished, I opened up all the windows to air out the place.

Mom was going to need breakfast to work off her hangover, so I pulled out some eggs I bought two days ago, along with some bacon and bread.

An old tune I knew well came on from Journey called *Don't Stop Believing* and I sang along while I laid some bacon into the heated frying pan.

Once the bacon slices were finished, I laid them on a paper towel and made the eggs and toast next. I wiggled my hips as I spread butter on the toast. Then I bounced my way to the fridge and poured Mom some OJ.

I put everything on a tray, along with two ibuprofen, and walked down the hall to her room. While balancing the tray in one hand, I opened her door to complete darkness.

Man, I was gonna trip or something. I set the tray down on her dresser and pulled open the curtains to let in the late morning light. The room reeked of sex, sweat, and cigarettes. I pushed back my disappointment and put a smile on my face.

"Mornin', Mom. Wakey, wakey. You gotta go to work in a couple of hours."

She pulled the blanket over her head. "Go away."

"Nope. You gotta eat and go to work. I'm too young to bring home the bacon, so instead, I brought you some actual bacon," I joked. It was hard sometimes to be happy around her. Mom didn't make it easy, but I tried. I had to keep up her spirits, so she didn't go off the deep end again and lose her job.

"Fuck off, Noah. My head fucking hurts."

I took a deep breath to shove back the hurt. She didn't mean it. Mom just wasn't a morning person, especially when she was hung over.

"No can do. You gotta eat. I made you eggs, bacon, and toast. There's some juice, and I brought you a pain reliever."

I pulled back her covers only past her head, not knowing if she had clothes on or not. "Come on. Sit up and eat. You gotta go to work. They said if you miss work again, they'll fire you."

"Let them. I'm so fucking tired. Working and caring for your ass is exhausting."

More hurt filled me, and I tried not to get upset. She barely took care of me with all her drinking and screwing.

"It's cool. It's almost over. In a couple of years, I'll be workin' and makin' my own money. Then I can get my own apartment. For now, you gotta deal."

"Fuck! Fine! Bring me my food and get the fuck out."

When she shifted in bed, sitting up and keeping the blanket up to her bare chest, covering herself up, she groaned and rubbed her head. Smudged dark makeup covered her face, and her bright blond hair was a tangled mess, but when she got out of the shower and dressed, I'd fix it for her.

I put on a fake smile as if she didn't repeatedly stab me with her words and brought the tray over to her.

"One hour," I sing-songed. "Then you need a shower."

When she started eating, I left her room and closed the door behind me. My smile dropped from my face, and I headed to my room. I sat on my bed, curled my knees to my chest, and cried.

I hated it here. The apartment was gross, and it smelled. Mom was always drunk these days and sleeping with too many men. That meant I had to take her to another check-up and get her tested for STDs. I had to learn how to drive on my own early since she couldn't half the time. God, so embarrassing, man.

She hadn't always been so bad. When I was younger, she used to take me out to the beach on the weekends and teach me to surf. Mom always drank, I think because she had me so young and my father was never in the picture, so she struggled. She might not have known who he was either. Mom was a surfer and party girl when she was younger. Now, she was just a mean drunk.

I had to keep convincing myself that she didn't mean her words. That there was good in her deep down inside. If I didn't... who knew what the fuck I'd do.

I'd gotten really good at taking care of myself and her, but I was so tired. She wanted freedom from me, and I wanted freedom from her. Just a few more years. When I graduate high school, I'd be totally done. Then I could live the good life with surfing, weed, and love.

But I couldn't abandon her. She chose to have me and took care of me when I was younger. I'd probably always help her.

I opened my nightstand drawer and pulled out a half-smoked blunt and a lighter. Mom had tons of them lying around and never missed them when I'd swipe a few. I put it in my mouth and lit up, inhaling the sweet, sweet smoke. After a few puffs, I relaxed, feeling better already. Some people preferred that fast shit you inject or snort. But I liked the chill weed gave off. It helped me deal with Mom and my stress, but it didn't leave me with withdrawals or hallucinations.

The song, 'Don't stop believin' ran through my head as I sang to myself and I toked up, though the song was long over.

Once I worked up a decent buzz, I looked at my old clock radio. Her hour was up.

Reluctantly, I got out of bed, put out the blunt, and headed to her room. I knocked on her door and walked in, praying she had clothes on. She sat on the edge of her bed with a towel wrapped around her and her long blond hair dripped down her shoulders and arms while she stared at the floor.

She didn't eat enough, so she was skinny, but the alcohol gave her a little tummy.

I took the brush from her hand, sat behind her, and brushed out all the tangles. Then I did her hair in two French braids. Some friends of mine who were girls showed me how to do women's hair. Once her pain reliever kicked in, and she had her coffee, she'd be almost normal. Nice even.

"I'm gonna make your coffee now. I laid out your work uniform on the chair."

She said nothing when I left to brew her coffee. She worked as a sales clerk for a golf club store. It paid decently, but it was never enough. Hawaii was too expensive to live for a single parent, but we got by. Barely. We'd do better if she didn't drink so much and go out all the time. The men she spent time with probably bought her a lot of drinks, too.

I tried to remain positive. At least we didn't live on the streets, and though the apartment was a dump, we had a roof over our heads and food in our fridge. Some people had it worse.

I poured some milk into her cup and added three teaspoons of sugar, just as she liked it. When Mom came out fully dressed, I put a big smile on my face and handed her the cup. She took a deep sip and sighed.

"Thanks, baby. You're the best. I'll see you tonight. Maybe we'll order a pizza."

"Sweet! Love me some pizza," I said. She finished her coffee, gave me a hug, and headed off to work. As soon as the door shut, the smile left my face. We wouldn't be having pizza. We never had pizza. I always made us dinner and usually ate alone.

Since Mom headed to work and the apartment was clean, I grabbed my worn and well-loved shortboard to catch some air at the beach. School was tomorrow, but I was caught up on my homework. Weed and surfing were my life. My stress relievers.

I took my bike and hauled my board with one arm down to Sunset Beach. When I arrived, my friends were already there. All but one. Malo. He and I had gone to school together since Kindergarten. We'd been besties ever since. But he moved away during eighth grade. Now that I'd started high school, I really missed my bestie.

"Dude!" Mason yelled, waving at me to come on over.

I dumped my bike in the sand and walked over to my two friends.

"'Sup, brah," I said, fist-bumping them.

Mason had blond hair like me, but a little darker, wavy, and fell to his shoulders. He was taller too. Nhan's parents came from Vietnam, but he was born in Hawaii.

"You're late, man," Nhan said.

"Yeah, I had stuff to do." My friends didn't know shit about my home life. It wasn't something I liked talking about.

"Ready to catch air?" Mason asked. "The waves are fuckin' pumpin'."

"Definitely, brah."

I shielded my eyes with my hand and looked out at the pumpin' waves. The barrels looked sick, and I couldn't wait to get in there. That was one thing I was grateful to my mom for. She taught me how to surf. Surfing was my fucking life. If I didn't have that, I'd die.

We all grabbed our boards and ran into the surf. I hopped on my board and paddled out to where the sweetest waves were. I didn't bother waiting for the right wave, taking one right after the other. That's how perfect they were.

The waves were big but not so big that I couldn't catch air on my shortboard. If the waves grew too high, you needed a longboard to enjoy the ride.

I was the first to pop up and take off, hugging the curve cresting over me. Once I shot out of the barrel, I twisted my body and crested over the lip, catching air. I did a quick spin and came down hard, almost slipping before I regained my balance.

This was the life. Man and ocean, battling it out together for dominance. Today, I fucking owned it. I was king and master of the waves.

When we got tired, we dragged our limp bodies out and fell onto our towels.

What an awesome day once I got past Mom. It was early October and the season with the fewest tourists. Though we survived on tourism, it was nice to have the beach to ourselves. This was our world that Bennys, non-locals, didn't understand. Tourists liked the show, but they didn't understand the life and culture.

Soon, the competitions would start, and I'd be there to watch when I had the time. I always wanted to compete but never felt good enough. Taking care of Mom took most of my free time unless she was at work, making it hard to train.

"Bruh, hello..."

"What?"

"Dude, I've been trying to hand off the blunt."

"Damn, dude... Can't miss out on that. You always got the best shit."

I took the blunt between my fingers and brought it to my lips, taking a long hit. I held it for as long as I could before releasing the smoke. "Sweet..."

"How's Clarissa?" I asked Mason. My dude was big, and girls dug him. Clarissa had been his girlfriend for the past four months, which was a record or something.

"Banging. I mean that literally, bruh. We did it this weekend."

My eyes opened wide. "Brah... no way! Was it totally epic?"

"I guess. It was like awkward and shit, man. I mean, I got some, right? But her, not so much."

"You gotta go down on that shit," Nhan said as if he was an expert, though I was pretty sure he hadn't lost his virginity yet like me. "Gotta lick the pussy."

I didn't know shit about sex. I mean, I looked shit up on the internet, but it's not like any of it was probably real. All I knew was what they taught us in middle school, and they definitely didn't teach us how to please a girl. The only thing I knew was that I liked girls and boys. I'd gotten boners looking at a sexy girl or a sexy dude. It didn't seem to matter. Another thing I hadn't told anyone about.

"Any girls you like, Noah?"

"Cha... there are like tons of cuties at school." Tons of cutie guys, too. It was like I had a whole buffet of people to choose from. Though, I hadn't even kissed anyone yet. While I thought several kids were cute, I wasn't really all that interested either. I wanted someone I could be with for a super long time, not just get my rocks off. I was a relationship kinda dude.

"Ugh, don't remind me we have to go to school tomorrow, brah," Nhan complained.

Little did my friends know I loved school. Shit. Did I have friends who really knew anything about me? Malo did. He knew everything about me, but he left last year.

And I needed to get back home to get dinner ready. I hated being the fucking parent sometimes.

"Gotta blow, bros."

"See ya in the manana, brah," Mason said.

After fist-bumping goodbye to my friends, I hopped on my bike to head back home.

CHAPTER FIVE

Noah

I WAS ONE OF THOSE WEIRD KIDS WHO LIKED SCHOOL AND HATED breaks and holidays. School gave me a desperately needed break from my home life. Breaks from school meant I had to do what I did today, almost every day, and I was so fucking tired. And holidays just sucked.

I yawned and sipped my coffee from my thermos as I chilled in the school hallway before class started, leaning against some lockers. My mornings started too early as I had to make my lunch and help Mom before I left for school. I barely made the bus on time this morning.

Someone plopped next to me and bumped my shoulder. "Morning, sleepyhead."

I glanced at Suzi and gave her a smile. "Mornin', sis." She was a pretty girl with long sleek black hair and almond-shaped dark brown eyes. "How's it hangin'?"

I grabbed her hand and kissed it. We weren't dating or anything, especially since she was more like a sister to me. My friends were used to me being touchy. I had so little affection in my life, and I craved it in any way I could get it. My friends didn't seem to mind, though I was more careful around the dudes. They could be weird about it sometimes.

She combed away my long bangs and looked at my face. "Dude, you got bags under your bags."

"Man... had to be up early." Suzi didn't know about Mom either.

I yawned again and drank more coffee.

"I'm spillin' tea," she said. "There's some new kid in school. He's supposed to look real dope. Rumor has it he's repeating the ninth grade."

"Bummer."

"Yeah... but he's supposed to be super cute. Ana said she saw him walking into the school this morning, lookin' all bad boy and shit."

"Cool, man. If I have a class with him, I'll say hi. Make sure he's got some friends and shit."

"Yeah, me too. Alright, gotta go to geometry class... Ugh, hate that fuckin' class.."

"See ya, Suz."

She pecked my cheek and ran off.

I had to get to class too. I stood and tossed my backpack over my shoulder, and headed to biology. Too bad I didn't have an easier class first thing in the morning, but at least it wasn't P.E.

There were ten minutes to spare before class started, so I made my way to the back of the class where my desk was and plopped in it. I stretched out my legs and shoved my hands into the pockets of my hoodie as I waited for class to start.

I must have dozed off because the door slamming shut startled me awake.

"Class, I'd like to introduce you to a new student," said Mrs. C. We all called her that because her name was Greek and no one could pronounce it. "This is Zayden Beckett. Zayden, please have a seat. There's a desk next to Noah in the back row. Noah, time to wake up. Don't think I didn't notice you dozing."

The boy was tall with dark brown hair that fell in his face as he looked down at his feet. He stood there awkwardly, looking like he wanted to bolt out the door. He wore an oversized hoodie in navy blue and black joggers. This must have been the boy Suzi talked about. Cool. I'd hit him up with some convo to make him feel at home.

When he sat down next to me, I reached over and tapped his shoulder with the back of my hand. "Dude... 'sup. I'm Noah."

He looked back at me with the most intense, gorgeous eyes I'd ever seen. I held my breath, looking at them. They were golden embers of fire, and they popped with his really dark hair. Fucking hell... he was gorgeous. Suz wasn't wrong. My heart stopped for a moment, and I lost all words. While pretty, he looked supremely pissed off. I guess I'd be, too, if I had to repeat a grade if the rumors were true. What happened to him?

Instead of saying anything, he faced the front, stretched his long legs out, and pulled his hood over his head, completely ignoring me.

Okay then. I guess he didn't want to be friends.

I shrugged and focused on learning about neurons.

By third period, I saw him again in my P.E. class. He stood in the far corner by the lockers, away from everyone, as he changed into his gym clothes. God, he still looked pissed off at the world. I doubted he was mean, but something had happened to him. And he looked so lonely all by himself, hiding away from everyone. When he took off his shirt, he had wiry muscles, but he was pretty skinny. Too skinny. Like his ribs stuck out, type of skinny. The poor dude. Nah, he seriously needed a friend.

"Hey, look. It's the new kid." Someone said. It was one of our school bullies, and he had his sights on Zayden. Shit.

Normally I stayed away from those losers because they scared me a little, but my body tightened, and my heart rate went up with this need to protect the new dude. I knew what it was like to get picked on.

He walked over toward Zayden with two other boys and cornered him. If Zayden was afraid, he didn't show it. In fact, he looked doubly pissed with his scowl and fisted hands.

"I remember you from last year. You weren't here long. What happened to you?"

"None of your business," he mumbled in a deep and sexy voice.

"Aww, did you fail all your classes and have to repeat the ninth grade? You stupid, brah?"

The room filled with tension between all four boys. I wasn't a fighter, but Zayden needed someone in his corner. Besides, I hated those jerks, picking on me and making fun of my Goodwill clothes, surfer hair, and the way I talked.

I quickly stood between the bullies and Zayden with more toughness than I felt. "Leave him alone, bruh. It's his first day, man. Do you dudes always need so much attention? Don't you have enough kids to pick on without addin' to your list?"

"Fucking stay out of this, Noah."

I folded my arms and refused to budge, feeling suddenly too small. I wasn't nearly as big as these boys. "No. Leave him alone."

A whistle blew, and we all turned to see the teacher watching us. "Finish up and get out into the gym. Now."

Eric bumped my shoulder hard when he walked away with a stupid smirk on his face. I got knocked back into the locker but righted myself.

"Jerks... Hey, you okay, brah?"

Zayden looked down at me without so much as a smile. "I can take care of myself."

Such a salty boy. It didn't hurt my feelings or nothing because all I had for him was pity, along with curiosity about what happened to him. He was definitely hurting. I knew how it felt.

I put on my biggest smile and nodded. "I'm sure you can. Anyway, those guys are jerks. They pick on me, too. Well, see you out there, dude."

While we played volleyball, I couldn't stop looking at Zayden and his angry face. I wasn't sure if it was anger as much as a need to keep people away. He seemed so withdrawn, which weirdly made me want to get to know him more. It was like approaching a feral animal, so I had to be careful. But if I could handle my mother, I could handle Zayden Beckett.

After gym was lunch break, instead of searching for my friends to eat with, I hunted down the new kid. He'd probably be sitting alone.

When I found him, he was sitting at a table completely empty of kids as if he had put a force field around himself with a neon sign that said don't approach. He wore his hood over his head to hide his face, but it wouldn't keep me out. Some kids needed that extra push to get them out of their shells or break their walls. I sat down across from him, and he looked up and rolled his gorgeous eagle eyes. Seriously, I had no idea eyes like that existed.

"You just keep insisting," he said, but there was no anger behind his words. No bite to his bark.

I beamed a smile his way, which was my force field breaker. "I'm persistent like that. It's the story of my life, brah. It's how I survive."

His face softened when he looked at me again, and he was so much prettier when he wasn't pissed off at the world.

"Why?" he asked.

"Why what? Why do I keep botherin' you?"

"Yeah."

I winked at him. "Because you're new and need friends, and I'm a pretty good friend. You can talk to me, or we can just sit here. I'm okay with either, dude, but I'd rather talk."

Zayden looked down at his lunch, picking at his sandwich but not eating. He was too skinny and needed to eat, not waste his meal. I was skinny too, but not like him. He looked like he hadn't eaten for a while.

"Hey, you wanna eat somewhere else? There's hardly anyone outside on the bleachers. I like eating there sometimes when I wanna be alone."

He looked up and scanned the cafeteria, then nodded at me.

I smiled and stood up, packing up my lunch again as he packed his.

I itched to grab his hand as I led him outside, but I didn't want to spook him. He was kinda talking, and I wanted him to get more comfortable with me before I pulled my weird touching shit.

The day was sunny and warm and a little too breezy from the trade winds coming off the ocean as fall and winter came. It's why the North Shore had all those surfing competitions this time of year.

We opened our lunch bags, and I took a bite of my peanut butter and jelly sandwich. I was sick of them, but the food was cheap. I had to get creative when grocery shopping.

And he still didn't eat. "Zayden, dude... not to be your mama, but you should eat. You need it."

"It's Zay."

"Cool, Zay. Love your name. But eat, man."

"I don't want to be here," he blurted, slinking his body down over his thighs and grabbing his legs.

"Where? At school?"

He nodded.

"They say you're repeatin' freshman year."

"Yeah."

Getting information out of Zay would be like trying to ride a double-up. While a fun ride, catching one wasn't easy, but if you did, it was rad as hell.

"What happened?"

"Nothin'. I... just missed most of last year. Everyone I went to school with before is now a grade ahead of me."

"So, you were definitely at this school before as those boys said?"

He nodded again.

No one would miss almost an entire year of school over nothing. Something definitely happened, but I let it go. Like any feral animal, you had to approach them slowly and with caution. Get them to trust you. Then you could pet it. Not that I'd pet Zay. Stupid analogy, but still, I had to be careful. He was talking, and I didn't want him to stop.

He grabbed his lunch, still staring at the food that sat on his lap.

"Don't make me do the airplane."

He looked up at me with watering eyes that had me melting for him. Poor dude. Zay was definitely hurting, though he tried really hard to hide it, which explained all his angry faces today.

"Huh?"

I took a deep breath with a big smile and tried to do my best to cheer him up. "The airplane... duh. If you don't eat, I'm gonna have to feed you your sandwich by pretendin' it's an airplane. Ya know... like they do with little kids."

He raised a brow with not even a smirk.

I snorted a laugh at his reaction. "I'm teasin', bruh. But you should eat."

Zay finally took a small bite of his sandwich and chewed slowly. I wasn't sure why that made me so relieved. After taking care of Mom for so long, I guess that need rubbed off on other people.

He only ate half of his lunch, but at least he ate something.

Before we headed back to class, I pulled him into a hug. Fuck it. He needed one. He stiffened and then pushed me back. Not hard, but it wasn't gentle either. His animal eyes went wild as he looked around to see if anyone saw us. I sighed, hoping he wasn't some homophobe because that was a deal-breaker for me in my friendships.

"Dude, no gay stuff. I just thought you needed a hug."

At least he looked guilty for his reaction. "Sorry... nothing against gay... stuff. You... surprised me."

I shrugged and smiled. "It's cool. I'm a hugger."

"Sorry," he said again, rubbing his neck. "Uhm, I feel like an idiot, but... I... forgot your name."

I threw my head back and laughed. God, he was so cute. "Noah Ellis."

We shook hands, and he finally cracked a smile for me. It was small, but it was something. And a start.

During the last period of school, we had Spanish class together. At that point, I just assumed we were fated to be friends. We didn't sit close together, but I popped him on the shoulder and winked at him when I walked by his desk. He was wide-eyed, then smiled, which fucking melted my heart.

Progress!

After school, I rushed to meet Zayden as we filed out of class and headed out to leave for the day.

"Yo, Zay... wait up."

He tossed up his hood as he turned and kept walking, glancing around as if trying to avoid someone, but he slowed down for me.

"Wanna hang out at lunch again tomorrow and meet some of my friends?"

"I... dunno."

I bumped his shoulder with mine. "Come on. My buds are awesome, brah. They'll love you."

"I don't know how since I barely talk to people. I haven't really socialized like in a really long time... Not like with friends, ya know?"

He hadn't socialized? What did that mean? Had he been alone all that time? Now I really wanted to know this dude's story. "Trust me, man. They're cool."

"I guess."

"Sweet! And you should come with us to the beach, man. Do you surf?"

He nodded. "Yeah, I'm not too bad at it."

"This is gonna be bitchin'! You'll see. You're gonna have tons of friends before you know it."

We stopped outside and moved out of the way of the rushing kids. He looked away, rubbing his hooded neck. "Ah, thanks for this, Noah. I know you didn't have to... be nice to me."

"Dude... it's all good. You seem cool, and I'm pretty sure we're meant to be friends."

He raised a cute thick brow. "How do you figure?"

"We have like three classes together. Yep, someone wants us to be friends and shit."

"I don't believe in that fate stuff."

I shrugged. "You don't have to. Facts are facts."

He puffed out a laugh and shook his head. "Fair."

"So, see you tomorrow at lunch?"

"Sure."

"I'll give you details on where to meet up on Saturday, then."

He nodded and walked off to his bus.

Yep, Zay and I were gonna be awesome friends.

CHAPTER SIX

Zayden

I'D ONLY BEEN BACK IN SCHOOL FOR A WEEK WITH A FUCK TON OF catching up since I missed about six weeks of the new school year, and I wasn't about to be held back a second time because fuck that. It was embarrassing enough being in ninth grade again.

To make things doubly hard, I'd seen Duncan around in the hallways in between classes. I hid under my hoodie whenever I saw him close by and avoided him at all costs. I couldn't face him. He probably forgot about me, anyway. I wasn't important or anything, but still... It was mortifying.

But each day was better than the before, thanks to Noah's insistence that we become friends. He pushed, but he wasn't obnoxious about it. He was way too laid-back for that. He had a sweetness about him, and fuck, he was really cute, too, with his bright blond hair like the sun personally blessed him or something. He also had really pretty gem-like green eyes that stood out against his tanned skin. His smile was as sweet as he was.

Noah just made it easy to become his friend. At first, when he hugged me on my first day of school, I freaked out, afraid someone would see us, and we'd get in trouble. After Mom and Dad's reaction, I had no idea how people would react, so I needed to keep any feelings towards guys locked up tight as shit.

But as I got to know him, I realized he was just a really touchy dude. He hugged guys and girls alike, held their hands, and kissed girls on the cheek. God, he was like the fucking happiest bro I had ever met, always wearing a smile. He made it impossible not to like him, and I needed a friend.

While he was my friend, my attraction to him grew too fast. I had to shut that shit down and never show it. Even if he was touchy, that didn't mean it was gay and shit.

I closed up the shop on Friday night, and when I counted out the till for the day, I brought the money to the office to give to Kel to recount and make sure I did it right. I was still learning the ropes around here. Honestly, I was surprised at how much Kel and Jon trusted me after I stole from them.

"Kel?"

"Yeah, Zay," he replied absently as he sorted through the cash.

"Uhm… I know I got some hours and stuff tomorrow for work, but, ah…"

He looked up at me. "Need something?"

"Yeah, uhm, I've been making some friends and—"

Kel beamed a smile. "That's great news, Zay. I'm so glad to hear that."

"Yeah. So, they want to know if I can meet them at the beach to surf tomorrow, and I figured I could get some training in while I did."

"That's fine with me. I can handle the customers tomorrow. It's good to hang out with friends now and again, but just be aware that you're going to be busy soon with driving lessons, taking CPR classes, and getting in training to be certified to teach. But you've been working a lot after school until closing, so sure, you can take a break."

"Thanks, Kel."

"I've also decided to not compete this year. I... need to train, but..."

He focused on me once more with concern in his eyes. "What's going on? I thought you really wanted this."

"I... do. It's just... I'm not fit enough, and I didn't realize how much weight I had lost in the past year. It's been super obvious in gym class how skinny I got."

I fed myself while homeless, but it wasn't like I could have three meals a day or eat healthily. I noticed my clothes had gotten baggier, at the time, but I hadn't realized how much I'd lost.

"You'll bulk up soon enough, but that shouldn't keep you from competing."

I probably could've competed, but it was embarrassing. People would stare or, even worse, ask questions.

"Yeah... Anyway, I want to maybe do some smaller competitions early next year, then maybe I'll be strong enough for a bigger one."

"If that's what you want. Sounds like a solid plan."

God, I loved Kel and Jon's support. My parents weren't bad to me, not until they kicked me out, but they never encouraged me to do much of anything other than pray and get good grades. I wasn't sure what I did to get the help and protection I so desperately wanted and needed, but I wouldn't question it either.

"Oh, before I forget." Kel dug around in his desk and pulled out a small box. "New phone."

I swallowed and tentatively grabbed the box. "You got me a phone?" God, did I sound ungrateful? No, I was surprised and extremely grateful. It was totally unexpected. I opened the box to find a smartphone. A nice one. "This... this is too much."

"It's not. You need it in case we need to get a hold of you. And that way, you can also stay in touch with your friends. Maybe even take some pictures and make some memories. Or join a social media site."

"Thanks, Kel."

"You're welcome, and have fun tomorrow."

After lunch, I rode my new bike down to the beach, which wasn't too far from the surf shop, carrying my board under one arm. On my back, I carried my backpack stuffed with my wetsuit, a towel, and water.

I dropped my bike next to a pile of other bikes and made my way to the beach, scanning the area to find Noah. He wasn't hard to miss with his bright blond hair made from salt and sun.

He turned as if sensing me, and his face lit up with a smile, making my heart beat a little faster. Noah was the fucking sunshine on a cloudy day. I had no idea how he did that but I had to shut down that shit because it only made my infatuation for him grow. I gave him a shy smile and a small wave.

He's only a friend. He's only a friend.

When I reached the small group, Noah stood and gave me a hug. His shirtless smooth skin was warm from the sun, and he smelled like pineapples, coconut, and saltwater. He looked good, too, with his wiry muscles, and I really liked his surfing necklaces and beads.

"Brah, I didn't think you'd come, but I'm happy you're here," he said, sitting down on the blanket.

"I said I would."

I sat down with him and smiled shyly at Mason, Nhan, and Suzi. "Hey."

Suzi sat next to me, smiling. She was really pretty, but I had my eyes on someone else. "Hey, Zay. Glad you could come."

I smiled shyly again. "Thanks."

Nhan just reached over and held out his fist that I bumped it back.

"'Sup, Zay," Mason said, lighting up some weed, took a drag, and handed it to Noah.

"Dude… my man always knows what I like," he said.

Mason chuckled. "I've got you covered, baby."

My man? Baby?

Were they together? I felt a surge of weird jealousy hit me, but that was stupid. For one, Noah wasn't mine. Two, I would never tell him of my growing crush. I barely knew him.

Should I ask about it, though? I could play it off casually, right? It was just me getting to know people. God, I'd hardly talked to anyone for a year except during surfing lessons, and we didn't chitchat much. I got so lost when it came to social shit, and I hadn't exactly been Mr. Extrovert while previously in school, anyway.

"Sooo, you two are… together?" I asked. Fuck, the heat crept up my face. The question sounded so stupid once I said it out loud.

Noah looked at me wide-eyed and snorted a laugh. Soon, he was rolling on the towel, holding his stomach, and cracking up.

"Screw you, Noah," Mason said, laughing with him. "You'd so go gay for me, and you know it."

That turned into another fit of giggles from Noah. "Dude… Mason is like my bro, man. Nah, I'm not seeing anyone."

I couldn't help but laugh along. Noah was infectious, but in a good way. It made me drawn even more to him.

"I've gotta girlfriend, too," Mason said. "She couldn't make it today."

The laughter was a good sign. That meant people who weren't straight didn't freak out. And I didn't hear any snide comments about being gay being played off as a joke, as a lot of kids seemed to do in school.

When Noah sat up, wiping away his laughing tears, his shoulder rested against mine, sending waves of weird electricity through me that I hadn't felt since Duncan. My stomach knotted up, and I eased gently away so he wouldn't notice.

"Come on… let's surf. I'm bored," Suzi said.

Everyone stood and put on their wetsuits. I slipped mine over my boardshorts but paused before I took off my shirt. Noah had seen my body already because I didn't have a choice but to get undressed during gym, but this was at the beach where everyone would see how bony I was. The weight slowly returned as I ate more, but it wasn't enough yet.

My face burned, so I turned my back to them while I debated on removing my shirt or not.

Noah must have sensed my unease or the fact that I had a tight grip on the hem of my T-shirt but hadn't removed it yet because he placed a gentle hand on my shoulder. More electricity sent a shudder through my body that I couldn't hide.

He leaned in, so others didn't hear. "Dude, you're fine. No one cares, brah. Trust me." He gently gripped my arm in encouragement, and when I turned to him, his smile was bright and with reassurance. "You look good."

I nodded and quickly tugged off my shirt and zipped up my wetsuit before anyone really noticed… hopefully.

We jogged out toward the water with our boards, and I looked at the conditions. The waves weren't massive, but big enough to get some good shredding in.

"Pumpin' waves," I said.

"Cha, man. This is gonna be rad."

We ran into the water and hopped onto our boards. It had been a while since I surfed just for fun. Usually, it was to survive or train. Now I wanted to catch air and do some spins and tricks just for me. To feel the power of the waves as they propelled me into the air or curled over me like a cocoon.

Surfing was freedom. Freedom from pain and suffering. At least for a little while. It was just you and the swells.

The day was crowded with surfers, so we had to float in the line-up away from the swells to wait our turn. Too many surfers at once would cause injuries.

God, the waves were peeling… perfect. Riding was going to be smooth and sweet.

"Go first," Noah said when it was our turn. "Let's see whatcha got."

I nodded, paddled fast, and caught the first wave. The glide was smooth, as expected, and the water was crystal clear. I carved the water with my board like a sharp knife in butter, then I did a wrap-around, hitting the lip of the wave and catching air. With a quick spin, I landed and pumped my back leg to pick up the speed, getting ahead before it closed out. I rode with the water curling over me, forming the barrel. When I picked up speed again and burst out of the barrel, then I carved, hit the lip, and exploded into the air again.

Fuck, this was epic. This was my element. This was my world. My happiness.

The water broke, and I let the board carry me to shore, still standing. I turned to watch the rest of the gang, seeing it was Noah's turn, and he was pretty damned good too. But after he caught air and landed, his board slipped out from underneath him. *Oof.* But we all fell. Even the best of us.

After an hour, we dragged our noodle bodies out of the water.

"Brah! Your moves were fuckin' gnarly, man!" Noah said to me, out of breath, unzipping his wetsuit. Then fist-bumped me.

"Dude, totally. Your moves are epic!" Suzi said, falling on her beach towel.

"Thanks."

"So, do you like to compete or something? You're good enough, man," Mason asked.

I nodded. "Here and there."

Noah offered his fist again, and I bumped it with mine. "Dude, you should totally do the Volcom Pipe Pro in January."

That was a massive compliment, but I couldn't compete in that, not quite secure in my abilities. "No way. I'm... not good enough for that one. That's like the biggest one, and I'm out of practice surfing the pipeline. Plus, I'm no pro." It was the same pipeline that destroyed my board.

Nhan snorted a laugh. "Could've fooled me."

"Thanks. I'm not bad, but I'm no Kelly Slater or Jack Robinson. Volcom has some of the best surfers in the world competing."

"With practice, you could be, brah."

I shrugged. "Maybe." I wasn't really confident going all pro with my surfing. These people who won did surfing day in and day out. They traveled the world, hitting surfing competitions. Plus, they had sponsors. That wasn't a possibility for me, and I was okay with that. I didn't need to be some champion. As long as I got to surf.

I pulled out my phone from my bag so I could take pictures of everyone. It was time I started creating happier memories, and today was amazing. The best time I'd had since that day with Duncan... before my homophobic parents ruined everything. Now I wanted to remember this day with new friends.

"Can I take pictures of you all?"

"Totally!" Noah said. "Me first."

Everyone was so tired but full of smiles and sun-kissed skin. Maybe I'd open up an Instagram account and post pictures of my friends and shit. My parents had never let me go on social media at all, and I had never had a smartphone before, just a cheap one so they could reach out to me.

When I held my phone to take his picture, Noah stuck his tongue out and made a peace sign. I smiled, shook my head, and took a pic of him. Even in that pose, he was fucking cute with the crystal blue water and white sand behind him.

Then I got a group shot of all three of them giving the Shaka sign, also known as *hang loose*. Noah even took a couple of pictures of me. Then we took a selfie together with his arm wrapped around my shoulder, sending zings through my body again. I tried not to read too much into it or let myself feel more than I wanted, but it was hard to ignore.

They passed around a blunt again, and this time I took it and inhaled to see what it was like, but I coughed and sputtered instead, making everyone laugh. I felt my face heat, laughing it off. When they passed it back to me, I shook my head.

I was on my back, soaking up the sun. "You should come by the surf shop sometime," I told Noah, who lay down next to me on the towels with our shoulders touching with closed eyes and a small smile on his face. I tried not to think about his warm skin baking in the sun against mine.

"Is that where you work? That's cool."

"I live there too."

He sat up, turned to face me, and rested on his elbow. "Dude, you live at a surf shop? How cool is that? That's so fucking rad."

"Yeah, it's pretty cool, I guess. I haven't been there for too long, but the owners are totally nice... I guess they're my foster parents now. I don't have to... Well, I have my own room and bathroom. They also gave me that sweet surfboard. I'm about to take some classes to learn how to teach surfing lessons and shit."

"No way. That's like a fucking dream job. Does it pay well?"

"Yeah, not too bad." More than I was making on my own, that was for damn sure.

"Hey, when you head back, can I go with you and check it out? Mom's workin' late."

"Yeah, cool."

I had to admit, hanging out with Noah longer made my day, and so happy that it wasn't over yet.

Noah and I said goodbye to his friends, then we headed back to the surf shop on our bikes an hour later. It was just as well since rain clouds were rolling in from the mountains like a white blanket being spread across the horizon. As winter approached, so did the rains.

We parked our bikes out front, and I led Noah inside.

"I've been by here lots, but I've never been inside. This place is amazing, brah. I always get my surfin' needs at Goodwill or a thrift store. Can't afford much."

"Yeah, I do that, too. You can get some pretty cool stuff for cheap."

He gave me a big smile, and I took him upstairs to show him my room. "Well, this is it. This is where I live and work."

"Bruh... this is sweet. Your room's totally big. You should decorate it. Put up some posters or somethin'."

"Yeah, I haven't been here that long. I'm not sure what to do with it yet."

"I'll help if you want."

"Sure. Come over whenever."

I took Noah back downstairs to the office to meet Jon. Kel was probably giving surfing lessons since he took over my shift today. I knocked on the office door and opened it when Jon said to come in.

"Hey, Zay. How's it hanging? Have a good day?"

"Yes sir... Er, I mean, yes, Jon. This is my friend Noah from school."

"Nice to meet you, Noah."

The two shook hands. "Same, brah. You gotta bitchin' place here."

Jon's smile was crooked. "Thanks, Noah. You're welcome to stop by anytime."

After some chatting, we went in search of Kel on the beach. But Noah grabbed my arm and held me back before we made it outside. I turned to him, rubbing the back of his neck, looking nervous.

"What's wrong?"

"So, ah, do ya think they... uhm, need help or somethin'? I could use some work. Things have been... tight lately."

I shrugged. "I have no idea. All we can do is ask, right?"

"Right."

We reached the beach and watched Kel surf. He was alone, so he must have been done with his lessons. He was pretty damn good, too. He rode fast and hard, but when he caught air and landed, he was graceful as a cat. Kel made surfing look easy.

"Dude, he's awesome."

"Yeah. This is actually the first time I've seen him surf. He's usually out here doing dawn patrol before I even wake up."

When Kel came out of the water, he pulled off his wetsuit and dried himself off.

"Brah, your foster dad, or bro, or whatever, is like a DILF. He's hot."

I snorted a laugh and shook my head. Kel was definitely hot. He looked like a supermodel and was fucking fit. But... yeah, way too old. "Dude..."

"What? I got eyes."

Kel walked over to us with a smile on his face and looked directly at Noah, and held out his hand. "Hey, I'm Kel."

"Noah Ellis."

"Nice to meet you."

"You were kickin' it out there."

"Thanks. You surf?"

"Yup. Every chance I get, brah."

"Noah's wanting to know if you need any more help, Kel," I said.

"Yeah, anything part-time or whatever. I'll take anything. Money's been… tight lately at home. I can clean, organize, cook, whatever, man."

"Okay, Noah. Let me talk to Dad about it and see what he says. We might have something available."

"Thanks, man. I'll be forever grateful."

Just then, the sky opened up and dumped rain on us.

CHAPTER SEVEN

Noah

When the rain came down, we all rushed back inside the surf shop, laughing and drenched. I shivered as soon as the air conditioning hit my wet skin, and Zay wrapped his arms around his body, shivering as if that would warm him up.

"Let me drive you home, Noah," Kel said. But I didn't want to go home. I had such an amazing day with Zay. He opened up like a flower today. He still had some shyness, but once he surfed, it was like he turned into a different dude filled with confidence. It brightened up his whole face, making him beautiful.

I wanted to spend more time with him and not go home to my depressing life. Once I saw Mom, my awesome day would be forgotten and ruined. It was the weekend, and Mom didn't have to work tomorrow, so I didn't have to be there to make sure she got her ass up. She could sleep off her hangover the entire day for all I cared. Ugh, but I did care. That was my problem.

I scratched my wet head and looked back and forth at Zay and Kel. "Can... I hang out here a bit longer?"

Kel's eyes softened as he looked at me. "Is everything okay at home, Noah?"

Huh? How did he pick that up? I rubbed my neck and nodded. "Uh... yeah."

"You sure? Your desperate need for cash and now not wanting to go home tells me a different story."

Smart fucking dude. "It's cool. I... money's just tight. But..." I shrugged, playing it off. "I just want to hang out more."

"That's fine, but I'm about to close up for the night and head home. I won't be able to take you back."

"Why don't you just stay here," Zay said, which made my heart beat a little too fast. *Yes, please.*

I looked back at Kel. "Would that be okay with you?"

"It's fine with me as long as you let your parents know."

I could call Mom, but there was no guarantee she'd answer. I guess I had to try because if she needed me and I wasn't there, she'd get upset.

"Okay."

"Well, you boys have fun. I need to get the store ready for closing. Oh, and Dad left some dinner in the fridge, Zay, but there should be enough for the both of you."

"Thanks, Kel," Zay said.

I followed Zay upstairs to his room. He opened up a drawer and pulled out a couple of T-shirts and basketball shorts. "These should fit," he said, tossing me the clothes.

He led me to the bathroom and handed me a towel. "Get dried off in here. When you come out, I can toss your clothes in the drier."

"Thanks, brah."

I removed all my clothes and tossed on the shorts and T-shirt, free-balling it since I hadn't worn underwear under my boardshorts. Then I got all weird and lifted his shirt by the neck to my nose and inhaled. It smelled like laundry detergent. Too bad it didn't smell like him.

When I finished, I stepped out and handed him my clothes. He was dried off and dressed already.

Once our clothes were drying, we headed to the little kitchen, where he pulled out a large container from the fridge and opened it. "Hungry?"

"Yeah." Surfing and weed always made me hungry.

"It looks like spaghetti and meatballs for dinner tonight."

He reached into the fridge again and pulled out another container. "And a salad."

I sat at the little table for two while he heated our dinner in the microwave and pulled out some plates and silverware from the cabinets. I tried not to stare at him moving around the kitchen like a pro with his back turned.

Sure he didn't have tons of weight on him, but he was hot no matter what. I hated that it made him so insecure today at the beach. He still hadn't told me what happened to him, and I didn't ask, hoping he'd open up eventually. I didn't want him to go back into his shell again after he finally came out. And to see him laughing today made my heart stupidly happy.

When the food was ready, he put the salad and spaghetti in front of me and sat down with his own food. I took a bite of noodles, sauce, and meatballs, groaning. God, that was fucking good. I cooked, but only basic stuff. If I made spaghetti, it came out of a jar. This meal was like homemade or something.

"So good," I breathed between bites.

"Jon probably made it. He's a pretty good cook. I've only started to learn to cook so I can take better care of myself. I used to just eat..."

What was he about to say? I waited to see if he'd finish, but he left the words hanging in the air, desperate to be completed.

After we ate, Zay pulled out a pint of vanilla bean ice cream and two spoons, then we sat on his bed watching TV, eating directly out of the container. I wasn't paying much attention to the movie as we leaned against each other while his touch electrified my body. I tried not to stare at him, sucking on his spoon, but I watched him out of the corner of my eye. My heart beat a little fast when his tongue licked off the ice cream on his full lips. God. I had to stop fantasizing about his tongue. I doubted he was into dudes.

When the movie ended, he turned off the TV and turned to face me. I looked into his amber eyes, trying to read him. Why was he looking at me weirdly?

"Noah?"

"Hmm?"

"Why do you need money so much? And when Kel said he'd take you home, you looked... super disappointed."

Did I show that much on my face? I thought I'd played it cool. Ha! I guess I'd never be good at poker.

I didn't tell anyone about my home life. Not that I didn't trust my friends, or they'd make fun of me, but it was seriously embarrassing. I mean, who took care of their drunk mother who always had a string of dudes sleeping with her? I just didn't want anyone to look at me differently. A happy Noah was more interesting.

Zay probably had his own story. He slowly opened up, and I doubted he'd be ready to talk, but maybe he would eventually if he could trust me. To do that, telling my story could help him.

I sat up, turned to face him, and crossed my legs. God, I needed a blunt. But that meant I had to go home and take some of Mom's weed. I stared at my bare feet and shrugged.

"It's... embarrassing," I finally said.

He placed a hand on my leg, sending another wave of chills through me but removed it too soon. "Don't be. Do you think this is something I'd make fun of you for or something? Because I definitely wouldn't."

I shook my head and sucked it up. "Nah, brah. Ugh, fine. So, like I never knew my dad. Mom... likes guys. A lot of guys. She used to be this hot surfer chick, so the dudes liked her. She got pregnant with me when she was seventeen, and her parents kicked her out of the house for it. I'm... not sure why she didn't have an abortion or put me up for adoption. Whatever. She kept me. If the dude who got her pregnant knew of me, he never came around or helped." I shrugged.

I'd often wondered who my dad was as a kid, imagining him super rich and didn't know about me. But when we met for the first time, he'd have me live with him and tell me how sorry he was for missing most of my life. Stupid fantasy. Yeah, I didn't tell Zay that part.

"She was okay at first, takin' care of me and stuff. She taught me how to surf when I was really little. The only good thing she's ever done. But as time went on, she drank more and more. Sometimes she does drugs. Too many dudes come and go from our apartment. It got to the point that she wasn't doing much for herself or me, so I had to grow up real fast. I pretty much do all the chores, cookin', grocery shoppin', and paying the bills. She pays the ones I can't, but it sucks, man. I've got to totally nag her."

Surprisingly, Zay grabbed my hand and held it in his. Not in an intimate way but comforting. It took all I had not to weave our fingers together. He probably did it, knowing how touchy I was.

"I'm sorry, man. That's hard to do all that on your own."

I gave him a grateful smile that he wasn't judging.

"Yeah... I spend most mornings trying to get her ready for work and fed. She can be... mean when she's like that. But once you get her going and caffeinated and shit, she opens up and isn't so bad."

"So, that's why you're here? A little break?"

I looked up at his animal eyes and smiled because he so got it. "Yeah. She doesn't have to work tomorrow, so I just wanna take a breath. I'm just so..."

"Tired?"

Shit, this boy... How did he know?

"Bruh, exactly. Like I'm the parent, man. If she wasn't so... mean all the time, maybe it wouldn't be so bad. And she keeps losin' her jobs no matter how hard I try to get her there on time. And I can't control her while she works. This job seems okay so far. She works at a shop at a golf store. It pays pretty well, not that we've got much to pay for. Still, we don't have much in savings and... I just want to make some money, so one day I can get a place of my own."

"Dude, that must be so hard. I'm sorry about your mom. You're... so nice. To me, anyway. She should treat you better and see how great you are. I hope Kel and Jon have something for you to do."

"Me too, brah. I'm likin' it here already, and Kel is super cool."

"He and Jon are really nice."

I yawned and stretched, reaching my arms to the ceiling. Zay's eyes looked straight at my exposed abs as my shirt climbed, but he glanced away.

What did that mean? It meant nothing. People look and glance away at things all the time. It was just wishful thinking that Zay had a crush on me like I was crushing on him and that maybe he was even a little bit attracted to me.

"I... don't have any extra blankets or anything and the floor is hard. If you... aren't weirded out; you can share my bed. It's big enough."

"Thanks, man."

Definitely *not* weirded out by sharing a bed with this cutie.

Since we had spent all day at the beach, Zay let me use his shower before bed, and I just put back on the old clothes he lent me.

We crawled into his bed, and Zay rolled over onto his side, away from me. Bummer. I tucked an arm under my head and stared at the ceiling, wondering if this crush I had on Zay would grow and what I was gonna do about it. I've had crushes, but they were stupid middle-school ones. Zay and I hadn't known each other very long, but this crush felt... real. Like it could end up being more for me. How did that make me feel? A little scared because if he was straight, and I made a move, it could ruin our new friendship, especially with him finally opening up. No way I wanted him to shut down again.

Ah, well... I'd just keep playing it cool and see what happened. Maybe I'd get lucky. I was due for some.

I woke up more comfortable than I had in a long fucking time. And well-rested. My eyes fluttered open to warmth and pressure against me.

When I looked down at the bed, my heart caught in the air like when I surfed over a wave. That moment you're up high, and everything is suspended in time before it comes crashing down.

Zay slept curled up, facing me with an arm draped over my stomach, and a pillow tucked between us. He was probably hugging the pillow, but I ended up wrapped around it, too. His eyes were shut, and his mouth was slightly open, looking cute as fuck. I didn't want to move and wake him up, so I just lay there, watching him sleep like a weirdo.

My finger hovered over his arm, dying to touch him but I dropped it. Would he freak out if he woke up all snuggled against me? I was sure as fuck freaking out but in a good way, pretending he was my hot boyfriend, and he was tired from fooling around.

Nah, I didn't want to risk him waking up and freaking out, especially if he was straight. He was already itchy with tension as it was. So, I gently eased his arm off and slipped out of bed to go hunt down some coffee. Hopefully, someone drank it around here.

I couldn't find any in the small kitchen, and I didn't even see a coffee maker. Bummer. I padded downstairs to see if they had some to make in the office. But when I reached downstairs, Kel had walked into the store.

"Oh, hey, Noah. How'd you sleep?"

"Good, man. Just huntin' for some coffee."

"Right, Zay doesn't drink it. Come on, and I'll make you some Kona."

"Sweet."

I followed Kel into his office and sat down in front of his desk while he turned on a pot of coffee. Soon, the small space filled with a mouth-watering aroma. Before, I only drank it, so I wasn't so tired at school after taking care of Mom, but now I loved it.

When it was finished brewing, he placed a steaming mug in front of me with some creamer and sugar. I doctored my coffee while he sat down across from me. I could tell he wanted to talk but was waiting for me to take my first sip, which I totally dug. He seemed like a chill dude.

Once I took a sip and sighed, Kel dove right in. "Tell me what's going on, Noah. The truth this time."

"Dang, dude. How'd you know?"

He blew out a laugh. "You don't exactly hide it well."

"Damn. I better work on that. Yeah, it's cool. I don't really talk about it, but since I told Zay last night, I figure I can tell you. Mom is... hard to deal with and she drinks too much and shit, spending money on goin' out and drinkin'. Too many dudes at the house and all. Not only that, but I gotta take care of her. I cook, clean, pay bills, and shit. I'm only here because I gotta breathe, man. She's off of work, so I don't have to rush her out the door. That's why I stayed the night, and I'm lookin' for work. We need money for groceries and bills and stuff."

"I'm sorry to hear that, Noah. No one should have to take care of their parents at such a young age. It forces you to grow up too quickly."

"Tell me about it. I... love her, I guess, and want her to do well, so I can't really walk away. At least not yet, but it's hard, ya know?"

"I can imagine."

"People make fun of me sometimes for being a total surfer dude, but I'm not stupid. I make pretty good grades and I work hard."

I took another sip as I waited for Kel to tell me to fuck off or hire me.

"Thanks for being honest with me, Noah. I talked to Dad last night about you, and we agreed if you were honest about everything this morning, especially with you being only fifteen, we can hire you for some work."

I sat up straight with a big, stupid smile on my face. "Seriously, brah?"

He laughed at my excitement. "Seriously."

"Dude, that's fu... rad, man. What will I be doin'? Cleanin'? Organizin'?"

"Keeping the store neat will be part of your job. But we want you to work the register too. Look, giving surfing lessons is new for us, but business is picking up in that area. I don't have the time to take it all on, so Zay is going to help with that as soon as he's certified. If you want to teach, we can get you set up with training too. With three instructors, we can increase the number of students, which will bring in more money to the shop."

My jaw dropped. Dream. Fucking. Job. "Hell, yeah, dude."

"Great. We can start paying you ten dollars an hour, and once you get certified to teach and learn CPR, we can bump your pay."

"That much? Whoa. I was expectin' like five an hour or somethin'."

"We'll get you all set up and give you some hours. Just let me know what days work best for you."

"All of them."

Kel laughed and shook his head. "Let's not overwhelm ourselves. Pick three or four days a week. You also need to care for your mom, right?"

And there went my mood. "Yeah."

"Look, I know it's hard. I can tell you really care about her, so I doubt you want to completely give up on her. Besides, you're also legally bound to her, not us."

"I really appreciate this, man."

"You're welcome, Noah. And thanks for being a friend to Zay. He needs them."

"Right? That's what I've been sayin'."

We shook hands on it, and he told me he'd get some paperwork together for me to sign.

Ten dollars an hour. So, cool. I had no plans of giving Mom that money. I'd pay some bills with it and get us extra groceries. And it'd be nice to eat something for lunch other than peanut butter and jelly.

Now to find Zay and give him the good news. Not only will I have a job now, but I got to spend more time with him. Life was definitely looking up.

CHAPTER EIGHT

Zayden

January 2017

I TOLD KEL I WOULDN'T DO ANY COMPETITIONS BECAUSE I HADN'T felt strong enough. But I had been too insecure about my body and weight. Most surfers were buff, strong, and broad. Surfing uses all your muscles, especially your upper body. But as the months passed, I bulked up. A lot of that had to do with Noah's insistence that I eat more and Jon's rich cooking.

It took forever to get used to eating more but once I did, I put on the weight and bulk I needed. Now I wasn't so mortified by my skin and bones. And with Noah being Noah, he talked me into finally doing a surfing competition. I signed up for a small one because I wasn't ready to surf with pros despite Noah's insistence.

I'd been practicing basic maneuvers and innovative ones. I'd be judged on sticking to the classics, creativeness, and combinations along with my speed and power. If I could add degrees of difficulty, even better.

The prize pool was ten thousand dollars, but one person wouldn't win it all. Several winners would. The women had their own prizes and competition. If I won, it wouldn't be tons of money, but enough to put away into savings for a rainy day.

I had no limit on how many waves I could ride. It all depended on how much my body could take. But I'd probably do about five. Then the judge would discount the highest and lowest score out of all my waves, awarding me the average total of all the other waves.

The day was cool and cloudy with some drizzle. Not a perfect day for a competition but the waves were pumpin'.

I slipped on my wetsuit, keeping it around my waist until I was ready as my stomach turned. Good thing I only ate a light breakfast. I hadn't competed since the winter of 2015, so I trembled a little with a flipping stomach, turning into knots while my heart beat too fast. I took several deep breaths to calm the fuck down.

Noah stood behind me and started rubbing my shoulders. I tried not to think about him touching me other than to get me to chill. "Brah, relax. You're gonna be awesome. Those waves are gnarly, and you're gonna rock them. Just think of this as you just havin' fun out there and not a competition. It doesn't matter if you win or lose. Right?"

"Right."

And it didn't. I had to remind myself that it wasn't the end of the world if I lost. I was doing this for fun. Yeah, that didn't help my nerves.

Kel, Mason, Nhan, and Suzi also showed up to give their support. They set up a canopy in the sand in case it started pouring.

I looked over at them, and they all gave me thumbs up.

"You can do this, Zay. But just have fun, yeah? And when you win, I get braggin' rights as your best bro."

I threw back my head and laughed. He was so good at getting me to calm the fuck down. "You already have those rights."

Before we could say anything else, they called us to get started.

Breathe. All you have to do is don't miss the fucking swell.

At least we were all amateurs. I didn't have pros around me, which would've made me want to throw up what little breakfast I'd had.

Doing my best to shut off my mind, I ran out into the water, carrying my board, and jumped on, paddling out just past the swells. Most of the waves were good, so hopefully, I'd get in some epic moves. They were even big enough that I'd get in some tube riding.

I immediately paddled with the first swell with another competitor, which was fine as long as we didn't interfere with each other. The first thing I did was ride the barrel as the water curled over me. I hunched over, pumping my back leg to pick up my speed. As soon as I burst out of it, I dropped down the wave and did a bottom turn heading back up. Once I hit the lip of the wave, I cutback by changing my direction and going back to the breaking point of the wave.

I pushed my board to flow with the wave as it was crashing and pumped hard for another bottom turn deep into the trough of the wave before the whitewater. I crouched low, pushing with my back leg for power, and moved forward as I climbed up the whitewater. Right when I reached the top, I pressed close to my board and twisted my body in the opposite direction.

My mind got lost in the zone. The competition was long forgotten as I focused on all the moves I knew so well that I mostly used muscle memory to do them.

That was the end of my ride when the wave was depleted. I simply sunk down and hopped on my board again as I paddled out for another.

After I burst from the tube again, my back leg pumped and pumped my board like a rotor, propelling me forward. I needed the speed and power for this move. I bottom turned, twisting my body up the lip of the wave before it curled over and caught air, doing a three-sixty turn. When I landed, I nearly fell back, but I caught my balance for another bottom turn and cutback.

I rode two more waves, and I saved my best for last. I'd been doing really well so far, but I was getting fucking tired after being out here for thirty minutes.

My board caught air, and I had enough power to leap off of the wave a few feet, needing the height to do a three-sixty counter-clockwise, called an *alley-oop*. It wasn't an easy move, but I'd been practicing. And I landed perfectly. Thank fuck. If I fell, that would have been game over.

With a few easier moves, I was done.

My muscles burned as I paddled my way back to shore. As soon as I stepped onto the sand, Noah came barreling at me. Before I could react, he jumped on me and gave me a massive hug. I wrapped my arms around his tight body and held him back as his feet dangled. Then I quickly set him down before things got weird.

"Brah! Holy shit, dude! That was fuckin' epic!"

I laughed despite still being out of breath and needing to sit. His excitement was always infectious. Soon the rest of the group came toward me, all patting my back and fist-bumping.

Kel then pulled me into a hug. "That was amazing, Zay. You outshined most of the surfers here, and believe me, I was watching. That *alley-oop* was absolutely perfect, saving it for last. The judges will take note. But it's tight with another surfer, so I'm not sure you got the most points or not."

"That's cool. Thanks."

After catching my breath, drying off, and chugging a gallon of water, we awaited the results. It took a while since there were a lot of surfers.

When they tallied the score, I came in second place with the other dude that Kel mentioned placing first. It was close. He got nineteen points, and I got eighteen. A perfect score was twenty. I may not have been the top surfer, but I did my best and not bad since I'd been out of the loop for so long.

Now I was three thousand dollars richer.

Kel took us all out to dinner that night to celebrate. He was so fucking nice to pay for my friends too.

When we got back, Noah and I piled into my bed to watch some TV and ate some ice cream which became a regular thing for us, and probably why I put on extra pounds.

We finished the rest of the ice cream, and I set the container on the nightstand to throw away later and dumped our spoons in it.

Noah was quiet and yawned, while I was still too hyped up from today. My body was tired, yet my mind was alert like I'd had five cups of coffee. I hadn't even expected to win today, and that I came in second left me reeling with excitement.

Soon Noah's head landed on my shoulder, and he grew heavy, like when the body went limp and sagged. I looked down to see him sleeping. A weird urge to kiss the top of his head hit me, but I held back. No good would come of that. But that didn't stop me from staring at him as he slept. He was so fucking adorable, inside and out.

I was grateful yet disappointed that Kel eventually bought a bed for Noah, too, since Noah had been staying here so much. I loved sharing a bed, but it led into too much temptation.

There was only one thing for me to do right this moment, and that was to make Noah sleep in his own bed. As much as I'd love to share, my need for him was too much, and I didn't trust myself.

"Hey," I whispered and nudged his head with my shoulder. "Wake up, No. Gotta go to your bed."

He mumbled something and nestled in tighter to me.

Dammit.

Hugging him was one thing. Snuggling was quite another, and it was giving me a fucking chub.

"No, come on. Time for bed."

I pushed him a little bit harder and shook him. He blinked his eyes open and looked up at me. Then his eyes widened, and his face turned a cute shade of pink.

"Ugh, sorry, man. Didn't mean to fall asleep on ya."

"It's okay."

His eyes turned downcast when he pulled away and slipped out of my bed. It took everything I had not to reach for him and pull him back into me. When he climbed in bed and pulled the covers over him, I laid down and rolled over, away from him.

My crush was becoming almost unbearable with this need to touch him all the time. The only thing holding me back was my fears. Fears of getting outed. Fears of losing my friendship. Even worse, fears he'd hate me.

I'd just have to suffer with pining.

CHAPTER NINE

Zayden

April 2017

AFTER I TOOK A SHOWER AND BRUSHED MY TEETH, I CAME BACK INTO the bedroom, ran, and jumped on top of Noah to wake him up before school.

"Oof... Brah! Fuck! Why you gotta do your bestie like that, man?" he gasped and laughed.

"Because I want to make sure my bestie gets up on time."

He shoved me off of him so hard; I landed on my back on the floor, laughing.

After he tossed a pillow on my face, he crawled out of bed and scratched his bare, beautiful back. I stopped laughing and swallowed hard as I watched him slip the same hand down his blue boxer briefs to scratch his ass. The band pulled down far enough to expose two cute dimples above the curve and a tiny peak of his crack. He left the room to wash up, leaving me with a fucking semi.

"Down, boy," I muttered.

With Noah staying at the surf shop so much, it took him a long time to get past the guilt of not being there for his mom day in and day out, but as he got more tastes of freedom and lots of long talks with me, along with some tears, he finally relaxed more. That and his mom would constantly demean him whenever he wasn't there for her, guilting him and telling him she took care of him when he was younger. It took its toll on him while it pissed me the fuck off. Noah was a sweetheart, and anyone who couldn't see that could fuck right off, even if it were his mom.

Noah didn't stop caring for her completely. He would go over to the apartment twice a week to clean, pay the bills, and prepare his mother some meals if she remembered to eat. Surprisingly, she managed to get up on her own and drag herself to work. Maybe Noah not being there left her no choice but to pick her drunk ass up.

Because he spent so much time still caring for her, working, and going to school, Noah was always tired. At least in two months, we'd be out of school and ready to teach surfing lessons.

His being at the surf shop all the time made me like him more and more, and not just the friendship kind. My crush grew daily, but I still hadn't said anything. I was so afraid after what had happened to me. My parents caused enough damage to keep me silent about my sexuality. He was probably straight, anyway, though I wasn't one hundred percent sure because we never talked about it, and he never dated a girl or a guy.

The best thing about being Noah's friend was that he showed me what real kindness could be like. Sure Kel and Jon did that too, but as my best friend and being around him all the time, I calmed the fuck down. He kept me from floating away in my pain and anger. Noah showed me how much good was out there. That it wasn't all horrible like my parents or his mother. If he suffered her and still came out as an amazing person, then I could get the fuck over my parents and my abandonment. Noah was someone I aspired to be. Chill, caring, and forgiving.

But that also didn't mean that I could easily let go of my fears about my sexuality. What started out so good and open turned out destructive. That openness ruined me in the end. Abandonment wasn't something easy to let go of despite my best efforts.

Noah came out of the bathroom with a towel wrapped around him and headed straight to the dresser to pull out a pair of briefs, slipping them on underneath his towel. He wasn't exactly shy. I internally groaned and looked away before he caught me staring like a nutjob.

I drove us to school in the beat-up pickup truck Jon and Kel bought for me after I passed my driver's test. It wasn't fancy, but it was more than I had. I'd be forever grateful to those two men. They kept their promise of protecting me and taking care of me, even taking in Noah, even though he had a home already.

"There's some summer dance next month," Noah said. "You wanna go?"

"No."

"Come *on*, brah. All our friends will be there."

I didn't want to go. I'd manage to avoid Duncan all year. It helped that he was a grade higher than me, and the school was big, so with a hoodie over my head whenever he was close, he never saw me. If he saw me around, he never reached out to me, which was fine by me. We didn't date all that long, and if he were anyone else, it wouldn't have been a big deal, but in that short period, I'd had my first kiss, discovered my sexuality, and my parents kicked me out over it. So, Duncan had a big effect on my life, and I didn't want to hash that shit out with him or have to explain why I had to repeat the ninth grade. I didn't want to risk seeing him there.

"I know." How could I tell Noah the reasons for my not wanting to go? We were best friends. Why couldn't I just explain it to him? Tell him my story? Fucking fear was why.

"Dude, it'll be fun."

"You don't seem like the school dance type, Noah."

"Dude, anything where I can party and hang out with my bros is my type."

I laughed. "Fair."

"So, you'll come?"

"I guess."

"Sweet!"

It was just hard to say no to Noah. Now, I just had to hope I didn't run into Ducan.

School was uneventful yet again, and just the way I liked it. My grades were good, I had cool friends, and a decent home life despite it not being conventional.

I was in the newly renovated kitchen. Kel and Jon expanded to have a small sitting area with a sofa, TV, and gaming console. They also converted the other room and added another bathroom. They asked if I wanted my own room, but I was totally cool sharing mine with Noah. And it had nothing to do with my crush. *Lies.*

I pulled out some chicken drumsticks, Adobo seasoning, potatoes, carrots, and onion. After preheating the oven, I chopped up the vegetables, spread them on a baking sheet, and rested the chicken on top, sprinkling everything with olive oil and seasoning.

Noah cooked sometimes, but I enjoyed making meals while he didn't for obvious reasons. He always cooked for his mom, so I didn't mind doing it for us.

I played a video game while I waited for dinner to cook in the oven. Noah was at his mom's place, checking on her, but he'd be back in time to eat.

After an hour, dinner was ready. I pulled it out of the oven and set it on the stove to cool, then searched for Noah to let him know it was time to eat. He should've been back by now, but he hadn't stopped to say hi.

I headed to our room, opened the door, and walked in. Noah wasn't in there, but the light in the bathroom was on, and the door was cracked open. I paused my hand on the door, about to knock, when I saw Noah with his back to me and his pants and underwear pushed down past his ass. His taut, smooth ass. He had his head down and was breathing hard with slapping noises, obviously rubbing one off.

I instantly got hard at the sight, straining through my shorts. I needed to leave. To give him some privacy, but I couldn't look away. My feet were glued to the ground. I swallowed the forming lump in my throat as my heart beat a little too fast and my face flushed with heat. Arousing heat. I ached between my legs, pulsing with need. I'd had hard-ons before but never like this. His sounds and knowing what he was doing made me throb.

Turn around and go. Now. Stop staring like a perv.

A groan escaped him, and my dick jumped, asking for more. I must have moved the door because it creaked. My heart stopped when Noah suddenly turned around wide-eyed. He was still hard in his hand as he looked at me. We both stared, not saying a word. I still couldn't walk away, while he said nothing, unmoving.

I needed to run. I needed to leave. But all I did was stand and stare. Then I glanced down at his heavy dick resting in his hand, glistening with pre-come.

Fuck. So fucking hot.

To my shock, instead of him telling me to fuck off or slam the door in my face, he stroked himself again. Right in front of me. My eyes laser beamed straight at his movements, watching him slide his hand up and down. Up and down. Pumping. Stroking. Pulling. It was the hottest and scariest thing I'd ever seen. My mouth turned dry, and the swelling between my legs was beyond painful while I tried to keep from punching out my hips, seeking out his touch. I cupped myself while he watched my movements. *Fuck, did he see?*

Noah's eyes fluttered closed, and his mouth slacked open as he groaned and threw his head back. Soon his hand and stomach were covered in his release as he continued to tug and pull until his balls were empty.

When he looked at me again, his eyes were glazed over, and I fucking panicked. I ran out of there as fast as I could, tripping over some shoes and landing hard on my knees. I scrambled up, and ran into the kitchen, resting my back against the wall as my heart beat the shit out of my chest.

Holy shit. I shouldn't have watched him. Why did I stay? Why didn't I walk away? I invaded his privacy like some sort of pervert. But he didn't stop either. He kept going as if he knew I'd enjoy watching him. I rested my hand on my still-pounding heart as my face turned to fire.

"Stupid, stupid, stupid," I mumbled, berating myself as I hit the back of my head against the wall as if I could pound the memory right out of my brain, pretending I didn't just witness Noah jacking himself off for me.

What would happen to our friendship now? Did I ruin it? Would he even talk to me? Yell at me? Why did he finish? Maybe he was caught up in the moment. I got myself off enough to know how easy it was to shut everything out as you came. Sometimes consequences went out the window. I cupped myself, which was still fucking hard. Despite my mortification and guilt, the entire thing turned me the hell on. Any feelings I had for Noah beyond friendship kicked up to about a thousand degrees. And there was no unseeing Noah masturbating. That wasn't even the part that mortified me. It was my actions.

He probably hated me now. But I should apologize to him, right? Right. I'll do it during dinner.

After I calmed the fuck down—barely—I grabbed two plates and piled them high with vegetables and chicken. By the time I put them on the table, Noah had walked in. I was jittery as hell as I quickly glanced at him to see his face beet red all the way to his ears, which turned my face into a burning flame.

I looked away and sat down to stuff my face with food. Noah sat across from me and picked at his chicken.

"Sorry!" we both said at the same time, making us laugh awkwardly with faces still beet red.

My face didn't stop burning through the entire meal and well into bedtime. As I lay in bed, tossing and turning, trying to sleep, all I could see in my mind was Noah stroking himself. That vision was seared forever in my brain, and I liked it. The longer I thought about it, the harder I got.

My dick had been demanding why I'd been ignoring it after that glorious vision, so I paid attention to it now. I reached under the covers, slid my hand underneath my briefs, and grasped myself, imagining it was Noah's hand. As quietly as possible, I stroked to completion with visions of Noah and his beautiful dick. It was the first dick I'd ever seen besides my own, so maybe I was a little biased.

After cleaning up with some tissues, I rolled over and tried to sleep. Eventually, I did, with dreams of Noah and me doing things I'd never done before.

CHAPTER TEN

Zayden

Things had been super fucking awkward for the past month between Noah and me after I caught him masturbating and him putting on a show for me… and me staring like a freak. We didn't stop being friends or anything, and we still joked around and surfed, but nothing was quite the same either. Both of us kept our distance from each other. Where Noah was usually touchy and had no problems sitting close to me, now he stayed away, which made me feel like I was missing a part of myself. We really needed to deal with this. We'd never go back to how we were until we did.

The Sunday afternoon was rainy, so Noah sat in the kitchen, playing video games as he usually did when he didn't have to work or couldn't surf. I headed in there with shaking hands and a pounding heart, unsure exactly what I wanted to say, but we needed to fix this shit between us. Ugh. We weren't broken, but I wanted to go back to the way things had been between us before. Enough of this awkwardness.

"Yo, we need to talk, Noah."

He didn't even turn around as he shot up a bunch of zombies. "Later, brah."

"Now."

He huffed and ignored me.

Instead of getting angry, I tried to see things from his side. I just came storming in, making demands. It was only because I was nervous as fuck, so I calmed my tone.

"Please, dude. Can we talk?"

He sighed, put his game on pause, and turned on the couch to face me. I sat down across from him as my mind went fucking blank. God, how did I approach this? It was so embarrassing. My face burned again for the hundredth time, but I took a deep breath and sucked it up.

Noah must have sensed what this was about because he wouldn't look at me as he picked at his fingernails. His long blond bangs fell in his face, so I couldn't tell if he was blushing as much as me.

"So, ah... I, uhm... shit. I owe you an apology," I squeaked out. Not very eloquent, but I said it.

"For what, brah?"

Since he still wouldn't look at me, I assumed he knew exactly what I was talking about.

"Dude, you know what I mean. I'm tired of this weirdness between us. That was my fault. I... don't know what possessed me to... watch you. It was wrong and completely inappropriate."

His green eyes finally glanced at me. He wore a guilty face but gave me a small smile. "If you were inappropriate, then so was I. God, I don't know why I finished when you caught me. It was like... I needed you to watch. So weird. I'd been so fuckin' mortified since, brah. Like afraid to talk to you and shit. I thought you hated me."

Was that what he thought? "Shit, all this time, I thought you hated me."

"No way, brah. Never. We're like total best besties."

I laughed, loving Noah's made-up terms. It's what made Noah unique, among other things.

"Thank god. I think so, too."

I wish I could tell him how turned-on I was when he rubbed one off in front of me. How hard he made me. And I wasn't about to ask if he saw me tenting through my shorts. He probably did, though.

Noah suddenly came at me in a rush and pulled me into a hug. I smiled and hugged him back, grateful to touch him again. It was as close as I'd ever get to have him.

"Thanks for gettin' the balls to talk," he said when he pulled away.

"I was nervous as fuck."

"Yeah, me too, but I'm glad we got this shit fixed. I'm so sorry, Zay."

"I'm sorry, too."

Thank god that was out of the way, and we fixed our shit. Now things could go back to normal.

It was the end of the year school dance and so not my thing, but Noah wanted me there, and he was my best friend, so I'd be there. We walked into the gym that had been decorated with streamers, banners, balloons, and a disco ball in the center with colored lights beaming at it to put discs of dancing light on the floor and walls. The music was poppy and so not my jam. Give me some classic rock or alternative any day.

Noah and I wore Hawaiian shirts and boardshorts. Nothing fancy, but more than what we usually wore, which consisted of worn T-shirts and hoodies. He had his hair combed away from his face, and he looked so cute now that I could really see the green of his eyes. But I liked floppy-haired Noah the best.

"Dudes! You look totally cute!" Suzi said, running up to us with

Mason and Nhan in tow. She was dressed in a really cute short black dress that flared out at the bottom but was snug at the top, with the short sleeves falling off the shoulders.

"So do you, sis," Noah said. "Who knew you'd clean up so good?"

She gave him a playful shove and then spun around to show off. When we all applauded, she curtsied.

I pulled out my phone and took a bunch of pictures of us for my Instagram to post later. After the pictures, Suzi dragged Noah and me to the dance floor. I wasn't much of a dancer—at all, really. I'd never been to a dance before, and I didn't do it alone to music either, so I swayed awkwardly. But Noah looked pretty damned good. His dance moves were amazing as if he'd been dancing his whole life. He was bold and confident like always, uncaring of what others thought.

After dancing to a couple of songs, we headed towards the snack table to get some cookies and punch. We ate and drank as we people-watched, laughing at some dancers or were in awe at how good other students looked.

"Bro," Mason said to get our attention and leaned in, tapping the front pocket of his shirt with his hand. "Got some of the good stuff tonight."

"Dude, sweet!" Noah said.

I rolled my eyes at his perpetual need to toke up. But I also understood it. Noah started doing it pretty early in life as a stress reliever from his mom. If it helped him cope, who was I to say he couldn't do it? While I didn't normally smoke the stuff, I would tonight. Why not? It was a party, right? As long as we didn't get caught and I had no competitions coming up.

Mason led us out of the gym, making sure teachers and parents didn't catch us. Then we made our way down the halls and out the back to an area where they wouldn't see us and far enough away, so no one smelled the smoke.

Mason lit up and took a long drag before handing the blunt to Noah. Once he inhaled, he passed it off to me. I didn't toke often, but it was often enough now that I didn't hack up a lung when I inhaled. I took a long drag and handed it off to Nhan. And so it went as we passed the blunt in a circle until we finished it.

Noah leaned against the facade of the building and rested his head against it, exposing his Adam's apple. I had the weird urge to lick it, but I shut that shit right down.

Fucking weed.

"Dude, that was smooth," Noah said.

"So, what's up with you two," Nhan asked, eying Noah and me.

I shrugged while my stomach flopped around. Could he tell I had a crush on my bestie? *Play it cool, Zay.* "What do you mean?"

"Dude, you two have been off lately, but you seem okay now. Did you two have a fight or something?"

"I don't get it." Well, I did, but I didn't realize we were that obvious. I glanced at Noah, who quickly eyed me and then looked away. Yep, he thought the same thing I did.

"Brah, you two are like attached at the hip, then one day you were all like barely acknowledging each other," Mason said.

Suzi nodded in agreement. "Totally."

Noah and I quickly glanced at each other again. "Nothin', man. Nothin' between Zay and me. We're good."

They eyed him like they didn't believe him, but we weren't about to spill what happened last month. No fucking way.

"Ah, how cute. Look at the little stoners. Fucking losers."

My stomach suddenly clenched as that old rage I hadn't felt since the beginning of the school year built up. I'd been picked on way too much, so my reaction was almost visceral. Hell, so had Noah. But things finally slacked off, so I thought they'd forgotten about us or finally left us alone.

I turned to face them, no longer afraid since I'd bulked up and grown taller. But as I turned, my heart stopped.

Duncan.

Fuck.

I'd been doing so good at avoiding him. But how stupid to assume I could do it forever. I still had two more years to go before he graduated.

While I was shocked, he didn't seem to be, proving he knew I had been here all along. God, I was such a fucking idiot.

"Zayden," he said. "I knew you were here at the school, but I never expected you to hang out with these... types of kids."

"You knew I was here the whole time?"

"Yep. You clearly thought you were doing a good job avoiding me under those hoodies, so I avoided you too."

All those residual feelings I had for him since he had such an important role in my life washed away and morphed into anger. Did he turn into a fucking bully too? Why was that necessary? He was the popular kid. He didn't need the attention.

"What do you know of it, Duncan? You hadn't seen me since the beginning of freshman year... your freshman year. Things change."

He stepped close to me as his friends backed away, staying quiet. I glanced at them, untrusting, then back at Duncan. We were about the same height now.

"Has it been a year and a half already? What happened to you that day at the beach when your mom took you away? I never saw you again."

My fucking eyes watered, and I quickly glanced away as the memory slammed into me. All that pot I'd smoked and feeling good was instantly gone.

Duncan took another step toward me, and I backed away. That didn't stop him from getting closer.

He scanned my face, then down my body. "It's... strangely good to see you. I didn't expect it to be, despite seeing you hide in the hallways. You... look so good."

What was the point of this discussion? We weren't together anymore, and I would never go back with him if he hung out with those losers. "Why are you with these jerks? You're gay and open. You, of all people, should care more and understand."

"I'm not their mama."

"You could be a role model being the popular kid at school."

All my friends said nothing as Duncan, and I had our back-and-forth. This wasn't what I expected. I honestly had no idea what to expect, especially with him looking like he was still into me, making me uncomfortable. I liked Noah now. The two boys just didn't compare. Duncan had charisma and was fun and confident. Noah was sweet, kind, empathetic, and funny. He liked everyone.

Duncan dragged the backs of his fingers across my cheek a little more intimately than I'd liked. As if we were still boyfriends. When I pulled my head back, fingers weaved through mine. Protecting. Claiming.

"Zay doesn't like you touching him, Duncan," Noah said.

Duncan dropped his hand and looked directly at me, holding hands with Noah.

"Is this your boyfriend, Zay?"

"No," I said.

"Yes," Noah contradicted at the same time.

He huffed a laugh. "Which is it? Now that I see Zay, I'm thinking about dating him again."

Shit, shit, shit.

His wanting to be my boyfriend again was the least of my problems. My heart raced because he had just outed me right in front of everyone. Sure, I was sort of out during that short period we dated, but it seemed everyone forgot. Or at least they never said anything. And I certainly hadn't told my fucking friends. Even Noah didn't know.

I shook off Noah's hand and glared at both boys.

"I wasn't out, you fucker," I said to Duncan. Then I glared at Noah. "You have no right." God, I hated Noah frowning and looking sad, but dammit, I didn't ask him to do that. Duncan outed me. Noah outed me. Only *I* got to do that.

Duncan smirked. "So, you're not dating him. Good. Besides, you've been out since I outed you with our first kiss in front of the entire school."

My hands fisted, ready to deck him. "So it was just a game to you? You did that on purpose to out me? I liked you. I trusted you."

"It wasn't a game, but facts are facts. You've been out for a while now, Zay."

I poked Duncan hard on his chest. "Not to my friends. I wasn't ready to say anything. Do you have any fucking idea what I went through when my mom found out! Do you! And now everyone fucking knows."

At least he had the intelligence to appear guilty.

"What happened?"

"You shouldn't have fucking said anything! It wasn't your fucking business! You had no right! Fuck, fuck, fuck." I paced in a circle as panic filled me, unable to look at anyone or face my friends. My heart raced as a thousand scenarios flashed in my mind about what would happen now, and none of them were good.

"Zay, I'm—" Duncan started.

"Don't! Don't you dare!"

I had to get out of there, not wanting to see the disappointment on my friends' faces. I lied by omission because of my fear. They'd either hate me for being what I am or hate me because I didn't trust them enough with my secret. Either way, I was fucked. On top of it, what my parents did to me that day filled me with so much hurt and fear.

So I ran.

CHAPTER ELEVEN

Noah

I HAD TO GET A RIDE BACK TO THE SURF SHOP FROM MASON SINCE ZAY took off without me in the truck. God, my poor bestie. He looked rough after facing off with Duncan. I often wondered why Zay would be under his hoodies sometimes in the halls at school, and now I knew. He thought I didn't notice it happened whenever Duncan was around, but I never asked him about it. I wondered if something bad had happened to my bro, but he never talked about his life before living at the surf shop. He was a damned bank vault. I tried not to push him and to respect his boundaries.

Honestly, I never would've imagined Zay and Duncan together. I just assumed Duncan had bullied Zay or something. The two boys were completely different. But what did I know? My bro was probably a different kid then.

I shouldn't have pretended to be his boyfriend. I'd only meant to protect Zay because I saw how much he tried to get away from Duncan. Maybe if I were his boyfriend, Duncan would've backed off. I didn't think I'd outed him because Duncan had already done that. What a dick.

To be fair, it looked like the other dude still liked Zay. But when he touched my bestie's face, weird jealousy and anger took over. That was new. Did I really try to help Zay? Or did I react from jealousy? Staking my claim like some stupid caveman? It wasn't like I had any claim to Zay. We weren't like boyfriends or anything, and me wishing it didn't make it so.

But now that I knew he was gay or whatever, my interest in him blew up. Seriously… mind fucking blown, and my crush went from a little pining to all-out want. I felt safe telling him about me. Since he was out now, my plan was to out myself to him. That would make my bro feel better, right? And maybe I'd have a puny chance of having him. Ugh. It's hard when your love interest is your best bro. It could risk our friendship.

Instead of heading inside, I shoved my hands in my pockets, tossed off my sandals, and headed toward the water. Zay liked to sit in the sand and listen to the waves and shit when he was stressed or needed to be alone.

Though it was dark, the full moon cast a glow over Zay, sitting cross-legged, staring at the water.

He was my feral Zay again, tightly wound, and who knew how he'd react? So I slowly approached him and quietly sat next to him. We needed to talk, and he needed to stop running, even from his head.

"Go away, Noah."

I leaned back on my hands in the sand and stretched out my legs. "Nope."

"I don't want to talk."

"Dude, we've been besties for a while now, and you haven't told me anything about yourself. You like never talk. I literally know nothin' about you other than the type of guy you are. Who's quite amazing, by the way. I've told you *my* embarrassing shit. You can trust me."

"I know…"

"I'm… sorry Duncan outed you, brah."

"Yeah… Are you… do you hate me?"

I scoffed. "Seriously? If you think I'd hate you for being gay or liking Duncan or whatever, then you don't fuckin' know me, bro."

He sighed and made piles of sand in front of him. "You're right… I'm sorry. I just get so—"

"I know. You get wrapped up all in your head."

"Yeah."

I bumped his shoulder. "Would it make you feel better if I told you a secret of mine?"

"You've told me lots of secrets, and I still can't…"

"It's okay, dude. I get it."

"God, you're such a good friend, Noah. More patient than I deserve. Fine… what's your secret?"

I gave him a big smile and bumped him again. "I'm bisexual."

He finally looked at me with wide eyes that glimmered in the moonlight. "Seriously?"

"Yep."

I breathed out a sigh. "So am I."

"Dude! See, we were made to be like best buds. I haven't told anyone, either. I dunno. It's not an easy thing coming out, even if you trust that person, so I totally get it."

Zay picked up a seashell and threw it far into the water. "I didn't even know I was bisexual. I mean, I liked girls and didn't think much about dudes. Not until Duncan. He asked me to be his boyfriend one day, and I just said yes. He was so cute, and I really liked him. How did such a popular boy like someone who was a nobody?"

"Brah, you're not a nobody."

"You know what I mean. I'm not Mr. Popular. Anyway, not long after, he just kissed me right there at school in front of everyone, essentially outing me. But no one gave a shit, ya know? Then again, he was the popular boy. I thought it was so awesome. I could like boys or girls out in the open, and no one would care. It made me feel brave and strong. God, I fell hard for him."

He picked up another shell and tossed it. I waited him out, giving him time to gather his thoughts. Shit, I was just happy he was talking about himself. But then he stopped throwing shit and wrapped his arms around his folded knees.

"We were at the beach one day, surrounded by friends. His friends, really. I was having so much fun getting to know people, having a boyfriend, and surfing. I had forgotten the time, so Mom came to find me and bring me home."

I had an idea of where this was going. His mom didn't know. My mom didn't know I was bisexual, either. Not that I cared that much about what she thought, but I didn't want to listen to what she thought about it, either. I told her very little about myself, and she never cared enough to ask.

"My... parents are... were... super religious. They taught me early on that homosexuality was a sin, but honestly, I never really paid attention. Going to church, reading the bible, praying... it was all just chores to me. Not once did I look at others and think badly about them. Even when Duncan kissed me, all I thought about was that I just liked it and wanted more. It didn't feel wrong. How could that be evil or a sin, right?"

"Exactly, bro."

"God, they were so angry, No. Mom called Duncan a sinner in front of everyone. I was fucking mortified. Then she made me pray and pray until Dad got home from work, but I didn't. I was so scared. What were they going to do to me? Little did I imagine what would happen. I had thought I'd be yelled at and grounded for a long time."

"Dude, you didn't go through that... conversion shit, did you?" My heart pounded at the idea. I'd heard horror stories, unable to imagine my Zay going through that.

He shook his head. "No, I'm not sure if what I went through was any better, though. I got angry with them, Noah. I told them there was nothing wrong with me. That was the wrong thing to say. In return, they kicked me out of the house."

"Wait, what? Dude, you were what? Fifteen?"

"Yeah."

"Bastards! What did you do?"

"What else could I do? I left."

"But... how'd you survive?"

"The only way I knew how. Surfing. I had my board, and I'd teach whenever I could. I'd sit on the beach all day, waiting for anyone willing to shell out some cash for a quick lesson. I also did a couple of local competitions, but I only won one. They helped me earn enough to tide me over for a while. I had money and a place... sort of. I'd found this old, abandoned concrete shed. It was the size of a bedroom, I guess, but it had a lock, and I lived that way for a year."

"Was that when you finally came to live at the surf shop? Did Kel find you?" He lived on the streets for a year? No wonder he was so skinny when we met. Even if he could feed himself, it probably wasn't nearly enough.

"Not quite. Everything was fine... if you could call a kid living on the streets, fine. At least I wasn't starving and had shelter. Then my surfboard broke on the lava rocks while training on the Pipeline for the next competition. My money maker was gone."

He hunched over, staring at the sand, so I took a chance to stroke his back in soothing circles.

"I pulled out the last of my money and headed toward Ohana Surfing Club because it wasn't that far to walk to. When I got there, no one was around. I was looking at the boards, intending to buy one, and I needed a good one to win, but fuck... they were too expensive. I didn't have enough cash. Still, no one came around, so I just took the board I wanted and ran. But a few days later, the cops found me and arrested me."

"Bro, no way. I can't see you stealing, but I totally get it. So you stole from Kel and Jon? How'd they not get pissed, man? I mean, they're cool and all, but still."

"I don't know. I still ask that every day. Kel came to the police station, and he had a long talk with me. The deal was I had to serve community service to work off the board, but once I did, I gotta keep it. They... fostered me, too; otherwise, I would've been tossed into the system. Well, being with them was still in the system, but it was more than I could've hoped for. It took me like two seconds to agree to their terms."

"Kel and Jon are amazeballs. They're so nice."

Zay was still hunched over when his body suddenly trembled and shook under my hand that still rested his back. My heart ached for him as he cried. I was a big-time crier and hated it sometimes. The curse of feeling other people's pain. But I didn't mind doing it for my bro.

"They *are* amazeballs. I... sometimes wonder if I deserve it."

"Don't say that. Of course, you deserve it. You're such a good person and my bestie. And I'm not besties with just anyone."

I pulled him into a hug as his tears soaked through my shirt. He finally wrapped his arms around me and rested his head on my shoulder. "I hate them, No. I hate them so much. All this happened because I wanted to love a boy. How is it wrong to love someone?"

"It's not, boo."

"I hate them, but... I miss them too. They're still my parents. Does that make me weird?"

"Nah, bra... not weird at all. I feel the same about my mom sometimes. I sometimes think even when our parents are shit, we want them proud of us or somethin'."

When I sniffed, he sat up and looked at me. The tears glistened on his face from the moonlight, and I hurt so much for my dude.

We rested our foreheads together with our arms still wrapped around each other. I'd never felt this close to Zay, and not just because of the little distance we shared. But deep inside. I wanted to wrap him up in my arms and keep him safe and happy forever. But what I *really* wanted to do was kiss him. More than anything. Would he freak out now that I told him my secret? Would he even want me that way? He'd been so jumpy about his sexuality earlier, so who knew?

I nuzzled my nose against his to get his attention. He opened his eyes and looked at me. God, we were so close as his warm breath puffed against my face. My dick stirred in my shorts, reminding me of that day I rubbed one off in front of him. I still couldn't figure out why I did that, and I never told him I saw how hard he had gotten when he watched. I definitely noticed. It was hot as fuck, even if it mortified me afterward.

I nudged my mouth toward his, and he drew closer. Yes. This was it. I'd finally get to kiss my Zay. My best bro.

But it was like cold water in the face when he instantly pulled back and shook his head. "I can't," he said, standing up and walking away, leaving me disappointed and hard as a rock.

I could have sworn he liked me more than a friend. The signs were there, but he was fighting it. Probably still afraid, even if I did know the truth about him. My feral animal. I was going to have to be patient and slowly work up to more with him. Hopefully, he'd get past his fear because I really wanted Zay more than anything or anyone. And I think he wanted me too.

CHAPTER TWELVE

Noah

"So, the plan is to kiss me and tell me you've liked me for a while now. You've got to make it believable," I explained to Suzi over video chat.

She rolled her eyes. "Dude, Zay's not gonna go for it."

I finally outed myself to my friends since I told Zay. It felt good to get everything off my chest to everyone, but mostly I did it for Zay so that he wouldn't be so alone. They didn't care, and I didn't know why I expected them to. It was still scary as shit, though. Everyone had a damned opinion on who you could and couldn't love.

"He definitely will."

"Noah, just ask him for a fucking kiss."

"We almost kissed once, sis, and he ran. I need to approach this another way. I know he likes me, but he's afraid. My bro only needs a… nudge." I didn't tell her Zay's story since it wasn't mine to tell, but since they knew he was bisexual, I didn't feel like I said something I shouldn't have. Plus, I needed help to get Zay's walls to crumble. I mean, he wasn't mine, and seeing Duncan touch Zay had my jealousy in a rage, so maybe jealousy could blow up Zay's defenses.

I'd be lying to myself if I ignored the worry that Duncan would eventually convince Zay to be his boyfriend again. I couldn't have that. Zay was mine… or would be. Hopefully.

Maybe.

"Okay, so we go to this party, and you want me to start flirting with you."

"Yep."

"Then I try to kiss you, and you're expecting Zay to intervene and stop it?"

"Correctomundo."

"Dude, this isn't gonna work. What if he gets pissed at me? What if he says fuck it and lets us kiss? You need to talk to him, brah."

"Ugh, I can't. He's already twitchy."

"You're going to make him more twitchy, No."

"That's the plan."

She scratched her head and shook her head. "Dude… whatever."

"Trust me. It'll work."

"If you say so."

I hung up the phone with Suzi and headed back inside to get ready for the party. After showering, I dressed in an old vintage T and some boardshorts and did my best to fix my hair. I probably needed it cut soon as it fell down close to my jaw. I put on a couple of surfer necklaces to finish the look.

When I headed into our bedroom, Zay had his shirt off with his back to me. He'd put on a lot of muscle and, in the past school year, had grown taller and broader. My bro was sexy as fuck. I pulled my eyes away from his strong back and grabbed two blunts out of my underwear drawer that Mason had made for me.

"I'm not sure I wanna go, dude," Zay said, rolling his shirt over his head.

"You gotta go. I need my bestie bro there." *Please don't change your mind.*

I put my hands together to beg and plead, giving him puppy dog eyes. When he laughed, I knew I had him. Shit, I was just grateful it wasn't awkward around us after we almost kissed.

"How can I say no to that face?" he asked.

"Exactly! I'm adorable, brah."

He laughed again, making my heart flutter. I put my hand to my chest when he wasn't looking and smiled.

Please let this plan work.

We arrived at the small house crowded with kids and thumping with loud music. The party was fucking pumping. Some dude in his junior year in our school threw it when his parents went out of town, so there was alcohol, too. I grabbed a beer though I didn't plan on getting drunk. Never drunk. But Zay stuck with soda since he drove.

I tried not to stare at how good he looked. He had his usual thrift store vintage T-shirt, but he wore ripped jeans that fit snugly around his perfect ass and perfect package, not that I'd seen his package yet. He towered at over six feet now, too. And as soon as we walked in, all the girls stared at him, whispering and giggling. They'd been doing that a lot lately at school, too, since he bulked up. It wasn't only his body, but those intense eyes and chiseled face that made me flutter like one of those girls whenever he pinned me with those eyes spun from fucking gold.

I must have sighed like some fangirl because he looked at me with a raised brow. Before I got all flustered, Suzi ran toward us.

"Boo! There you are," she said, giving a hug to Zay, then she turned and pulled me close to her and gave me a peck on the cheek that lingered long enough to show it wasn't quite a friendly kiss.

Let the games begin!

I excused myself for this petty behavior being only fifteen. Fine, I'd be sixteen soon, but still—hormones and shit. And this was Zay we were talking about. The cutest boy in school and my best bro.

Zay scrunched his brows at Suzi but said nothing. Okay, so we'd have to work harder on this.

I lit up a blunt and stood extra close to Suzi with my arm wrapped around her, and passed the blunt to her. Again, Zay looked back and forth at us, totally fucking unfazed. Ugh. Then again, I was a touchy dude. Maybe my bro just brushed it off.

I leaned into her and pretended to whisper something, and she giggled in perfect timing.

"Dude, what's going on with you two?" Nhan asked from behind me. If I didn't know better, he looked kinda pissed at me. What was that about?

Great, he was about to foil my plans.

"Nothin', brah," I said.

He folded his arms with a furrowed brow. "It sure doesn't look like nothing."

Then again, this could help because Zay just wasn't catching on. Before Suzi was about to lean in and pretend to kiss me, someone called Zay's name, and I instantly recognized the voice.

Hell no. Duncan does not get to draw my bro's attention away.

Duncan stood in front of Zay, who was suddenly tense, but he didn't run like the last time we saw him.

"What do you want, Duncan?"

"Can we... talk privately?"

I untangled myself from Suzi, getting that now-familiar feeling of jealousy. Duncan was beautiful, smart, and popular. All the things I wasn't. Not that I was stupid or ugly, but I was more like the boy next door kinda dude. Duncan was like model worthy. And I definitely wasn't popular, though I didn't think my bestie really cared about that stuff.

"Why?" Zay asked.

"Please?"

Fuck. Duncan was going to be trouble for me. I could feel it.

"Fine," Zay said. He looked back at me and then at Suzi, frowning. "I'll be back."

Duncan led my boy outside, and I handed the blunt over to Suzi and stupidly followed without being seen. It was like I had no will of my own. I had to hear what Duncan wanted to tell Zay. If it was to get back together, I was gonna be super upset.

Jeez, where'd this possessive, jealous shit come from? I was supposed to make Zay that way, not me.

They walked over toward the side of the house where there were only a few kids, so I stopped at the edge of the house to eavesdrop like a creepy stalker. Not like. I *was* being a creepy stalker.

Zay stood with folded arms in his defensive posture. "What do you want?"

"To say I'm sorry."

"For?"

"Saying that shit about you in front of your friends. You're right. I need to do better. I want to."

"Good. You should because kids look up to you."

"You're right."

"Is that all?"

"Come on, Zay. Cut me some slack. I'm trying here. I know we weren't together long, but when you left, I thought about you a lot, like what happened to you? Were you okay? I would've talked to you sooner, but you were obviously avoiding me."

Zay's body relaxed, which I very much didn't want.

"It's embarrassing. I don't want to talk about it."

"Because you missed a full year of school?"

"Yeah."

"So you didn't go to school at all?"

Zay shook his head. "It's why I had to repeat the ninth grade."

"Did your parents do that to you?"

"Look, I don't... want to talk about this, okay? Let's just move on. We can be friends, but—"

"I want to be more than friends, Zay."

Tell him no. Tell him no.

Zay said nothing, staring at the ground and kicking dirt with his shoe. My heart pounded, and I swallowed hard. Was he going to give in? No, he couldn't. Zay was mine. Not Duncan's. Duncan had his chance.

Duncan lifted Zay's chin up and slowly leaned in to kiss him. My heart stopped, and before I could even think about what I was doing, I rushed over there, grabbed Zay by the shoulders, and spun him around. I placed my hands on his face with wide golden eyes and pulled him into a kiss.

My Zay. Not Duncan's.

That kiss belonged to me.

Hello, possessive, needy, controlling Noah. Nice to meet you.

My bro didn't pull away or get angry. Instead, Zay closed his eyes, wrapped his arms around me, and eased into our kiss. His arms were warm and comforting, like a familiar, old blanket that reminded you of home and safety.

I had yet to kiss anyone, so I was sort of a noob, but Zay had, and he slowly took over. And when he inserted his smooth, warm tongue into my mouth, I died.

I wanted to cry. To laugh. My emotions were all over the place, but the strongest emotion was relief. I took a massive risk, and it paid off. I whimpered and grunted in his mouth like a weirdo.

My first kiss with Zay.

My Zay. My Zay.

I clung tightly to him, fisting the back of his shirt, afraid if I let go, he'd realize our mistake and go back to Duncan.

"Are you seriously dating that... stoner, Zay?" Duncan asked, pulling Zay away from me. No, not pulling. Yanking. Well, it felt like it, anyway. Like those scratching noises from records when they skip that they use in movies all the time.

Zay looked me dead in the eye, and I died again when he said, "Yes."

My bro, now my bae, turned to face Duncan and put a hand on his shoulder. "I'm sorry, Ducan. It's just... it's been a long time. Noah's amazing and my best friend. He's helped me through a lot of shit and has always been there for me when I needed it most."

Duncan gave a small smile and nodded. "It's cool. Good luck, you two." With that, he left Zay and me alone to figure out our shit. I was sure a talk was coming. Yes, he kissed back but would he be pissed now that he'd had time to think about it?

"I'm sorry as fuck this took me so long, Noah. Thanks for pulling my head out of my ass."

Wait. What?

He grabbed my face and pulled me into another heart-stopping kiss. His mouth was still sweet from the soda he drank, and he smelled like deodorant and all things Zay. He had his own unique smell I could never describe but I always tried to inhale whenever he was close. It had an earthy smell, like the forest after a hard rain.

"You're welcome," I said when we came up for air. My brain was set to stupid mode right now.

He gave me a big, bright, and beautiful smile. Then he burst into a laugh and lifted me off my feet, holding me tight.

"And thank god you did. Not because of Duncan, but I thought you and Suzi were going to get together, and I was fucking losing my ever-lovin' mind."

Ha! My evil plan had worked, after all.

I wrapped my arms around his neck when he set me back down on the ground, though I was still floating on my high that I got to kiss Zay.

"I tried to make you jealous. Stupid, but I wanted you to see me more than your bro, dude."

He smiled again, not mad at me at all. Thank fuck. "Well, it worked," he said.

"I thought it backfired since it was Duncan that made me super jealous."

"Good. I should probably tell you I've always seen you as more than my bestie bro," he said. "I've always had a crush on you, No."

I pressed a hand to my heart and smiled, though I think my brain wanted me to cry a little, or it wanted to dance, or to short-circuit. It was so hard to tell. "Aww. Me too. So, you're not mad?"

"Nah, not mad."

"Good. Wanna dance?"

"I fucking hate dancing, but I'll do it for you. But before we go, another kiss first."

"Yes, please."

The third kiss was no less sweet than the first. I just followed his lead as we explored our mouths and tongues. The scruff on his face made my guy stir to life. I didn't know why it was so hot, but it was. Maybe because he was so close to being a man.

"How stupid of me to think I could resist you, No. The only thing that held me back was my fears from what my parents did to me but no more."

I was seriously melting. God, this boy.

I grabbed Zay's hand and held it. We've held hands many times as friends, but this was our first time as boyfriends. And just like that, with one kiss, we were together, and I'd never let go.

I wasn't familiar with this possessive side of me. This need to hold on and claim him to the world as mine, mine, mine. But I just rolled with it, which ended up working out in the end.

We headed inside the house toward the cleared-out living room that was converted into a dancefloor. I didn't know what song was playing, but it didn't matter as long as I was dancing with Zay. It wasn't a slow song, but that didn't stop us from swaying to the music with his arms wrapped protectively around me and my arms holding onto his neck. I rested my head on his shoulder, facing his neck so I could breathe him in as we moved.

While my heart beat wildly, I was completely at ease with him. This was how it should've always been. We were a perfect fit.

I looked up at Zay. "This doesn't bother you? Dancin' in front of all these kids?"

He shook his head. "It would have bothered me a couple of weeks ago, but my fear was just leftover shit. My parents aren't here. They aren't in my life anymore, and they have no say. The rest of these kids? I don't give a shit about them anymore. I only care about what you think... and our friends."

I bit my bottom lip and smiled. That meant back at school, we wouldn't need to hide and pretend to be something we weren't. We could be open. Kids would probably tease us and maybe bully us, but as long as we were together, we could deal.

Someone bumped into us hard, nearly knocking us apart. Speaking of bullies. I scowled, and Zay growled that vibrated into my chest, which had my nuts tightening. I loved his protective side.

"Isn't this fucking adorable? Stoners finding love—"

We turned to find one of Duncan's loser friends who'd always picked on us, but instead of having to confront the asshole, and to our surprise, Duncan grabbed him and put him in a headlock.

"Enough. Leave them the fuck alone. You know damn well I'm gay. You bullying them means you're bullying me. And you don't want to bully me because I will knock your shit out."

"Hey! No offense, man. Whatever."

The boy left, leaving Zay and me jaw-dropped. Duncan gave us a curt nod and walked away.

"I guess the dude isn't so bad after all. He seems to have listened to you," I said.

"So it seems. Good."

I pressed myself up to Zay again, holding him tight as we swayed to the music again.

Best day ever.

CHAPTER THIRTEEN

Zayden

Our first kiss happened three weeks ago. I'd never known Noah to take control or to be possessive before. He was the most laid-back dude I knew. But I loved that side of him. He definitely had more balls than I did. As soon as he pressed his lips to mine, any residual fear I had from exposing myself again washed away. Everything vanished, leaving only Noah and me kissing. It felt right. It felt perfect. Remind me why I was so afraid.

The school year ended, and Noah's sixteenth birthday had passed, so we could relax and just focus on surfing, making money, and making out. We curled up in my bed just in our underwear, watching TV late Saturday night. Noah was snuggled into me with a leg draped over mine and swirling his finger over my bare chest. He was my perfect other half, all nestled in like he'd always belonged here, in my arms, pressed up against my body.

It took no time at all to fall into each other as a couple. Maybe because we'd been friends for almost a year, but I also believed we became such good friends because we were made for each other. It was corny, but I couldn't help but believe that. We fell into each other like the sun and the moon. Two different personalities revolving around each other for balance and righting the world. Like we made a whole person when we were together. He was so easygoing and patient, and my complete opposite.

I kissed his messy blond head, and he looked up at me with a sweet smile and tropical green eyes that I never got tired of staring into. I slid down the bed and faced him, running fingers through his hair, then dragged them along his necklaces and down his chest as we stared at each other. My hand moved to the back of his head and gently fisted his hair to pull him into a kiss. Noah turned into an amazing kisser with the perfect amount of tongue, lips that weren't overly firm, but not sloppy-soft, and there was very little spit.

He slipped his knee between my legs, and I groaned as I got hard. Noah must have noticed because he smiled on my lips.

"Someone woke up," he said, making my face burn.

"Ugh. My dick loves to betray me at the worst times."

He snorted a laugh and wiggled his knee, making me groan again. "I think your dick is behaving exactly as he's supposed to."

Apparently, Noah found pleasure in torturing me. We hadn't fooled around beyond making out yet, but if he kept this up, I wouldn't have a choice but to relieve us, or hide out in the bathroom yet again, which was growing fucking old.

I also discovered Noah was the bolder one between us. He had no problems sneaking in kisses or cuddles whenever he felt like it. But that shouldn't have surprised me after that day he rubbed one off in front of me. Or claimed me in a kiss at the party. It was probably my fears trying to force their way in, but he always put me at ease. Noah was good at that.

He wiggled my dick some more, making it ache. "Keep this up, and I'm going to make you give my guy some relief."

"Promises. Promises."

I raised a brow and laughed, but my smile faded when he grabbed my hand and placed it between his legs. My heart thumped in my chest, and I struggled to find breath as I traced his length with my fingers over his briefs. He didn't feel too big or too wide. He was just right. Perfect. Just like everything else about Noah. There was a spot on his briefs that was cold and wet. God, why was that so hot?

Noah nuzzled his face in my throat and spread his legs a bit more. He gently thrust into my hand, silently asking to be touched more. His breath turned to pants and was warm on my skin. My hand trembled a little as I cupped him. This was the first time I'd ever touched a dick that wasn't mine. The heat emitting from his underwear was fucking unreal.

"More," he whispered. How could one word sound so needy, making me want to give Noah everything he'd ever ask for?

I swallowed and slipped my fingers underneath the waistband, grazing the coarse hair. Though it was covered, I knew it was blond because I remembered from our time in the bathroom when I couldn't take my eyes off of him stroking himself. My hand covered his length again, and the tips of my fingers grazed the soft, velvety skin. Noah gently thrust into my hand again, seeking more friction.

"Grab me... please." Again, such simple words. Unafraid to ask for what he wanted and needed. Brave words that I didn't have.

I wrapped my fingers around him and slowly tugged.

"Oh, god," he groaned when my thumb grazed over his tip. "Please, Zay... more."

How could I deny him when he asked so sweetly and breathy? Even if he hadn't, I still would've given him whatever he wanted. I lacked experience, but I used whatever I did to myself on him.

It barely took any time at all before Noah's body stilled and held his breath as wet warmth covered my hand. He gripped my hair, pulling it tight as he chased his orgasm with sweet-sounding grunts, moans, and whimpers. The entire thing didn't take but a couple of minutes, but it was a beautiful moment. That I gave him so much pleasure made me feel powerful, yet it was intimate and gentle too.

"Dude... your hand is so much better than mine."

I blew out a laugh. "Maybe it's just someone else doing it."

"Nah, just you, brah."

Noah rolled onto his back and slipped off his damp briefs, cleaned himself off with them, and tossed them on the floor. I swallowed hard seeing him completely naked for the first time, and he was totally unshy about it. His tan skin was smooth all over except where he wore his shorts, with whiter skin on his thighs. He had tight abs, and while his dick grew soft now, it was still beautiful.

I ached something awful for him, but I'd worry about it later. I'd rub one off in the bathroom tonight when he went to sleep. But my bold Noah had other plans. He tugged the band of my briefs and pulled them off, leaving me a little vulnerable and exposed. I had yet to be naked around him. While he was bold and not modest, I wasn't. It took everything I had not to cover myself up, though my dick didn't seem to care, craving attention.

"So pretty, Zay Bae," he said, calling me by the nickname he'd recently given me. I remembered when he first said it, giggling at the rhyme he made up.

My face turned to flame as I stared at the ceiling. And when he touched me, my back arched for more like I had no control over my body, making my face burn more. I tried to be brave like him and not hide my face in my pillows. Noah lay on his side, still naked, as he explored between my legs. He didn't rush to get me off. Instead, he touched, watched, and pressed his nose into the crook of my thigh to breathe me in. I couldn't take my eyes off his confident explorations.

I nearly jolted off the bed when he swiped his finger over the tip.

He looked up at me, filled with worry. "Is this okay?"

"Yep," I squeaked out.

His thumb swiped me again, and soon I was wrapped around wet warmth. My eyes widened as I watched him looking up at me. I nearly blew right then. Whatever he was doing to me was arousing as hell, but I didn't think it was really his intention. I think he just wanted to learn and figure stuff out. I was his blank canvas, and he, the paintbrush. Every stroke of paint revealed a picture. And I was all for it. But it was also fucking killing me, like he was teasing the fuck out of me. It was torture, and my nuts grew painfully tight.

"Fuck!" I cried out when Noah fisted me. My stomach was tight from holding back and keeping from blowing already, but I wasn't sure for how long I could hold it.

He rested his head on my stomach to watch as he played with me. Now I became his experiment, seeing how I reacted to what he did to me. It was so fucking hot yet so fucking painful because I wanted and needed to let go. Despite our inexperience, I had a feeling Noah was going to open my eyes to a whole new world sexually. He was fearless.

Fingers explored everywhere, then he lifted my dick and moved it around, and I would have laughed had I not been so fucking turned on.

"You're bigger than me," he said.

His comment calmed my nerves. My hand carded through his hair. "You're beautiful and perfect."

He rested his chin on my stomach and smiled up at me. "So are you."

He finally quit toying with me and gave me what I craved. He stroked and tugged, and if I reacted to what he did, he'd do it again and again. Noah paid close attention to all my reactions.

My back arched, and my body stiffened for the big release, making a mess all over my stomach and his hand. "Holy shit," I gasped. It was the strongest orgasm I'd ever had which probably had a lot to do with his foreplay.

"Whoa, Zay Bae. That was fucking hot."

I laughed as he swirled a finger in the wetness pooling on my stomach. And to my shock, he ran his tongue over my abs.

Holy.

Fucking.

Hell.

Slayed.

I was fucking slayed.

Where had he learned to do that? Or did he just follow his instincts?

I must have looked shocked because he turned red and gazed up at me with guilty eyes. "Did I do… something wrong?"

I shook my head. "No. Just… surprising. But it was so sexy."

He bit his bottom lip and smiled, crawled up to me, and kissed me. I tasted myself for the first time on his tongue. It was salty and earthy. With our naked bodies pressed up against each other, my guy fluttered back to life. Or tried to.

"This was fun. I want to do more," he said.

I brushed his bangs away to look at his beautiful green eyes behind dark blond lashes. God, this boy was perfect in every way. "I do, too."

Noah and I curled up on the sofa in the kitchen Sunday morning, wearing only our underwear, which seemed like our typical attire when we weren't working or surfing. We each had a controller and hunted opponents in an online gun game.

We walked into a building, cleared out baddies, and watched each other's backs. Someone kept firing at me, and I couldn't find them. My health was running too low before Noah took them out.

"Thanks, No."

"I gotcha, boo."

We almost made it to the checkpoint when someone took me out. Noah was trying to revive my character when he was killed, too.

"Dammit!"

"Wanna play again?" he asked.

"Nah. I'm video gamed out."

We put our controllers away and turned off the TV and game console.

"Whatcha wanna do?" He asked in a playful voice and waggled his brows.

I laughed. We'd gotten each other off for the first time last night, but he wanted more already. Hell, so did I.

I plopped back on the couch and pounced on him. My fingers found their mark on his ribs, and I wiggled them, making him giggle. "Stop, stop, stop."

"Nope."

Noah thrashed under me and tried to get me off, but I was stronger.

"Brah! You're... evil..." he gasped through his laughs.

"Aww, I'll be nice."

"Thanks, I'd rather have some other type of fun." He wiggled his hips, which made our dicks rub together.

Fuck. Touching our dicks together did weird things to me. I suddenly got all hot and tingly straight up my spine. Then it gave me an idea. I shimmied my briefs down over my ass and to my thighs, then pulled Noah's down too. I laughed at his broad smile and wide, hungry eyes.

I propped myself up on my hands and rolled my hips to rub us together. The heat, smoothness, fuck... the sensation was impossible to describe. What a difference when it was skin on skin, but it still wasn't enough. Apparently, Noah had a remedy for that by fisting us together. I thrust in his hand as he squeezed us, and... oh, that was nice. His dick was smooth as silk as he glided against mine.

"Dude, I like this," he said.

"Fuck, me too."

I kept moving, and he stroked us along until completion. I was the first to spill, but Noah followed shortly after. The heat of his dick against mine was amazing as it pulsed. That was when I imagined what it would've been like with him inside me. We weren't ready for that yet, but that didn't keep me from imagining it.

I still hovered over him, but my arms shook from the effort, and my muscles grew numb after that strong climax. But I leaned down and kissed him, shoving my tongue in as if I owned his mouth. I sucked on his tongue, and his hands forked through my hair. When we pulled away, we were both out of breath and a sticky mess.

His eyes were hooded from being blissed out with sexed hair and a crooked smile. So fucking cute.

I grabbed the paper towels sitting on the coffee table from lunch earlier and cleaned us up. And right when we pulled up our briefs, Kel walked in.

My heart froze, and Noah's eyes went wide with a bright red face. My face probably matched his.

Kel walked over to the microwave, not even noticing us, threw a container in there, then pressed start. Before he saw us, he leaned against the counter. He looked over at us and almost said something but stopped, eyeing us back and forth. Back and forth. As if trying to compute what he was seeing. You could see the moment he figured it out, and my gut plummeted.

Would he get mad? I hadn't said anything to him yet about Noah and me. We weren't related or even foster brothers, but Noah practically lived here, and we were co-workers. I wasn't sure what the rules were, but maybe I should've asked.

"Uh, when did this happen?" Kel asked, pointing at each of us.

Noah and I looked at each other, and he shrugged. "A few weeks ago, but we'd been crushin' hard for a while," Noah said.

"Cool. Cool. Okay, then. So, did you two… You know what? I don't want to know. Just be… safe. Be careful."

When his lunch dinged in the microwave, he pulled it out and took it with him back downstairs to his office… probably. He usually ate in the kitchen.

When he left, Noah and I burst out in laughter. Poor flustered Kel.

CHAPTER FOURTEEN

Noah

Zay and I climbed out of the truck in the parking lot at school. We tossed our backpacks over our shoulders, and he walked over to me, holding out his hand. I looked up at him and smiled, looking at the sweetest boy I knew. This was Zay's way of telling the entire school we were together, and he didn't give a shit what anyone thought. I couldn't tell you how happy it made me that he wasn't afraid anymore. I tangled my fingers with his as we headed toward our sophomore year.

We had U.S. History together, which was pretty cool. At least we had one class.

When we walked into the school, everyone looked taller and older.

Amazing what the sun and a few months did for growth. Zay and I grew a little too. Me more than him since he did more growing the last school year. I was a whopping five feet nine now and still not nearly as tall as Zay and probably never would be.

This summer had been amazing. The best summer of my life. The best year of my life. We did so much surfing and hanging out with friends, and I had no idea I'd love teaching surfing lessons as much as I did. It was a dream job, and I seriously wouldn't want to do anything else.

But because I had such a good summer, I felt more guilt than normal about not spending more time with Mom, and Zay kept reassuring me I didn't have to care for her night and day. Maybe she'd pick herself up and get her shit together on her own. I wasn't so sure.

I called her every other day. The calls were short, and she wasn't always nice, but at least she was doing okay and still working. I still visited twice a week to bring her groceries, make her meals, and pay any bills.

Sometimes I wished I didn't have her in my life and that Kel and Jon also fostered me. But then more horrible guilt would hit me for even thinking such a thing.

Zay and I hung out with our friends by our lockers until the bell rang, holding hands.

"See ya later, Zay Bae," I said.

He pulled me against him and gave me a little kiss. In front of everyone. Was I still a dude if I swooned?

"See ya, No."

We headed in different directions, and I probably wouldn't get to see him again until lunch. Then we had sixth-period class together.

Ugh. I was going to hate having P.E. first thing in the morning. I shoved my thermos full of coffee and my backpack into the gym locker, pulled out my gym clothes, and got dressed.

A boy leaned against the locker, facing me, while another was behind him, both smirking. *Here we go.* First day of school and my first class, and the bullying had already started. I rolled my eyes and slammed my locker shut.

Ethan Howard was the newest addition to the popular boy's club, though I'd known him since middle school. He was pretty hot with black hair and eyes, but those were his only good qualities. He'd always been a dick. I didn't know the other boy.

"Heard you're a fag now, Noah."

I wasn't about to defend myself to this douche nozzle, so I shrugged. God, I hated that term, though. *Stay cool, Noah.* "So?"

I'd hoped that once I admitted it, he'd have no ammunition against me, but I was so very wrong.

"We don't like faggots around here. I refuse to get undressed around you and have you checking me out."

I turned to face him, standing my ground. Then I folded my arms and looked at him up and down. "Yeah, trust me… there's no interest here. No one wants you, Ethan. So, don't get undressed. See how the teacher likes that."

"Yeah, that doesn't work for me. I have a better idea."

The two boys grabbed me by each of my arms. I tried to pull away, but they were bigger and stronger. I yelled for help, but the other boys ignored me because they either didn't care or were too afraid.

"Bruh! Let me fucking go." I tugged and pulled and fought. They dragged me with little effort as my socked feet slid on the floor tiles. My stomach clenched, knowing I was going to be hurting soon. And where was the fucking gym teacher?

They threw my back against the wall of the showers, sending a wave of pain up my spine, making me gasp for air. They turned on the shower head, instantly drenching me in my gym clothes in freezing water. Ethan got in the first hit to my gut. I wasn't a fighter. No one had ever taught me how to fight back, not that they gave me a chance. The first hit had me on my knees. With every breath I struggled to take, I inhaled water, making me cough.

"Don't hit him in the face," Ethan said. "Don't make it obvious."

He lifted me, and I tried to protect myself, but it was no use. He grabbed my arms and held them back.

"Hit him," Ethan demanded.

The other boy looked uncertain.

"Fucking do it before the teacher comes back."

The boy's face hardened, and he hit me twice more in the stomach. Ethan let me go, and I fell on my hands and knees on the wet tiles, desperate for air, coughing, and trying not to throw up.

"Maybe that will cure you of being a faggot. And if you tell anyone, stoner, we'll do this every day if we have to."

With one swift kick to my stomach to seal the deal, he spat on me and left as the water poured down on me.

I curled up into a ball in the corner as a wave of sobbing hit me, making my stomach hurt even more. I'd never been beaten up before. How could kids hate so much? I wasn't mean to anyone and bothered no one.

The bell rang, and I pulled myself up off the ground. Then I grabbed a towel and did my best to dry off, but it was no use. My clothes were soaked. I had no choice but to head toward the gym. I wiped my face, looking in the mirror. My eyes were red, but there was nothing I could do about it.

When I stepped out sopping wet for class, holding my gut with my arms, half the class laughed while the rest took pity though they never helped me. My stupid lip quivered, and I did everything possible not to cry like a baby in front of them. And my stomach hurt so much, making it hard to breathe.

"Noah! Is there a reason you're soaked?"

I had no answer for my gym teacher. No lie came to me. I looked over at my bullies, and Ethan looked all smug. The other boy's face was blank. There was no way I could tell the truth. They'd hurt me again.

"I, uh... ah..."

"Never mind. Get changed into dry clothes and come back. You'll have to sit out of class, and I'll have to mark you off for it."

The kids laughed again as I sulked off.

With trembling hands, I removed my wet clothes and dried off. I looked at my stomach, which was all red and splotchy and hurt so bad. I took a shuddered breath and pulled out my clothes from my locker. After I got dressed, I tossed my gym clothes into the washer the school provided. I grabbed my backpack, headed back to the gym, and sat on the floor to watch the students play basketball while I got a zero for the day.

When I walked into the cafeteria during lunch break, I was wary, looking around for my bullies. But as soon as I saw Zay, my eyes watered. I rushed over to him with my hoodie pulled over my head to hide my tears and sat, grabbing my lunch from my backpack.

"Hey, baby. How's school so far?" he asked. Such a simple question, but I pulled my hood tighter around me and buried my face in his neck so no one would see me cry.

He wrapped an arm around me. "What's wrong? What the fuck happened, No?"

"Nothin'." My shaking voice said otherwise.

Zay lifted my head and eased my hood off to my tears. His face softened as pain filled his amber eyes. I pulled away and buried my face in his throat again as he held me.

"What happened, baby? Talk to me."

I would definitely tell Zay, but anyone of authority? Hell no.

"Two boys. Ethan Howard and some other boy called me a faggot and then beat me up right before gym class," I gasped. "They threw me in the shower and hit me and kicked me. I tried so hard not to cry all day in my classes."

His body stiffened around me as he radiated fury. "Where was the fucking teacher in all this?"

"I dunno. The teacher made me change 'cause I was all wet, and I got a zero for the day."

"Fucking bastards."

He cupped my face, wiped my tears with his thumbs, and kissed my nose.

"Show me where they hit you, No."

I eased my hoodie and T-shirt over my stomach. It was bruising already.

Zay gently touched the darkening red skin with a scowl. He fisted his hands when he pulled away. "They're fucking dead."

"No! They said they'd hurt me again if I told anyone."

Zay stood up, uncaring. He was too angry. "They can't hurt you if they can't walk. Stay here."

Suzi arrived in time so that I wouldn't be alone. I explained to her everything that had happened and where Zay was going. We both held hands as we watched Zay face off with Ethan until Duncan got involved. Of course, they were fucking friends. He got in Duncan's face, yelling at him, but I couldn't hear what he said. Then Duncan got in Ethan's face. Zay yelled a bit more before he came back, still fuming and tightly wound.

"What happened?" Suzi asked him when he sat down.

"I'm taking care of this after school. As much as I'd like to beat the shit out of those two boys right now, I don't want to get expelled. I got mad at Duncan since he was supposed to get his friends to back off on the bullying. He's going to meet us later and deal with this shit."

I grabbed Zay's hand, making him soften. He reached over and wiped my tears again. "They won't bother you again, No."

"Dude, don't fight for me. You'll get hurt. Please. Just... let it go."

"Not a fucking chance in hell. They'll never back off until you show them you're not afraid. They need to pay."

"But... you're not a fighter."

His smile was small but full of love, and he kissed my lips. "I am now."

"We don't need to do this. Don't fight over me, Zay Bae. Please."

It was after school, and we met in the parking lot behind the football field so no one would see us. The rest of the students had already left on the bus or in their cars and headed home, while Zay and I made our way to the meeting point.

"I need to. What kind of boyfriend am I if I can't protect you?"

He pulled to a stop, cupped my face, and kissed me. "I will always do what I can to protect those I care about. You, Kel, Jon... You all are my family. No one will hurt my family. I'm not afraid, No."

"But I am."

"And that's okay, too."

He held my hand, and we walked again. When we arrived, the two boys who hit me were there already and waiting, looking smug as always. My sore stomach clenched in fear, and I felt the acid rise to my throat. I tucked my body behind Zay, hating my fear. Hating that I allowed those two boys to make me feel small and powerless.

God, this was like the first day of school, and already it was a disaster.

Duncan leaned against the athletics building with his arms folded while the two bullies stood and headed toward us.

Zay let go of my hand, and I walked off to stay out of the way as my stomach fought off nausea.

"If it isn't the two faggots," Ethan said.

Fuck, this was like one of those bad old after-school specials on TV.

Zay stood there unfazed as Duncan walked over and stood next to him. I blew out a breath, relieved that Zay had someone by his side, watching his back. I wasn't a fan of Duncan, but after the party, he proved he listened to Zay.

"I guess I'm a faggot, too, huh?"

"Duncan, we're okay with you, but—"

"Why? Because I'm popular? If I wasn't, would you put up with me?"

The two boys said nothing.

"I thought so. First, everyone in the group agreed that both of you are out. No one will talk to you anymore."

The other boy fisted his hands with wide eyes. "Hey, that's not fucking fair! Besides, it was Ethan's fault! He started it."

"Hey! Fuck you, Alex."

"No, fuck you. Beating up Noah was your idea."

"Just like you went along with it, dick."

"You both are out," Duncan repeated.

"Whatever. Bunch of fags," Ethan said, spitting on the ground at their feet. Then he stood face to face with Zay. My body shook, and my mouth went dry. "What are you going to do, Zay? Beat me up? As if. You fags are a bunch of pussies."

"If I have to. This isn't only about your bullying. You need to pay for what you did to Noah. No one hits him. Ever. He's the sweetest person you'll ever meet and didn't deserve what you did to him. You're a piece of shit."

Duncan clasped Zay's shoulder. "Be better than them, Zay. You taught me that. You're not a fighter. Don't turn into them. They will get theirs, trust me. Without me and my group, no one will talk to them. The entire school will know what they are. Sure, there are others who think like them but believe me, they are in the minority. Get your boy home and take care of him."

"No. They'll just hurt Noah again."

"Then they'll pay."

"Please," Ethan scoffed, but he didn't look as tough as he had earlier. There was uncertainty in his eyes.

"Noah is my family. No one hurts my family."

Ethan tried to stand taller and got in his face, but he wasn't as tall as Zay, though Ethan was tougher. My bae wasn't a fighter.

"You sure about this, Zay?" Duncan asked.

"Definitely."

"Fine, then let's show Ethan here how it feels to be helpless."

Duncan gave a hard stare to the other boy, who raised his hands and backed off. Then he stood behind Ethan, grabbed his arms, and pulled them back into a tight hold.

"Hey! What the fuck? That's not fair. I have a right to defend myself."

Duncan leaned into Ethan's ear while he struggled under the tight hold. "Wrong. Did you let Noah defend himself before you punched and kicked him?"

Ethan fought but couldn't get out of Duncan's grip. Duncan was bigger and stronger. Before Ethan could do anything else, Zay pulled back his fist and let it fly into Ethan's face. The boy's head slammed back, and his nose started bleeding. Zay shook out his hand and punched Ethan hard in the stomach. He tried to lean forward as he gasped for air, but Duncan still held him upright until he let him go and shoved him to the ground.

The other boy watched the entire scene and then looked at me. "I'm sorry. Really… I didn't want to. But pressure and shit. It's no excuse…"

I nodded, and he walked off, leaving his friend behind, bleeding on the ground.

Ethan looked up at Zay and Duncan. "Fuckers," he said nasally.

"Stay away from Noah, or any of my friends for that matter," Zay said.

"Whatever."

Ethan finally stood and skulked off. I was honestly surprised there wasn't more of a fight. But I guess when you hurt someone's nose, that was it.

When they were gone, Duncan approached me. "How are you feeling, Noah?"

I shrugged. "I'm alright."

"If it's any consolation, I'm sorry. I've picked on you too. You didn't deserve to get hurt."

With that, Duncan left.

I looped my arms around Zay's neck. "My hero."

Zay smiled and held me close. "I thought you didn't want me fighting."

"I didn't, but… you still protected me."

"I'll always protect you."

God, my heart fluttered at that. He made it sound like we'd be together forever. I hoped so.

CHAPTER FIFTEEN

Noah

It was the weekend after Zay's seventeenth birthday. My bae still hated being older than the rest of his class, but there was nothing he could do about it. At least, for now, no one was bullying us. But after getting beaten up, I spent a lot of time in Zay's arms as he held me at night, protecting me. More than normal. And though my stomach healed, I wouldn't be able to get the painful memory out of my head any time soon, along with the periodic nightmares.

It was Saturday, and we'd pulled our tired bodies out of the water in the late afternoon with our friends. We'd wrapped up some lessons earlier that day, and Kel gave us the rest of the afternoon off.

I inhaled some MJ, feeling totally chill, leaning against my bae's bare chest. Everything was right in my world. He wrapped his arms around me, and he kissed my neck. I angled my head, so he had better access. When he pulled away, I slipped the blunt between his lips, and he took a long drag.

"God, you two are so cute; it's disgusting."

I scoffed at Mason. "You're just jelly."

Zay leaned down, and I reached for his mouth with mine, which I opened so he could blow back the sweet smoke into my mouth. Then we kissed.

"Truth, man. It's been a while since I got laid after Clarissa dumped my ass."

Nhan and Suzi looked at each other weirdly. It wasn't one of those 'I have a crush on my friend' looks with shy smiles and fluttering eyelashes. Oh, boy. I knew how that went.

"Nhan and I have something to tell you," Suzi said.

"You two are dating," I said.

They both looked at me, jaw-dropped. "Brah, how'd you know?"

I winked. "Just a guess."

Mason tossed his hands in the air. "Am I the only single one now? Bummer. Now I'm like a fifth wheel, dude. I gotta find me a girl."

We all laughed when he started pouting.

Zay leaned into my ear, and his breath sent goosebumps down my arm. "Wanna fool around when we get back?"

"I would never say no to that, boo."

"Maybe we can try something new… eventually."

"What new thing do you want to try?"

"Sex." He said it so softly I questioned what I heard.

"Sex?"

"Yes." His face was red, but his eyes were determined. "We… need to talk about it, anyway."

I swallowed hard, instantly nervous yet excited at the same time.

"Okay. Yeah… I'm down with that."

"What are you whispering about over there?" Nhan asked, now holding Suzi close, who rested her head on his shoulder now that they came out as a couple. It totally explained why Nhan was all jelly at the party last summer when Suzi and I pretended to date.

"Sex," Mason said. "It's gotta be. Look how red their faces are."

"What are you talking about? I'm sunburned," Zay said, making everyone laugh. We all knew better.

We left our friends on the beach later that afternoon and headed inside the shop. Zay closed the door behind him when we stumbled inside, pressing me against the wall, groping and kissing. We probably needed a shower, smelling like sweat, salt water, and sunscreen, but I didn't care. I loved Zay's smell. His natural scent was best of all, and I inhaled him every chance I could. It was like he oozed pheromones or something.

He fisted my hair from behind, pulled my head back, and shoved his tongue down my throat. I loved when he got controlling, making me melt, and I was willing to give him the world if I could. Sometimes Zay was shy, but the more we fooled around, the more confident he got. I did too, but I wasn't afraid to explore with him. I wanted everything with him.

My hands slid under his tank top, feeling up his warm, strong, and smooth back. He pulled my head back more to nibble on my throat.

"Zay! Noah!"

We froze and turned to see Kel and a customer staring at us.

I sucked in my lips, trying not to laugh, but I snorted one out anyway.

"Can we *not* do it on the sales floor, boys?"

"Sorry, Kel," we both said and rushed upstairs to his chuckles and apologies to the customer. At least we weren't in trouble.

After our shower together and some needed orgasms, we curled up in Zay's bed with the TV on, but we weren't paying attention to it.

"Zay?"

"Hmm?"

"So about this sex…"

"Right. Well, I'm not sure we're ready yet. It's not like regular sex, ya know? We'll have to research it and see if it's even something we want to do, but I definitely want to do it with you… eventually."

"I want to do everything with you," I said.

"Then we will." It was just like Zay gave me whatever I wanted.

"Zay?"

"Yep, babe?"

He dragged his fingers over my shoulder, back and forth, as I rested my head on his chest, loving the sound of his steady heartbeat. He was comforting, protective, and strong.

"Do you think we would've met if we never came here to the surf shop?"

"Hmm, I doubt it since I was on the street. If Kel and Jon hadn't taken me in, I probably never would've returned to school. I had intended to keep studying as long as possible and then take the GED."

"True, I guess. We met in school, but what if like I never came here? Do you think we'd be boyfriends, anyway?"

"What's with these questions?"

"I dunno. Is it stupid to think fate and stuff brought us together?"

It was something I wondered about a lot. We became great friends, but we were perfect together. We never fought and were open and honest with each other once my boo got past his fears. I couldn't imagine myself with anyone else ever. If we ever broke up, I'd die. My heart would be too broken to be fixed. Zay ruined me for everyone else, and I was just fine with that.

He thought about my question and kissed my head. "I'm not sure about fate or if I even believe in it or not. But I want to. It's like sometimes I think Kel found me and brought me here to wait for you."

I sat up and hovered my face over his, wearing a stupid grin. "I totally love that," I said and kissed him. When I laid back down, I continued to play with his chest. "I love the idea of soulmates. That two people meant to be together are lucky enough to find each other in this big world."

"I like that, too, baby."

"I sometimes wonder if some soulmates never find each other. What happens to them? Do they live a life of loneliness?"

"Hmm, maybe. I don't know. I'm still not sure I believe in all that stuff, but it's a nice thought, though maybe not the loneliness part so much."

I snuggled into him more. The warmth of his body traveled straight into my soul. If I could get closer to him, I would. I hoped we'd be together forever.

"Zay?"

"Hmm?"

"Do you… have fantasies?"

"What sort of fantasies?"

"You know… the sexy kind."

"Yeah, I have all kinds of thoughts about you and me."

I smiled into his chest. "Me too. Is it weird that…" I paused, not sure if I wanted to tell him. Would he find me weird or creepy? But I trusted Zay enough to believe he wouldn't make fun of me.

"Go on. You can tell me anything."

I rested my chin on him so I could look up at him. "I had this weird fantasy while we were makin' out downstairs… ugh, so embarrassing. People watching us was kind of a turn-on. Is that gross of me?"

He rolled over onto his side and combed my bangs away from my face with his fingers, and smiled. "No, that's not gross at all. I'm not surprised you'd feel that way after rubbing one off in front of me that one time. I think you liked it."

I buried my burning face into the pillow. "Ugh, I did like it. You watchin' me was so hot."

He lifted my face and kissed me. "Don't be embarrassed. Do you want to fool around somewhere that might get us caught? Is that what you're asking?"

I nodded. *Yes, I would like that very much.*

"Then we'll do it."

My heart thudded as my eyes popped wide. "Really?"

"Really."

"You'd be okay with that?"

"Dude, I'd be okay with doing anything with you."

I climbed on top of him, straddled his stomach, and leaned down to kiss him.

"I love you," I blurted. Though my face burned again, I refused to take it back. I'd loved this boy for a while.

Zay, being Zay, was unfazed. He rubbed my chest and arms with a broad smile on his face. "And I love you." God, he said it with so much ease, which was so like him. "But if we're going to explore more, I want us to be open and honest, just like tonight, okay?"

"Definitely."

"But I think we should wait a little bit for sex. We've only been dating for a few months, even though we've known each other for a year. We have plenty of time to learn everything about each other. Is that okay?" he asked.

"Brah, just being with you is more than okay. As long as you love me, I'm just right. No. More than right. I'm perfect."

"Wanna learn some more about each other right now?"

I snorted a laugh. "Is surfin' fun? Duh. I'd never say no to you."

"And I'd never say no to you."

"Ugh, I still can't believe you're all mine," I said, squeezing him tight. "I won the boyfriend lottery, brah."

"I'm the one who won."

This time we sucked each other off at the same time. We curled up, facing each other in opposite directions on the bed. How different from a regular BJ, as if a BJ from Zay was regular. But to enjoy him and his taste at the same time he was enjoying mine had me coming in no time. And I loved that my reaction turned him on so much that he quickly followed.

I loved our BJs, but I knew we'd get better and better at them as time went on. And I couldn't wait for Zay to go down on me outside, risking getting caught. Shit, the very thought had my dick waking up again.

After a long day in the sun and having orgasms, I was beat. I grabbed one of his legs, not bothering to turn back around from our sixty-nine position, pressed my body against his, and dropped off to sleep.

It was still dark out when I woke up. I yawned and smiled, careful not to stretch, so I didn't wake my boo. Usually, I was his blanket, but now Zay was mine. His sleeping head rested on my chest, and he had one hand in my hair and his other arm wrapped around my neck. My body was sweltering because Zay was like a fucking furnace, but I loved when he got all snuggly. That it wasn't just me who needed to be close to him.

And he said he loved me last night. My sleepy grin widened as I wrapped my arms tightly around him and kissed his head.

My phone that Kel bought me because my other one crapped out buzzed. I'd wondered what woke me up. I tried to reach for my phone on the nightstand without disturbing Zay. My fingers pulled it closer and grabbed it. I swiped it open to see a message from Mom.

God, please give me a break.

The time read two-thirty in the morning. My gut sank in part with frustration and the other part with worry.

Mom: Need you whr r u

The fact that she couldn't type shit meant she was drunk… again.

Noah: What's wrong
Mom: Miss u

My eyes watered but not from being needed by my mom because she loved me. She missed me taking care of her and being at her beck and call. This wasn't the first time she'd done this.

Noah: It's late.
Mom: So tired feel sick pls

I wondered if I'd ever be free of her as I eased Zay off of me and climbed out of bed.

Noah: Be there soon.

I grabbed my shorts off the floor and a T-shirt that was Zay's, then headed to the bathroom to piss and brush my teeth.

When I came out of the bathroom, Zay sat up in bed, stretching. "What's going on, babe?"

"Mom."

"Shit. Did something happen?"

I shrugged. "Just being her drunk self." I opened up my phone and showed him the messages.

"I'll drive you."

I stiffened. While I appreciated the thought, I had yet to take Zay to my old apartment. It was fucking embarrassing, and the place wasn't even the worst part. He knew Mom was an alcoholic, but he'd never met her. I didn't know if I wanted him to see that part of my life.

Zay stood up, still naked and gorgeous, walked over to me, and grabbed my face. "Babe, it's okay. I don't care and love you no matter what. Let me take you so you can take care of her. I'll do whatever you need me to do while we're there. Please. You need someone to care for you, too."

I wrapped my arms around his neck and hugged him. "Okay." No, Zay would never judge me.

We got there after twenty minutes. I let myself in, wincing and worried about the state of the apartment. Sure enough, she trashed the kitchen, and the place reeked of stale alcohol, cigarettes, and old food.

Zay placed a hand on my shoulder as if telling me to try not to be embarrassed. "Go take care of your Mom. I'll be out here."

He gave me a quick kiss, and I headed to Mom's room, knowing I'd find the same thing I always did. Either she'd vomited in her bed, and I'd have to clean it up, or she'd be passed out on the bathroom floor. Telling her she needed help never did any good, even when she was sober and feeling guilty. Despite my age, I was smart enough to understand that addiction could push away rationality. I'd seen it enough in my life.

I didn't see her in her bed or her room, so I headed straight to her bathroom, and there she slept on the floor. Ugh. Even worse, she was naked. I fucking hated when she did that. She probably tried to take a shower and didn't make it. There was vomit in the toilet, so I flushed it and grabbed her robe lying on the floor. At least she didn't throw up everywhere, and one less thing to clean.

I squatted down and lifted her passed-out body to wrap the robe around her. It wasn't fucking easy when she was deadweight like this. I could ask Zay for help, but as much as I trusted him, this was mortifying.

"Come on, Mom. Wake up enough so I can get you in bed."

She moaned and mumbled something but still didn't move.

I stood and grabbed the cup to rinse her mouth out and filled it with water. After pulling her body upright, I poured some water down her throat, which she drank down on instinct.

"Let's go. Wake up. I need you to help me help you."

"Noah? Is that you?" she mumbled and slurred.

"Yeah, I'm here, Mom."

"Where have you been?"

The guilt gnawed at me and my eyes watered. "I've been… working." *And falling in love as you've been hurting.* I shut that thought down. I had every right to fall in love.

She helped me as I lifted her to stand and walked her to her bed. I took off my shoes and climbed in next to her. When she rolled over to me, I put an arm around her and held her. She reeked of alcohol, something I grew used to when I lived here, but now it just made me nauseous.

"Don't leave me, Noah." My eyes watered more with the guilt hammering me. Feeling angry. I was so torn. I hated leaving her like this, but I couldn't stand it anymore. It was so fucking exhausting.

"I have to work and make us money."

"Does that mean I can quit now?"

"No, you can't quit. I don't make enough for both of us."

"Oh."

I wiped the tears from my face and rubbed her robed back. I hated her, yet I loved her, too. What kind of person did that make me when I hated no one?

"I miss you…"

A sob caught in my throat. I'd spent most of my life needing to hear love from my mother and rarely got it. Usually, when she was this drunk, she wasn't so bad. It was when she was hung over that she was the meanest. So I tried not to take her words to heart, but it still hurt like fuck.

I didn't know what time it was when I woke up. It was late enough that the sun was peeking in through the blinds. Mom was rolled over on her side, away from me, so I climbed out of bed and went to check on Zay.

Not only did I find him sleeping on our gross couch, but he'd cleaned the entire apartment when I was in Mom's room. God, I loved my bae. My eyes refused to stop watering. Ugh, I hated being so sensitive sometimes.

I rubbed my eyes with the heel of my hands, kneeled in front of him, and watched him sleep for a little bit. Then I gently brushed back his long dark bangs and kissed his forehead, then his nose, and then his lips.

His eyes opened, and he gave me a tired smile. "Hey, is everything okay?"

"Yeah. Thank you… you didn't have to clean."

He put a hand on my face, and I leaned into it. "It's just one less thing you have to worry about, babe."

God, what did I ever do without him?

After I made some meals for her and left her a note with instructions on cooking, we went back to my new home.

Away from her.

CHAPTER SIXTEEN

Zayden

THAT MORNING, AFTER HE TOOK CARE OF HIS MOM, I SAW HOW NOAH fell into depression. I think it stemmed from not only being embarrassed by his mom but where he lived and the state of the apartment. So, I had an idea and hoped it didn't bring him down more.

"Come on. I want to show you something, and after that, we can grab some coffee."

"Okay."

I kept glancing at him as I drove. He looked so hurt and sad and tired, making me ache for him and to take away his pain. "Talk to me, No. What happened?"

He stared out the window as he answered. "Nothin' any different from normal. One minute she's loving, and the next, she hates me. She was too out of it to hate this time, but… It's… just hard."

"I totally get that, but I don't think she hates you. Alcohol changes a person."

"I wonder. I love your support, Zay, but I'm totally embarrassed, too. My apartment is so gross, and she always trashes the place. She doesn't fucking care about anything."

"Don't be embarrassed, baby," I said, but my words probably wouldn't have made a difference. All I could do was show him I didn't care and that I understood.

I pulled the truck to a stop, and we climbed out. While holding his hand, I led him to the back of the concrete shed I used to live in.

"Where are we?"

"You'll see."

Someone put a new lock on the door now, and they probably cleared it out of all my things since I hadn't lived there in a long time. I grabbed a rock and smashed the flimsy lock off. The door was rotting wood, so any lock wouldn't be hard to get off.

We stepped inside the tiny space, and I held out my arms. The opened door allowed the light to steam in, casting every corner into darkness while dust motes danced in the beams. I forgot how claustrophobic it felt to live here sometimes. But I suffered just to have a roof over my head and be in relative safety.

Someone completely emptied the place, which was fine. The stuff I left behind held no sentimental value to me. "This is where I lived for a year. No windows and it was dirty with bugs, but I did my best. I put a small, stained bed in that corner, and I put a cover over it with sheets and stuff that I bought at Goodwill. Over in that corner, I stacked crates to hold my clothes and stuff. I put up curtains and pretended I had a window, and I bought two camping lanterns so I wasn't in complete darkness. There was even a rickety chair in the corner. I'd shower at the public beach, and tried not to go to the bathroom outside, but sometimes I didn't have a choice. I had to do a prepaid phone thing, and kept it charged at the library or coffee shop that offered free Wi-Fi."

Noah looked around with sadness on his face.

I rested my hands on his shoulder. "I didn't bring you here to make you sad but to show you we all struggle. You shouldn't be embarrassed about where you come from. I'm not, but I used to be, so I get it. What you do is amazing, No. You're so loving, caring, and empathetic. You're doing your best for others while also caring for yourself. That makes you such a strong person, and I love you for it. Don't be embarrassed, and don't feel bad about your mother. You're an amazing son, friend, and boyfriend."

Noah jumped into my arms, and I caught him as he wrapped his arms and legs around me while resting his head on my shoulder. My big, adorable baby. "Thanks, Zay Bae. You always know how to make a bro feel better."

"And on to our next adventure in making my bro feel better."

I put him down, and he finally smiled at me.

"Yeah?"

I nodded. "First, we need to get you caffeinated."

After we left the coffee shop two blocks away from the shed, I took his hand and walked him through a section of a tropical forest I found a long time ago. There was a small beaten path, so people came through here, but not enough to make the place crowded.

There were some areas we had to climb, and the place I wanted to take him to was about a mile hike away.

"Brah, where are goin'?"

"It's a surprise."

When we finally reached it, Noah was jaw-dropped. "Dude, how'd I not know this place was even here?"

"I didn't either until I felt like hiking one day and followed the trail when I stumbled upon it."

It wasn't big, but it didn't make it less beautiful. The small waterfall, surrounded by a blanket of green and lush plants and trees, spilled into a clear pool below before continuing on its path to the ocean.

I wanted to take him somewhere beautiful to cheer him up, but I had another intention in mind. And because there was no one currently around, I grabbed the hem of my shirt and pulled it off. Next went my shoes, shorts, and underwear.

Noah's smile was crooked, and his green eyes that matched the landscape sparkled with humor. "Dude, you sneaky dog."

"Your turn, baby. Get naked, and let's go for a dip."

When he stripped down, my eyes bee-lined between his legs which was already hard for me. Did he guess what I had planned? Despite no one being around, that didn't mean people wouldn't show, so this was a perfect opportunity to fulfill his little fantasy.

Once he was naked, I reached out, and he took my hand, and I led him into the water. It was cold and fresh. The pool wasn't huge, but it was deep. We submerged up to our necks, and the cool water sent waves of goosebumps across my skin, and my balls climbed inside for warmth, but I loved cold water. Noah wrapped his arms around my neck and his legs around my waist. I swayed my legs and arms in the water to keep us afloat, with him clinging to me and kissing me. I opened my mouth, allowing his tongue entrance. It was warm and smooth with a lingering sweetness from the sugar he had put in his coffee earlier.

"Thank you for this," he said, making me ache for him. I wish I could take away all his hurt and pain. Make his mother get her shit together and love him as he should be loved. To see what an amazing son she had despite her best efforts to ruin him.

"Anything for you."

He raised a brow and smirked. "Anything?"

I smiled back and nodded. "Anything. Even that BJ you've been dying to have out in the open."

"I knew I loved you for a reason, boo."

Laughter bubbled out of me; then I kissed him again.

"Let's get out. I can't reach your dick underwater."

"Can't have you drowning now, can we?"

"You'd miss me."

"Definitely, Zay Bae."

We climbed out of the water, and I had Noah lean against a large rock. The sun kissed his tanned skin like sparkles through the trees. He looked like a blond god with his face basking upward toward the warmth. I probably should've taken a picture, but I did in my mind, capturing this moment of pure happiness.

As soon as I dropped to my knees in front of him, his gorgeous dick rose in salute. I smiled, never fully appreciating, until now, as he went from flaccid to hard, and it was a beautiful sight.

I grabbed it at the base, and when I looked up at him, I ran my tongue over the tip. He went from smiling to mouth open wide and groaning.

"That's so hot…" he breathed.

Noah was gentle when he combed his fingers through my hair, easing my mouth deeper around him. I opened up my throat as much as possible, but I still gagged a little. After I popped off of him and stroked him to catch my breath, I was back at it.

Noah wasn't wrong. It was kind of exciting to be out here, completely naked, as I went down on him. Anyone could stumble onto us at any moment. Maybe someone saw us and watched in the distance, hidden, as we put on our show for them. There was definitely something to this exhibitionist thing. We'd have to find new places to explore this where there was a small risk of getting caught but not arrested.

I played with his nuts and sunk him deeper into my mouth.

"God, Zay… so good."

I looked up at his head thrown back and his mouth slack. Such a beautiful vision to be able to turn Noah mindless and numb as he got closer and closer to his climax.

"I'm coming."

He didn't have to tell me. I could tell. We'd gone down on each other enough to be familiar with the swelling and heat of our cocks.

As soon as he came, I popped off to stroke him and opened my mouth to catch his release while I looked up at him. His eyes struggled to keep from rolling into his head, yet wide as he watched his come hit my tongue.

I swallowed and then stood, pulling him in for a kiss. He tasted himself and groaned again.

"That was so fucking hot, boo."

"I completely agree. Let's do that again sometime."

"Definitely. Thanks… for all of this. You're the best bae ever."

"Oh, this was for me too. I love sucking you off."

It was a pretty rainy day for May, so Noah and I worked the register today, though not many customers came in. No one except die-hard surfers enjoyed surfing in the rain. There were definitely no beachgoers.

Noah was straightening out the racks of boardshorts and T-shirts while I updated our inventory and sales on the computer when Kel headed our way.

"Hey, boys. I have some news."

"What's up?" I asked.

We both approached Kel. I stood with folded arms while Noah wrapped an arm around me and rested his head on my shoulder.

"Dad and I are fostering another boy. He's fourteen, and his name is Mateo Del Luna. It was fate. I stumbled onto him just in time as he was overdosing. I dragged him to the hospital before dumping him in a detox clinic, and I'd been watching over him for the past month."

"Poor little dude. So, he's okay?" Noah asked.

Kel nodded. "He's fine, but he's still got a long road to recovery. Addiction is a tricky thing. He'll be here in a few days. Dad and I are going to set up that empty room as an extra bedroom. Good thing we installed that extra bathroom. I can count on you to make him feel at home and welcome, right?"

"Definitely," I said.

"No problem, boss man."

Kel rolled his eyes and chuckled. "Mateo won't start high school until the Fall. He's been out for a long time. So, I'm going to get him a tutor to get caught up and have him pass some assessment exams, so he's not held back like you were, Zay. I wish I'd known to do that back when you came to live with us."

"It's cool. I hated it at first, but I may not have ever met Noah otherwise."

Noah reached up with his lips, and I kissed him.

"Good. Please watch over him. Not only to make him at home but when Dad and I aren't around... protect him. If he looks like he's going to bolt, call me immediately."

"Will do, Kel," I said.

By the following week, in the early morning, there was a knock on our bedroom door. Noah and I had stayed up way too late fooling around last night. I climbed out of bed and tripped over something with bleary eyes. I landed hard on my knee and cursed.

"What's goin' on, Bae?"

"Someone's at the door."

I grabbed some shorts off the floor and quickly threw them on, and then answered the door. Kel stood there with a boy a little shorter than Noah, with hair as dark as mine, but his eyes were almost black. He was emaciated with dark circles under his eyes, looking like I did when I used to live on the streets. And he looked nervous and twitchy as hell.

"Zay, you both should be getting up already," Kel said.

"Sorry, Kel, it was Friday night, and we got a bit carried away with the video games," I lied. He didn't need the details of what we were really doing. "Hey, new bro. You Mateo?"

The boy shoved his hands in his pockets and nodded.

"Come in and meet Noah, my best bro."

He looked at Kel for reassurance, who nodded for Mateo to go in. Noah tossed on some shorts, rubbed his sleepy eyes, and pulled the boy into a hug that was so like him. Mateo froze for a second but then gave Noah an awkward pat on the back.

"Nice to have another dude bro around here. You're gonna love it, man," Noah said.

"Kel and Jon are great," I agreed.

Mateo nodded again, staring at the floor. "Ah, thanks."

Kel laughed. "Thanks for the vote of confidence! You boys get cleaned up while I show Mateo around."

We said our goodbyes as Kel took Mateo away to show him around. I closed our bedroom door and got dressed.

"Poor little dude looks scared," Noah said.

"Yeah, I was in the same boat when I first came here. I wonder what his story is."

"We'll be his best buds, and hopefully, he'll open up. It also took you a little while to talk."

I grabbed him by the neck and kissed his head. "If anyone can pull someone out of their shell, it's you, baby."

CHAPTER SEVENTEEN

Zayden

It was my eighteenth birthday today, and I asked for only one thing. Sex. I'd been holding back long enough.

Noah and I have had an amazing journey together for over a year as boyfriends. I'd never imagine having a relationship with anyone and never fighting with each other. And we never, ever fought. Noah was just a beautiful soul, and it was impossible to get upset with him. Even Kel couldn't bring himself to get mad at him when Noah smoked weed in the shop after hours when he wasn't allowed to.

And Noah was so patient with me, even when I had my irritable bad days. He'd always find a way to make me laugh through jokes and pranks. And it worked every time.

But I was so ready for this, and so was he. It was Thursday, and school was tomorrow, so we'd probably be tired in the morning, but it'd be worth it. My actual birthday party with my found family would be on Saturday, leaving Noah and me alone tonight.

God, and I couldn't believe I was officially going to be an adult.

Noah and I had spent several months researching anal sex and prepping, so we were ready. When Noah asked how I wanted to do this, I'd surprised him by telling him I wanted to bottom. I think he expected me to top, and I planned on doing that too. But first, I needed him in me.

I'd surprised him so much he'd asked me why I wanted to bottom first.

"I dunno. I just want to feel you inside me."

He gave me the sweetest smile, kissing the tip of my nose. "I want to have you in me too."

I winked at him. "Wanna flip for it?"

He snorted a laugh. "Nah, we can do it your way first. I'm good either way. As long as we share."

"Oh, we're so sharing."

I lay on my back in bed, completely naked. We'd fooled around, warming up to the big finale, so I was achingly hard and so ready to have him in me, but we had more work to do.

"Hold your legs back, boo."

I grabbed my thighs and pulled my legs to expose my hole. Even after all our fooling around over the past year, this was probably one of the more vulnerable positions I'd ever been in. My face burned all the way to my ears.

Strangely, I calmed as soon as Noah started exploring me as was his way, running a finger around and around my tight hole. Round and round he went until he tugged a whimper out of me, getting lost in the arousing sensation. The touch promised more but not too soon. And definitely not enough. Not until I begged and pleaded for more. The area was so sensitive, making me needy for him to be inside me already.

"I love how you respond to all my touches with those cute sounds and panting. Fuck, and your dick bouncin' when I touch you a certain way is hot. And is it weird I find this freckle next to your hole adorable as hell?"

I breathed out a laugh, still blushing but thoroughly turned on. Noah was good at that. He excelled at bringing the most out of your body but unintentionally. He just loved to learn everything about me, which made him such a good lover, paying attention to the details, so he knew exactly how to please you.

"I love your body, Bae."

He poured a little lube into his hand and slowly inserted a finger while kissing my inner thigh. I bit my bottom lip and shut my eyes, accepting the burning pressure. Noah eased his finger in and out as he hovered over me, watching every movement, every reaction, making sure I had no pain showing on my face.

Everyone who didn't really know Noah assumed he was slow or stupid, but he was none of those things. He was just supremely laid-back. And the weed helped. I understood more than anyone he used it to keep his stress levels down. He also had some insecurity issues that cropped up here and there thanks to his mother's damage, but he hid it well. People should be so lucky to know the real Noah. And he was all mine.

"I like to play with your body too much sometimes, so I promise not to prolong your torture this time."

I grinned. "And I appreciate that, babe."

After he inserted a second finger and worked me, I felt adjusted enough. "I'm ready, No."

"You sure? Because I'm bigger than two fingers. And I gotta admit that I love watching my fingers go in and out of you. So hot."

It'd hurt no matter what, so I wanted to push forward.

"Yeah, I'm ready."

Once he had a condom rolled on, and he lubed us up, he hovered over me again, and gave me a deep kiss full of sloppy tongue. Sometimes I liked kissing dirty with a lot of spit, tongue sucking, and bottom lip nibbling. Noah was good at it. He knew the right kiss for the right occasion.

He pulled away from my face and stared at me with those gorgeous leafy green eyes blown black.

"Now, baby," I said. I could tell he didn't want to hurt me, but I trusted him.

He leaned over me again, nudged his tip in, and slid in about an inch before his eyes rolled back. It stung as he stretched me, but he sat for a moment, allowing me to adjust, relaxing my muscles that tried to deny him.

Inch by inch, he eased in as I gripped his upper arms, breathing through the sting, burn, and stretch. But him filling me with his dick was so hot; it kept me turned on and hard, allowing me to push back the discomfort. There was something arousing and intimate in having his cock in me, filling me, claiming me.

"Ugh, I'm gonna have to take this slow whether you like it or not, Bae. So tight... So good. Whoa... This is so not the same as a hand, even your hand. Fuck, and the heat..."

His breathy words pulled a whine out of me as he fully seated me.

"Shit. Am I hurting you?"

I must have had a pained look on my face. While uncomfortable at first, and it burned, it set me on fire for him. We were one and the same person and as connected as two people could get. But the cumulative sensations made me strangely and unexpectedly emotional. The surge of love I had for Noah skyrocketed right then.

I shook my head. "Only a little... just move before I die. Need you."

No matter how this turned out, or if he busted a nut in seconds, this was perfect. Just me and my Noah, united in a way we'd never been before. The sex completed us.

His slow movements were agonizing, dragging, prolonging my suffering and need. I wanted more of him. Harder. Faster. But we had to take our time and experience this in the way only Noah understood and experienced it best. Through exploration and learning.

I reached for his beautiful face with furrowed brows and beaded with sweat as he held in the need to let go while trying to give me pleasure and not to hurt me.

My fingers moved down and dug into his arm, meeting his last thrust when he hit that spot we read about. Holy fuck, that was nice. My eyes slid shut as stars sparkled behind my lids, and my back arched to suck him in deeper. I gasped and whimpered at the expected sensation, but nothing prepared me for how good it felt. Thank fuck for prostates.

"Zay?" His sweet voice was so full of concern.

I opened my eyes, grabbed his face, and pulled him into a deep kiss. "I'm good, baby. So good. This is perfect."

My words must have reassured him because he moved faster, making me groan as he kept hitting that spot. I arched my back and wrapped my legs around his waist, pulling him in for more and more.

"You're so beautiful, Bae."

My arms wrapped around his back, and my blunt nails dug into his skin as the first tingles traveled along my spine. We both groaned. Soon that familiar pressure grew as my balls tightened. I was getting close, and I hadn't even touched myself yet. I scrambled to grab my cock and began stroking. Fuck, that combination of him hitting my prostate while my cock was getting happy attention grew intense and addicting, and I was going to bust any second.

I could happily live forever in this place between desperate need and impending bliss.

The closer I got, the faster I stroked. Noah kept up with my pace, slamming into me. His mouth fell open, panting as he kept watch on me. Suddenly, my body froze, and I spurted come all over my chest and hand as my eyes rolled into the back of my head.

This was no fucking orgasm. This was nuclear. I'd never experienced such a strong and visceral reaction to Noah. That combination of pressure-reducing climax filled with love for this man.

"So hot…" he breathed and grabbed my thighs, pushing them back. With a few last hard thrusts, his body trembled as hot come filled the condom, searing me. Branding me. Owning me.

Out of strength and steam, he fell on top of me, and I wrapped my arms around his sweaty back and kissed his sweaty head.

"Fucking amazing," I whispered, dragging my nails gently along his back.

His softening dick slipped out, leaving me entirely too empty without him.

He nodded. "So amazing." He lifted his head with concern on his face. "Did it hurt?"

"Oh, my ass will be feeling it for a couple of days, but I loved it. You will, too, when you try it."

"Good, I can't wait."

A smirk appeared, though his eyes were hooded and tired. "You look wrecked, Zay Bae. It's a sexy look on you."

"So do you. This is only the beginning, baby. We're going to get wrecked often."

Mateo had only been living with us for five months when Kel and Jon took in another boy. I laughed when Kel told me the news. He and Jon, apparently, collected kids now. They wanted to help all those in need, but there was only so much they could do.

Kel lost his mom to suicide at age eleven, and then his older brother grew so distraught he left to head to the mainland. Kel hadn't seen his brother since, and that was about twenty years ago. Because Jon and Kel only had each other, I think they tried to fill some void in their lives. And they had so much love to give.

Levi Dawson was thirteen when he came to live with us at the surf shop. And how opposite he was from Mateo. Mateo was introverted and quiet, whereas Levi was outgoing and smart as hell. A spitfire. It took only some tutoring and passing several tests to get him settled in the eighth grade, even after being out of school for over a year. Mateo was smart too, but Levi blew us all away.

Even more surprising, the boy, whose parents had died in a fire when he was five and went to live with his piece of shit uncle, who pimped him out when he was eleven years old. Levi ran away when he was twelve and did the only thing he knew how to survive, and that was to prostitute himself. And survive, he did. He became so good at it; he hired one of his johns to pretend he was Levi's father and rented a studio apartment. Levi gave him freebies in return and paid for the place himself.

And that he had no residual trauma afterward was astounding. Or shit even lived through it. How no one physically hurt him was beyond me. Maybe because he took full control over his life, or he hid his pain really well. Surely he had underlying issues, right? Who knew? But Kel found him by accident soliciting an older man and practically dragged the boy here after Kel had the man arrested as a pedophile. Levi was so pissed at first to lose his income, but Kel gave him a better offer.

He and Mateo were sharing the room across from us, and I knocked on their door at six in the morning.

"Come on, guys. Time to get up."

Before I could knock again, Levi answered, scratching his thick head of floppy brown hair. His hazel-green eyes were half closed as he yawned.

"I'm getting up. Mat's a snooze fest over there, though. Another nightmare."

"Okay, I'll get him up. You get washed up. Breakfast is ready in the kitchen. We're leaving for school in an hour."

"Okie Dokie."

Levi picked up a pair of shorts off the floor, sniffed them, then shrugged and tossed them on. Gross. For as smart as he was, Levi was a slob. Noah and I tossed things around, but we always cleaned up after ourselves and never wore clothes that hadn't been washed in weeks.

When he took off for the bathroom to brush his teeth, I headed to Mateo's bed to wake him up. It wasn't unusual for him to have nightmares which made him tired in the morning. I wish he'd opened up, but he refused to talk about what happened to him. Kel told me to give him his space if he needed it, hoping Mateo would eventually trust us enough to help him. At least he received therapy.

I sat on the edge of his bed and shook him awake. "Come on, Mat. You gotta get up."

He rolled away from me and pulled the covers over his head. "Just give me five more minutes."

"Five is all you get. Breakfast is ready. You sure you don't want to talk about it?"

"No."

I sighed. "Okay."

I'd keep asking him, and hopefully, one day, he'd talk. I wasn't sure it was healthy to keep trauma so bottled up.

After we dropped off Levi at the middle school, I drove Noah, Mateo, and myself to the high school. Mateo was starting the ninth grade, and Noah and I started the eleventh. Only two more years, and we'd be done with high school. I had no idea what I wanted to do with my life yet, and I hoped I'd figure it out soon. Noah was content to continue to teach surfing.

Hell, it wasn't a bad job and paid pretty well, but eventually, I wanted to move out of there and get a place just for Noah and me. Hawaii wasn't fucking cheap, so I probably needed a better job. But college wasn't for me. I had no interest in going, and I definitely had no desire to rack up huge student debt that I could never pay off.

Mateo ran off to his classes, yawning all the way while I held Noah's hand and walked him to his first period.

He leaned against the wall next to the door of his class and looped his arms around my neck, pulling me into a kiss. We were out and proud, not giving a fuck anymore what anyone else thought. I loved Noah, and the world will always know it.

I gave him one more quick kiss before he went inside, and I rushed to my class so I wouldn't be late.

And this year, I had to make sure no one harassed my Noah or hurt him ever again. Last year, I'd made it clear to all bullies that I'd do whatever it took to protect him. Duncan and I intentionally spread the word about Ethan's broken nose because he messed with my boyfriend.

Seeing my Noah hurt like that still made me want to burn things.

Never again.

CHAPTER EIGHTEEN

Noah

LIFE HAD BEEN AMAZING FOR THE PAST THREE YEARS BEING IN A relationship with Zay. It seemed that was the way things were always going to be between Zay and me. We had both graduated high school, and I didn't think I had seen Kel and Jon so proud. They threw us a big graduation party at their house, allowing us to invite our friends from school. I didn't invite Mom. She wouldn't have cared. But I could brush it aside, having all my friends and found family supporting and loving me.

But life had also been chaotic with the newest additions to Ohana Surfing Club. Two girls came to live with us, forcing Mateo and Levi to move into our room, so the girls had their own space.

Moni was fourteen, and Rumi was fifteen when they moved in last year during our senior year. The two girls were wild, loud, and young.

They were both as sweet as could be, and I felt so bad for them. Moni's mom died, and her dad struggled to handle her while he grieved and worked three jobs. Granted, she was a handful and acted very entitled. Her dad knew of Kel and told him to take his daughter or else he'd kick her out. I never learned the details of why, but it didn't matter. What kind of parent did that? Zay's parents did too. A parent's love should never have conditions.

My mom wasn't always nice to me, and I knew I was a burden to her. Or I used to be, but she'd never kicked me out because of it. So Moni had been abandoned after losing her mother. Kel, because he was a saint, took her in when her dad legally waived his rights to his daughter. Moni cried so much the first few weeks, poor thing. And we did our best to console her. To show her that people loved her. Her newfound family would always take care of her.

Then came Rumi. Her parents were hard-core Japanese traditionalists. They planned out her entire life until she ruined it by getting pregnant by her boyfriend, upending their plans. Yeah, she'd been really young, but it happened. Her parents forced her to get rid of it only to disown her, anyway. She shamed her family.

Word had spread of Ohana Surfing Club helping kids in need and giving them jobs and a loving and stable environment. So she came to Kel and begged him to take her in. Of course, he did. It took Jon and Kel a lot of legal legwork to get her parents to sign over their rights.

So, he and Jon fostered the two girls. I was the only one who never got fostered, but I loved that I was still a part of this amazing family.

With Zay being twenty and me nineteen, we needed our own space. The surf club was crowded and loud. Zay and I had no more privacy to do what we wanted sexually. Even after being boyfriends for three years, we still couldn't keep our hands off each other. God, I loved that. We never got tired of it. Zay always made sure to show me how much he loved me. How was it possible to love someone more after being boyfriends for so long?

Our love was like our superpower. Whenever anything went wrong, we lifted each other up and held on tight until the pain went away. And we were so much stronger together. Two strong waves merged into one for a more powerful wave that could prove disastrous or become the ride of your life. Zay and I became a double up wave, and we were each other's wild rides.

It was late, and Zay draped his blanket over our heads while crammed in his bed as Mateo and Levi slept. I was used to sleeping with him, but we switched to smaller beds to make room for the other two boys. Zay and I were just too big for his single now. That didn't stop us from fooling around. We needed to be super creative and super quiet to get sexy alone time.

It was stuffy under the covers, and we sweated as Zay's cock slowly slid in and out of me with my legs folded back for maximum penetration. We'd both had sex so often that we barely needed prepping anymore. Just a good clean-up and some lube, and in, he eased his large, sexy dick.

I bit back a groan when he hit my sensitive prostate. Stars danced behind my eyelids, and when other needy sounds came out of me, Zay swallowed them with a kiss. Staying quiet was the hardest part because we liked to be loud when we made love before, when we had the room to ourselves, or when we went bold and fucked outside someplace where we weren't likely to get caught.

"You like my dick filling you, baby?" he asked in my ear like a whispering ghost, sending shudders and chills through my body, and I didn't know if it was from his naughty words or his breath tickling my skin.

I opened my eyes to stare at his darkened amber orbs and nodded. Zay kept his reading light on under the covers so we could watch each other get wrecked. His face glowed beautifully, and the sweat beading on his face sparkled like glitter in the dim light.

"Always," I breathed.

Zay pressed his forehead to mine and pumped faster, harder, and deeper. His fingers threaded to the sides of my head, gripping my hair painfully, but I loved the sting. A reminder that I was alive and in love with this man.

His kisses were controlling, owning me. Taking what he wanted as the scruff on his face left a delicious burn on my skin.

When he hit my prostate again, I reached between our flushed bodies and grabbed my cock, stroking it to the rhythm of his pumps.

"Come for me, baby. Show me how much you love me."

I squeezed my inner muscles that tightly wrapped around him, making him gasp for breath. He hit that delicious spot harder, and my eyes rolled into the back of my head. Blackness and stars were all I saw as the tingles traveled down my spine, pulling my nuts tight against me.

"Fuck…"

I stroked faster, and in seconds, I came all over my stomach and hand. Zay pressed back down on top of me, and our stomachs glided over my sticky mess. My fingers gripped his back when his cock burned like fire and swelled, filling me even more. Then his hot release hit deep inside, and the best feeling ever. I loved when Zay came in me, marking me, reminding me he owned me, and I owned him.

We eventually did away with condoms since we had been our firsts and had no interest in finding seconds with anyone else.

After cleaning ourselves up, we kissed once more, said we loved each other, and I climbed back into my bed, already missing my boo. I hated not being able to sleep with him all night. Maybe one day we'd get a place of our own.

Soon, life went from chaotic and wonderful before taking a downward spiral into hell. After fighting advanced prostate cancer, Jon was terminal. He refused any more treatment, leaving Kel to work his ass off at the shop, taking care of the kids and his dad at home. He was exhausted all the time and stressed. He didn't surf enough, not having the time. We all tried to make life a little easier on him, but how could we with his dad dying?

All of us were already grieving, knowing Jon would eventually leave us forever. He was the sweetest man and didn't deserve this. Kel had been more like a father to us than Jon because he was around more, but Jon was such a good man. How could life throw this disease at him? So unfair.

When Kel gave us the news, Mateo got pissed off and went surfing alone while Levi buried himself in schoolwork. Zay and I were left alone in our bedroom, so he held me as I cried. Zay, too, tried to hold it back, and while he was stronger than me, his eyes watered too. I straddled his lap and nestled my face into his neck as I tightly gripped him.

"Why does this have to happen?" I sobbed. "He's so amazing."

Zay slipped his hands underneath my T-shirt and rubbed my back in gentle strokes. "I don't know, baby."

"Why won't he get help? What if the treatments help him get better?"

"I know. He's so tired from all the treatment, but the cancer came back."

I sat up and wiped my nose with my hand. "He needs to fight harder. And he won't let us see him! He won't let us even say goodbye," I wailed like some infant, but I didn't care.

Zay pulled me back to him as I sobbed all over him. "He wants to die without us all fawning and crying all over him. I get it, but… you're right. I would like to see him too."

"It's not fucking fair, Bae."

"None of it is."

I'd just turned twenty, and Jon was still hanging in there while Kel did his best to keep us up-to-date on his condition. The stress of it all had me toking more, and I wore my smiles and laid-back attitude like armor. Not to hide my pain from others but to keep me sane.

It didn't help that Mom slipped again, calling me all the time for help. She'd been doing good for a while after finding some dude to put up with her longer than a one-nighter. But they broke up, and she went back to her old ways. Now that I wasn't in school anymore, it wasn't as hard time-wise to help her, but it didn't matter. It still emotionally drained me when my emotions were already hanging by a thread. She'd never get her shit together.

Kel walked into the surf shop in the early morning before we opened, looking super tired and stressed. He'd been gone more and more taking care of Jon. At least he had a nurse now who helped.

Zay and I sat behind the counter, getting ready for the day. I was on my phone scrolling through Instagram while Zay was updating the inventory. We had no one else on the books for surfing lessons until later in the afternoon.

"Zay, can you round up everyone, please? We need a family meeting, and it's mandatory. Everyone needs to drop everything. If they're still sleeping, wake them up."

I looked at Zay, who looked at me. His amber eyes looked like how I felt. Nervous. Anxious. My stomach twisted in knots. What was going on? What else could go wrong? Kel rarely called for a meeting.

"Uh, sure, Kel," he said and left to grab everyone who was still upstairs, except for Mateo, who spent most of his time in the workshop, repairing some old boards. He'd been hiding out there more and more lately, blasting old-school punk music. I hated that he kept withdrawing from us. After all this time, we still knew very little about Mateo.

Once Zay gathered everyone, we all headed outside on the beach to talk.

The first one to question everything was Levi, with bright hazel eyes full of suspicion. "What's happened?"

Kel pinched the bridge of his nose and took a deep breath. "So, to the point. There are going to be some major changes coming up. I… shit. Between my dad being so sick and the medical expenses piling up, I had to take out two loans on the shop. I'm currently spending more than I'm earning, and I can't fucking financially get caught up."

We all glanced at each other with the same look on our faces. The 'oh shit' face.

"Dude, are we out of a job?" Zay asked.

"No. Not if I can help it. A company has been hounding me to buy up the shop. There's going to be a boutique resort coming into the area."

We all groaned. North Shore had been a hot spot lately, with lots of tourists wanting to get the genuine surfer flavor. That meant lots of businesses had been trying to build up in the area, which also meant prices would go up around here, and it was already fucking expensive.

"We heard the rumors," Levi said.

"Did you sell?" Rumi asked.

Kel stood there stone-faced. It was hard to get a read on him. "Not exactly. The owner of the company made a deal with me instead. He wants to keep the shop open, and I would be a co-owner with him. I can pay off all my debts with his portion of the sale. But you should know that the place won't be the same. It will have to get a redesign to keep in line with the style and theme of the resort."

"What happens to us?" Mateo asked as we all nodded in agreement.

"Nothing. The deal was that you would keep your jobs. I make no promises, but I'll try to get you all pay raises, and I'll do my best to keep your living arrangements. If not, I will find a way to keep you all sheltered. But that's something I need to talk to Anders Stone about."

Levi reacted first, apparently, knowing who this dude, Anders Stone, was and his development company. He said Stone had been buying up property all over the North Shore.

Then Kel hit us with another whopper. He had gone on a date with Anders Stone, not knowing who he was at the time. He was the same hottie older dude who came into the shop a few weeks ago. Apparently, Anders made the buyout deal more tasty as long as Kel dated him. I had no idea Kel even liked dudes, not that we ever saw him date anyone.

"That's like extortion, right?" Mateo asked.

"What a dick move," Zay mumbled.

But Kel explained it was better than being completely bought out and us with nowhere else to go. At least he kept half the rights to the shop, and we got to keep working with a place to live. Kel said that

Anders didn't have to make this offer, and it was a good one. His only other choice was to lose everything eventually.

There was more arguing, suggestions, and discussions, but in the end, Kel had already decided and signed the contract, which made it a done deal. The lengths he went through for us and to keep the shop open broke my heart, especially with Jon dying. The rest of the kids felt it too. You could see it on their faces. It broke our hearts, but our gratitude toward this man soared.

We all gathered around Kel like a protective barrier and gave him a group hug. He fought back the tears, but he couldn't hide his emotion. "You know how life is. Like surfing, you need to roll with the swells until that perfect moment lifts you away onto a new adventure, hopefully, a better one than before. I love you guys."

CHAPTER NINETEEN

Zayden

SHORTLY AFTER OUR FAMILY MEETING ABOUT THE STATE OF THE SURF shop, we got to meet Anders Stone. He introduced himself, and since he was to be our new boss alongside Kel, we had to put up with him, but that didn't mean we had to like him. I took an instant dislike to him for setting up Kel on this dating thing and using the shop as leverage against Kel. Honestly, I wanted to fucking deck the dude, but I held back. Even Noah didn't like him, and Noah fucking liked everyone.

But it was Levi who tore Anders a new one when we finally met the older man. Only he had the balls to say something which was so like him; telling Anders what he did to Kel was a dick move.

To my surprise, Anders admitted his arrangement was shitty. He didn't just sit there and defend his lame-ass actions with lame-ass excuses. as I assumed. But then he turned to Kel and told him he was tearing up their dating agreement and allowing Kel to keep half the surf shop as promised with no conditions.

Kel was as surprised as we were. They headed outside for a brief meeting alone, leaving us to talk amongst ourselves.

"What do you think?" Levi asked. "He's a tool, right?"

Mateo nodded. "Yep. He shouldn't have done that to our Kel. Nice fucking trick. What shitty thing is he up to now?"

"Nah, bros... think about it. He likes Kel enough to give up the whole dating thing and help keep the shop open. It's kinda romantic," Noah said. I smiled, pulled him into me, and gave him a quick kiss on his head. "He's probably gonna try to make things up to Kel. Maybe he's not so bad."

Moni didn't buy it, but Rumi seemed to be on Noah's side.

I wasn't quite on board with Noah's thoughts about the man, but he was a more forgiving person. Only time would tell how good Anders really was. "We can complain all we want, but at the end of the day, this is all Kel's decision, and we need to accept it. If he wants to keep dating the tool, then let him. I don't want to hear you all bitching at Kel about it at all, got it? Kel has enough stress going on without us adding to it. Let's be supportive," I said, looking at each kid in the eyes. I wasn't their boss, but they treated me like their older brother, and I happily took on the role.

They all mumbled their agreement.

And as if things couldn't get worse, a few days later, all hell broke loose.

Jon had been rushed to the hospital for a stroke and died a few hours later. We all tried desperately to visit Kel. To tell him we loved him, but Anders denied us at every fucking turn. And again, I wanted to deck the dude, but admittedly, he was kind about it and explained that it was Kel who refused to see anyone. His grief ran too deep.

That was when I started the beach get-togethers at night. We used each other to lean on in our own grief.

I reined in my anger at Jon for not getting any more treatment and at Kel for keeping us from Jon and him while he grieved. The helplessness was fucking frustrating. Jon had been like a father to me, and none of us ever got to say goodbye. But I held back the tears except in private with Noah.

We all sat on beach blankets under the starry night and cool breeze coming off the water.

Moni leaned into the stoic Mateo. We all loved Moni, but he had the most patience for her, so she grew pretty attached to him. She was crying quietly as he had an arm wrapped around her. But he looked fucking angry and withdrawn. Mateo had gone silent since Jon's death and his nightmares at night grew worse. I fucking worried about him and kept a close watch to make sure he didn't slip back into drugs again.

Noah sat between my spread legs and lit a blunt. After he took a drag, he passed it to me, then around in a circle, it went except to Mateo, who refused to smoke weed. The rest of us smoked and grieved in silence.

As the night grew late, we headed inside, and I went straight to the bathroom, turned on the shower, and got undressed. I'd bottled up the pain, and now I needed to fucking explode. When the water turned warm enough, I stepped under the spray and rested my head against the shower tiles to cry. To finally release that pressure valve.

I hadn't noticed Noah coming in until he was in the shower with me and wrapping his arms around my waist from behind. I turned around to face him and cried into his shoulder. He held me tight with his own sobbing, sending shudders through me.

"I miss him so much, and I'm so fucking angry."

"I know, Bae."

"God, what would I do without you?"

Noah looked up at me with his face covered in tears and water from the shower. His green eyes were red-rimmed and in pain. He reached up and grasped my face. "No, Zay. What would I do without you? You're my everything."

More tears slipped out from his words, and I shook my head. "I love you so much, No."

"You know how much I love you."

Suddenly, Noah dropped to his knees and took my dick in his hand, stroking up and down my shaft in languid movements. It was his way of doing what he could to make me feel better, and I let him though I wasn't overly horny at the moment. But it didn't take long for me to get hard. He looked up at me as he ran his tongue along the entire underside of my cock, then curled it around my cock head, making me hiss. God, I never got tired of his mouth on me.

I fisted his hair and pulled his head back. He opened his mouth, knowing exactly what I wanted, and I slipped my cock in as far as he'd let me.

"My beautiful, Noah."

He moaned as I pushed deeper down his throat, but not so far that he choked. Noah reached around to my ass and pulled me into him even deeper. I slammed my eyes shut as he gagged around my sensitive skin, making me thrust, but he pulled back in time, ready for my reaction.

Soon he had me ready to explode. I pulled his mouth off of me by his hair and stroked myself. He opened his mouth again, allowing me to shoot my come on his tongue and face.

Once I was spent, I slid down into the tub with him and cleaned his face with a wash rag, and then we held each other until the warm water ran out.

I wasn't sure what I'd do without him. He was my everything. He was my rock. Someone I could always rely on to keep me from falling. But he wasn't wrong when he'd say the same things about me. We held each other up.

Noah and I were like a double-up wave. Together we were stronger and more powerful.

Noah and I stood staring out at the choppy waves. All surfing lessons had to be canceled due to the dangerous current, but these waves were made for us. We lived for big and challenging swells.

Both of us had been in a bit of a funk lately until Kel finally came out of his hole after grieving. He still hurt, but he slowly came around. And just when I thought he'd return to work, his brother Keo showed up after twenty-four fucking years and disrupted everything. Asshole.

Who the hell did he think he was that he could just come back into Kel's life like that and expect everything to go back to the way things were? All of us had Kel's back. If his brother made the wrong move or upset Kel further, we'd deal with Keo. He wasn't family anymore. *We* were Kel's family. Keo lost that right years ago when he left Kel to mourn his mother alone.

The good news out of all this was that Anders made me shop manager and, with it, a pay raise to twenty bucks an hour. The most money I'd ever made. Between Noah's and my salaries, we'd be able to save for an apartment finally.

"Brah, those waves are totally epic," Noah said, pulling me out of my stressful thoughts.

I glanced at the red flags along the beach. Yes, the conditions were dangerous, but we lived for these kinds of waves and surfed on them for competition. I knew these waters. Surfing them was my thing. And I knew how good Noah was too.

"Ready?" I asked him.

"Dude, I live for this."

We grabbed our boards and ran into the water, which was still warm enough before fall hit, so we didn't need our wetsuits. We quickly jumped on our boards and paddled out toward calmer waters.

Noah instantly hit a wave, and I watched him catch air and spin. He was amazing to watch. I'd tried to get him to compete, but he never felt good enough. Plus, he was pretty content with the way things were. Noah was just someone who chose to live the good life as much as possible. The surfing life.

I let him come back to me so we could ride the waves together. I rode the barrel, surrounded by the power of the water under my board. The roar of the water deafened all other sounds. When I exploded free from the white water as it crashed over me, I caught the lip of the wave and hit the air. When I landed, I fell off my board and came up for air. I looked around for Noah with a smile on my face at how high I got, but I couldn't see him.

I saw a spot of red from his board, but no Noah. He should've reached the surface by now.

Something was wrong.

Before I panicked, I ditched my board and swam toward the direction of his board, and that's when I saw him floating before a wave came crashing down on him.

No.

No, no, no.

Why wasn't he moving or swimming?

I finally reached him, and I shoved my panic aside to get him out of the water immediately. I flipped him onto his back and swam with him back to shore. It was a struggle, fighting the waves, but soon I saw Anders in the water with us, helping get Noah out. We dragged him onto some towels on his back as I gripped my hair and paced back and forth while panic blanked out my mind, and Anders inspected my boyfriend.

My best friend.

My life partner.

"Is he breathing?" But I didn't wait for an answer as my training finally kicked in, shoving Anders aside. "Forget it. Grab me another beach towel." When he did, I told him to roll it up as I checked Noah's pulse. There was a faint one.

I shoved the rolled-up towel under his neck and began CPR. My training took over, and I worked on chest compressions, then I tipped his head back and breathed into his mouth.

My heart was threatening to give out on me as my eyes welled, making everything blurry.

Please, baby. Please wake up.

Finally, Noah coughed and sputtered water from his lungs and out of his mouth. He didn't wake up, but he was fucking breathing.

"He must have hit his head, man. Dammit, the wave must have caught him off guard for him not to fall right. Noah's a pro."

"Don't move him," Anders said as he dialed 9-11.

I rode in the ambulance with Noah as Anders raced off to get Kel and bring him to the hospital. By the time we got there, they had taken my Noah away and refused to let me back there. It pissed me off, but I backed off because Noah was the priority. When they whisked him away, I sat still wet from the ocean and curled up in a chair, shivering and letting my emotions out finally, when a nurse came out and handed me a blanket.

Please don't let him die. He's all I've got. He's my everything. Let him live. Let him live.

Kel and Anders finally arrived, but they still wouldn't let me see my Noah unless one of them pretended to be his father. None of us were his legal family. And no way we'd call Noah's useless mother.

Kel was too young to be Noah's father, so Anders took up the role, thank fuck, which also swayed my opinion of him. After he took care of Kel while he grieved when he didn't have to, and now this with Noah, Anders instantly became family right then.

They told us his room number, and I took off running. I burst into his room to see his head bandaged up and him awake. I choked back a sob and rushed to his side, taking his hand and ignoring the nurse and doctor. He smiled up at me when I gently kissed his head.

"I thought I lost you."

God, I couldn't stop the tears, wiping my face with my free hand. When I pulled his limp body out of the water, I thought he had died for sure. Now to see him alive and smiling... I fucking lost it as the relief consumed me, as was the crushing weight that pushed me down and down until I knew Noah was alive and well. Now I could breathe again.

Anders and Kel finally walked in with me, smiling, and that my Noah was okay.

"Dude, I'm okay. Except my head feels like someone's been hammerin' me, and the room won't stop spinnin'," he said. "Was it at least a rad move that made me wipeout?"

I choked back a laugh. I hadn't seen his move, but I told him it was the most rad move ever.

The doctor explained to us that Noah had a nasty concussion and he needed to rest and not do anything strenuous for a few weeks. Anders and Kel talked to the doctor while I focused on my Noah, dragging fingers across his cheek. Then I leaned in to kiss him.

He reached for my face, and I leaned into his touch, then kissed his palm. "I'm okay, Zay Bae," he whispered.

Kel told us we could stay at his house because Jon's nurse was still there. That he'd pay her more to take care of Noah while he was in recovery. He also banned Noah from surfing for a month.

Before Kel and Anders left, Noah reached for Kel. "Please don't tell my mom. I don't want to get my... hopes up that she'll show up or... care."

God, that broke my heart. She should've been here, watching over her son, but she was probably drunk off her ass as usual.

"You got it," Kel said.

When the room cleared out, I crawled into bed with him, careful of all the wires, and stroked his face.

"Don't ever do that again," I ordered.

His smile was broad but tired. "Brah, no promises."

"Do you have any idea how lucky you are? Some surfers like you break their necks."

"I guess someone's watchin' out for me."

"And I am too. I'll take care of you, not just while you're injured, but forever."

Noah's smile was sad and tired. "That sounds really nice."

I kissed his bandaged head as he dozed off, and I fell asleep with him.

CHAPTER TWENTY

Noah

I crawled out of the bed I shared with Zay at Kel's place. We still lived there while I recuperated. It'd been four weeks since my tumble onto the sea floor. Four weeks without surfing. Four weeks without fucking. I loved Zay and Kel, but they'd both been too overprotective, and I was getting antsy, wanting to climb out of my own skin. It was a fucking drag. I was fine.

The morning was dark with rain, and the heavy drops sounded like thunder on the roof, reminding me of my mood. I stumbled into the bathroom to take a piss, and after I washed my hands, I opened the medicine cabinet and pulled out a couple of Advil. My head fucking pounded this morning, like most days, but I stopped telling Zay when my head hurt because he'd freak out again and try to drag me to the doctor. At least I wasn't dizzy anymore. And the weed helped, so I'd been smoking it more.

I just couldn't take being trapped, unable to do anything for another month. I was losing it, not used to holding still for long periods. You don't realize how much you do stuff and move around until you aren't allowed to.

But my head wasn't the only reason I woke up. I tossed and turned all night because I had to visit Mom. I hadn't seen her since before my accident. She had no idea what had happened to me, and I planned to keep it that way. She wouldn't give a shit. Besides, Mom would be too obliterated, anyway. Probably.

Mateo recently moved in, too, staying in the living room, while Levi, Moni, and Rumi stayed at Kel's bro's place. Keo and Kel had reunited and made amends, and I did my best to like Keo. He really stepped up when some asshats torched the surf shop in retaliation against Kel for selling off the shop and dating the enemy—the man who was building a resort into our community.

I got it. The resort would cause the cost of living to skyrocket and put the mom-and-pop shops out of business. But we were already poor here. And Anders would provide hundreds and hundreds of jobs, along with affordable housing. But to burn the shop down? What purpose did that serve? What did those men who attacked hope to accomplish?

The shop burned to the ground, and we all suffered over the loss, but Anders promised to rebuild. I guess it was a good thing he was rich.

I walked into the kitchen and made myself some coffee, and as I waited for my brew, I scrolled through my phone, looking at nothing, killing time and sick of being bored. Kel didn't allow me to surf, work, or play any video games as they had too much stimulation for my damaged brain. I spent most of the past month in bed reading or on my phone. It drove me nuts and made me so irritable I even annoyed myself. It wasn't like me to be this moody and depressed. But I knew as soon as I got to surf again and make epic love to my bae things would get better.

Tomorrow I'd go to the doctor for the all-clear. Fucking finally.

"Hey, babe," Zay said, walking into the kitchen with half-closed eyes, dark hair sticking out widely, yawning, and looking entirely too cute. My mood instantly improved at the sight of him. I wasn't sure how Zay could do that, like it was his superpower or something.

He dragged his feet over to me and kissed my head, then pulled me into a sleepy hug. I inhaled his manly, earthy scent and smells of sleep like a drug. It was my favorite, keeping me in a perpetual high from Zay smells.

"Hey, Bae."

"You're up early."

"Yeah, I couldn't sleep… Mom."

"Ah, right. I'll go with you if you want."

I shook my head. "Nah, it's all good. You gotta work."

As much as I loved Zay, and we'd spent almost every waking moment together since we'd been a couple, I needed a break from him. A break from his smothering and mothering. Seeing Mom wasn't the best break, but one stressor at a time.

"Maybe I should drive…"

I pressed a hand to his bare chest and took a deep breath to keep from getting upset or angry with him. I didn't want to hurt my boo. "I'm fine to drive, Zay. It's been four weeks now."

"I know, but maybe…"

"Stop! I'm fucking fine!"

Goddammit! These stupid fucking emotions.

I stormed off as my eyes welled with tears, not from anger, but from how I talked to my Zay. It wasn't like me. I was just suffocating here, but that was a shitty excuse. I was mean to my bae, and I never yelled at him.

The guilt had me stopping in my tracks. I turned to face him. "I'm so sorry."

Zay's surprised face softened, and he gave me a smile I didn't deserve. He walked over to me and hugged me. "Talk to me, baby. What's going on in that gorgeous head of yours?"

I wrapped my arms around his waist and rested my head on his shoulder. "I'm tired of everyone fuckin' babying me. It makes it hard for me to breathe."

"Oh... we only do it because we worry and love you."

"I know, but... it's been a month now. Y'all need to stop freakin' out."

"Okay, I'm sorry. It's just... when I thought you were dead..."

"I get it. I'd be the same, but still..."

He cupped my face and lifted it to look at him. "How about this? Once the doctor gives you the green light, we'll have some fun. Some real fun. Sexy fun."

He pulled me against his chest, and I smiled for the first time since I woke up. "Really?"

"Yes."

"Thank fuck. I'm tired of jacking off in the shower."

Zay laughed, and I enjoyed the rumble in his chest against mine. "You and me both, baby."

When I walked into the apartment, nothing had changed. The ever-familiar stale, lingering smell of alcohol, cigarettes, and old food remained the same. Honestly, I often wondered how Mom was still alive. She was young at only thirty-six, but still, her lifestyle wouldn't allow for longevity.

I headed straight to her room to get her up for the day, though it was late morning already. Her schedule that I kept track of didn't show her working today, which meant she'd probably be extra hung over. She probably partied last night, so I hoped I didn't walk in there to find her sleeping with some naked dude. It wouldn't have been the first time. No kid should ever see their parent having sex and shit.

God, this crap with Mom emotionally and mentally exhausted me, even with my breaks from her. She lived in my brain rent-free. I worried for her way too much. I hated her, yet loved her. The conflicting emotions wore me out, not to mention the extra work I needed to do with parenting my parent.

Sometimes, I just wanted to curl up in a corner and never leave despite my need to always slip a smile on my face and show the world that I was just fine. Only Zay fully understood me and never pushed or questioned me. He accepted me just as I was, and I wasn't sure I would've been okay if he hadn't been in my life, holding me up.

When I opened her bedroom door, holding my breath to what I'd find, she wasn't there. Or at least she wasn't in bed. She even drew the blinds open. My brows furrowed as I made my way to the bathroom. The only thing in there was humidity and lingering scents of body wash from a shower earlier.

Huh.

She must've dragged her body out of bed. Where did she go? She didn't have work today. Unless they called her in.

I could've texted her and asked, but I didn't bother.

After I opened up all the windows to air out the place, I headed to the kitchen to start cleaning the apartment. Then I'd work on bills and prepping meals if she had any food left. If not, I'd have to go grocery shopping.

As I turned on the faucet to warm the water, I started rinsing off dishes and putting them in the dishwasher. At least the ancient thing was still working. Once I loaded the dishwasher, I put soap in and ran it. I then hand-washed anything that hadn't fit in the washer.

The kitchen was finally scrubbed down, so I headed into Mom's room, gathered her dirty clothes and put them in the washer, made her bed, and cleaned her bathroom.

By the time I finished dusting and vacuuming, my head was pounding again. One of those throbbing kinds right at the front of my brain that sent shooting pains along the rest of my head. I rummaged through Mom's medicine cabinet and pulled out a couple of Advil again, and swallowed them dry.

I sat down at the kitchen table, rubbing my temples, and went through all of Mom's mail to find her bills. She'd put me on her bank account a while ago, so she didn't have to deal. It not only made it easier for me to pay the bills, but to put money into her account, and her job did direct deposit.

When I finished everything, my mood lifted a little. My headache was reduced to a small dull yet annoying ache, and I'd accomplished a lot. Plus, she hadn't been home, so I didn't have to deal with her fluctuations of cruelty and kindness.

All that growing positivity went out the window when keys rattled in the front door, taunting me of the impending drama about to start. My mood instantly deflated.

Mom walked in looking... strangely normal and not wasted, carrying two bags of groceries.

"Noah? I didn't expect you today."

Did she ever?

Instead of being snappy, I put on my shield and gave her a big smile. "I texted you yesterday that I had planned to come over, remember?"

Her eyes clouded over as she got lost in her memories, trying to recall our text. She'd been drunk at the time, judging by her unreadable texts.

"Oh, I..."

"It's okay," I blurted. "The apartment's clean, your clothes are in the dryer, and I finished paying the bills."

She walked over and kissed my head. "Thank you, Noah. You're the best. Always taking care of me."

I choked back my watering eyes and avoided her face, so she didn't see. "It's no problem."

"I miss you. You've been working so much."

With a quick swipe at my face to gather the annoying tears, I coughed away my pain. I didn't know which was worse. Her cruel words or her sweet ones. Her sweet ones gave me only a tiny taste of love and hope that I never got to have. She'd snatch it away like a bully as soon as she was wasted.

I hadn't only been busy at the shop, but with Zay. I'd never told her about him. It was weird, but I felt if Zay got to know her, she'd ruin him somehow. Contaminate him. I didn't want or need her to say something mean to him. He was beautiful, and he'd had enough cruelty in his life.

"I gotta go," I said before I started sobbing. Ugh, I'd been particularly emotional lately, and I hated it. It had always been that way, but it was worse since my injury, making me more sensitive than usual. It was probably because I'd been babied and cooped up for far too long.

I gave her a little kiss on her cheek, walked to the door, and gripped the handle about to leave before Mom stopped me.

"Don't you want to stay for lunch? Or... I got some ice cream. It's your favorite... uh, coffee, right? We could share."

My back was turned to her, but I heard—no, sensed—the need in her voice. I couldn't do this. If I got close again or had just a tiny bit of hope, she'd just crush it like an ant underfoot as she always did. It was getting harder and harder to deal with, and I no longer trusted her with my heart.

"My favorite is vanilla. Anyway, some other time, Mom."

I left before she could talk me into it.

I dragged my crushed soul back to Kel's place, took a shower, and made an early dinner, making extra for when Zay got home. Kel had spent most of his time over at Anders' house, so I never made some for him.

Because Zay was much better at cooking than me, he had made dinner for us when we lived in the shop. But since I'd been home for a fucking month, and to keep from being bored, I took over.

Tonight I made hamburgers and fries. Not exciting, but it was food. Zay liked my burgers, anyway.

I didn't hear him come in over the frying of meat on the stove, but he wrapped his arms around my waist. A chill swept up my body because he was soaking wet from the pouring rain, yet my tense muscles eased with his touch. His other superpower. The one thing I could count on with my boo was that he loved me and always showed me how much.

"Dude! Off," I giggled from the cold wetness, but suddenly my emotions plummeted now that my bae had come home and I was safely in his arms after my rough day.

God, I was such a fucking mess.

He pulled away to dry off, but I turned in his arms and yanked him back. With a spatula still in my hand, I wrapped my arms around him, let loose the dam of my pent-up emotions, and cried in his chest.

What the fuck was wrong with me? It wasn't unusual for me to be sensitive, but not this sensitive.

"What's wrong, baby?" His soft and tender voice sent ripples of sobbing through me. The tears had been more of a catharsis than being upset. His reassuring voice made me feel whole again.

"Nothing. Mom. Everything. I dunno."

Zay lifted my face by my chin and pressed soft, tender kisses all over my face, kissing away my tears. "You're home now with me. Someone who loves you more than life itself."

God, I needed to hear those words. Fat tears rolled down my face, and he wiped them away with his thumbs and a sweet, understanding smile. The longer I lived with him, showing me how love was supposed to be, the more upset I got with my mom, feeling the full effects of her neglect.

Zay reached around me, turned off the stove, pulled the spatula out of my hand, and set it on the counter. Then he tugged me out of the kitchen and into the bedroom.

"Fuck the doctor tomorrow. We're doing this now. You need some lovin', baby."

Yes, I did. Desperately so.

Zay removed all his wet clothes and dropped them on the floor with heavy plops, and then he stripped me down. Once we both stood naked, he pulled my face into a deep, all-consuming kiss, thrusting his tongue into my mouth. I knew this kiss. A kiss that meant he'd take charge and take care of me.

When you spent most of your life caring for someone, having another person take care of you for a while was soul-cleansing. It was like Zay erased all the bad and replaced it with new, sweet memories.

"Lie on the bed, baby," he said when he pulled away.

"Zay..." I whispered as I fell into the bed, not knowing what I even wanted to say.

"I've got you, No."

He grabbed my thighs, pushed them back to expose my hole, and swiped his tongue across the sensitive muscle. My body instantly relaxed as I let my mind get swept away like a wave with a perfect barrel. My cock wept at its intentional neglect while Zay ate my ass.

Strong fingers pried me apart, and as I loosened for him, his tongue dug deeper. He nipped, licked, and sucked while I ached, wanting to come now but wanting this to linger forever. I was on the cusp of needing to be consumed for longer yet wanting to let go of everything and come to his warm and wet mouth.

I reached for my dick to stroke, but he looked up and shook his head. "That's mine," he said, so instead, I combed my fingers through his thick hair and held on for the ride.

After tongue fucking me for a while, making me nice, loose, and relaxed, Zay pulled away and grabbed our lube from the side table and slathered his dick and mine. I was so fucking sensitive already; I nearly blew at his touch and had to force it back with all the power I had.

"God, you look so wrecked already. So beautiful," he whispered and leaned in for a quick kiss.

"Please... hurry."

We hadn't had sex in a while, so he edged his fat cockhead in slowly, working me, filling me with the beautiful burn, and I was desperate for more. I could take it.

"In me already."

I took in his crooked smile and blown-black amber eyes, loving him and needing him. He was my everything. With one thrust, he was fully seated. Thank fuck. It hurt a lot, but I breathed him in, allowing me to adjust. I was full of my Zay Bae. We became one again. While I loved all our foreplay or sometimes doing kinky play, having him inside me was the best. It was the closest we could get to each other, and my mind and soul filled with love for this man.

Zay hovered over me, gripping my head as he slowly pulled out like a threat to end things before he slammed home, forcing my back to arch for more when he hit that perfect spot. My eyes slammed shut to take in every thrust, every touch, his manly smell, and his breath on my skin. I whimpered with pleasure, and from finally getting to make love.

Usually, our lovemaking was sweet and gentle, but Zay took me away from my pain and filled me with lust and need. This was exactly what I needed. For Zay to take over and remind me I belonged to him and he belonged to me. That I was loved and cared for.

CHAPTER TWENTY-ONE

Zayden

THE EVENING BLEW A DELICATE BREEZE WITH A BRIGHT BLANKET OF stars. The tiki torches cast a warm glow on us as we sat on the beach, sharing a blunt and drinking beer I'd bought now that I could legally buy alcohol. Noah and I rarely drank for obvious reasons, but we sipped a little beer while having a beach party, something we do every weekend now.

The surf shop was still being rebuilt, and we had two new members of our group and a little family, Lucy and Mia Stone, Anders' daughters. Mia was super sweet and smart. Way more mature than our shared age of twenty-one. Lucy was nineteen and a firecracker, but she had a sweetness to her, too, if not outspoken. The two girls not only had different personalities, but they barely looked alike. Mia shared her father's appearance with his brown hair and leaner frame. Whereas Lucy looked like her mother, curvy with long red hair.

Noah sat between my legs, taking a long drag from the blunt as I kissed his neck. He'd been doing much better now that his doctor cleared him to do whatever he wanted, which was tons of surfing and sex. The whole concussion injury and not being able to do anything stimulating took its toll on him. It killed me as I watched him grow more and more depressed, losing his bright light. Thank fuck, it was all over now.

After he passed the blunt to Lucy, he craned his neck and puckered his lips. I smiled and kissed him.

"Which one?" he whispered.

I raised a brow to clarify what he meant.

"Mat... do you think he's into Mia or Lu Lu?" he whispered, so no one heard us.

I glanced over at Mateo and held back a laugh as I watched him practically drool at the Stone sisters. It was nice to see him not so stressed. Pining was so much better than mentally withdrawing.

Noah turned around to straddle my lap and wrapped his arms around my neck. He pressed his lips to mine, and with a quick swipe of his tongue on my mouth, I opened for him. I loved how he wanted to kiss all the time, and he was so fucking good at it. And I also loved how open he was, unafraid to show the world how much we loved each other. But it was also his need to exhibit his sexuality.

We came up for air, and he pressed gentle kisses on my throat, then moved up to my ear. I slid my eyes closed as my cock swelled in my board shorts, but he blocked it with his body, so I didn't care.

"Let's make a bet," he said, nibbling my lobe.

"What sort of bet?"

"Guess which one Mat's obsessin' over. If I win, I want a BJ right here on the beach."

"It has to be at night, No. We don't want to get arrested."

"Deal."

I would've done it whether or not we bet, but this was fun, too.

"What do you want, Bae?"

"I don't know... I have everything I could ever want, baby."

"Aww. I love you, too." He pulled my face into another kiss.

"Dudes... do you ever stop making out?" Levi asked. It was a rhetorical question because we never did, and he knew it.

Noah rested his head on my shoulder, looking at Levi. I couldn't see his face, but I knew he'd have a teasing smirk as if Levi had just dared him to show how much more he could put on display.

I moved my mouth to his ear, so no one heard us. "If I win, the next time we sit together behind the counter at the shop while we're working, you'll suck me off. No one will notice you down there, but I'll feel you consuming me."

His body stiffened, and he slowly turned to face me. "Dude, remind me how I lose in this little game of yours? So hot, boo."

It was definitely more for Noah, but I didn't mind. I really did have everything I ever wanted from him.

"Who's your pick?" I asked.

"Lu Lu," he said, which was his nickname for Lucy.

"I think it's Mia. Lucy seems like she'd be too much for Mat. Mia's also a psych major. She'd understand him."

"Nah, man... Lu Lu will have Mat wrapped around her little finger. He needs someone to own him."

"Kiss on it?"

He pressed his lips to mine to seal the deal.

"Can I have a beer?" Moni asked.

"No," I said.

"But I'm bored!! You all get to drink and smoke. What do Rumi and I get to do? Cart your butts around as designated drivers. Lame!"

If I let the two girls drink, and Kel found out, he'd have my head. While Lucy, Mat, and Levi weren't legally allowed to drink, Moni and Rumi were even younger. No way.

"Don't be that way, MonBon," Noah said. I had no idea where he got half of his nicknames. "You'll get your turn soon."

She rolled her eyes but, at least, stopped complaining. Rumi never complained and was busy chatting it up with Lucy. Both girls seemed to have hit it off.

Levi stood up, brushed sand off his ass, and walked over to Noah and me.

"'Sup, Lev," Noah said.

Levi looked around at the group, then leaned into us. "Can I ask you all a question?"

"Anything," I said.

"So, like... I'm lusting after someone that maybe I'm not supposed to. Well, it's more than a crush. Actually, there's no maybe about it. I really shouldn't, but I can't help it."

Noah leaned in closer to Levi with a mischievous smile and a sparkle in those green eyes. "I like it already."

Levi had started college early since he skipped a grade after some more placement testing. He was going places. Probably more so than the rest of us. Even if Kel hadn't found him prostituting himself, he probably would've done well for himself, like starting his own male brothel or something. It would've been funny had it not been accurate.

"It's... my adviser. He's... older, obviously. He's so fucking hot, too. Shit, I hope I don't have daddy issues. Fuck, I probably do." He shrugged and smiled. "Oh, well."

We all laughed because that was so like Levi to think of such a thing.

"Anyway, he's hot, sexy, wise, and so fucking smart. I keep trying to flirt with him, but he gets all stiff and huffy and ignores it. Ugh, as if that doesn't turn me on more. What can I do to get him to like me?"

I grasped his shoulder and gave him a brotherly shake. "Dude, I hate to break it to you, but you're only seventeen. He's not gonna touch you. Even if you were older, he probably couldn't because of university rules. I think you're shit out of luck, brah."

"Ugh, I was afraid you'd say that. I know. I've been racking my brain to find ways out of this taboo dilemma I've found myself in. And I mean, with him and me together without getting into trouble. But nothing's coming to me."

"I get that you like him, and even if you find a way to reach him, do you really want him to risk his career over your crush?"

He looked at me as if I had just sprouted a tail. "Crush? Crush? This is no crush, I assure you. Crushes are for juveniles. I'm stupidly obsessed with the jerk."

"Dude, wanting him is cool, man, but this is super risky."

Levi deflated and heaved out a dramatic sigh. "Yeah, I don't want to see him fired. But god, it's so fucking hard to keep my hands to myself. I just want to sit on his lap, ride him for eternity, and call him 'daddy.'"

Noah snorted a laugh.

"Isn't there a boy at school who's more your age?" I asked.

"As if. They're stupid and boring, and all they do is party. No, thanks. Anyway, I'll… figure it out."

"Are you sure you're only seventeen?"

He huffed. "Unfortunately."

Levi stood and headed off to talk to Mat, leaving Noah and me shaking our heads and laughing.

"He definitely has daddy issues," Noah said, making me burst out into a laugh.

The morning grew late, but Noah and I didn't have anywhere to be, so we snuggled into each other, not leaving the bed yet. Sometimes I loved just to touch and explore without involving sex. To be intimate without having to get each other off.

Noah curled into me with a leg draped over mine, and I had a leg between his. He looked at me, watching his fingers dance over my face, trailing through my morning scruff, outlining my jaw, then dragging up and along my brows.

"You're so beautiful, Bae. Your eyes are magical like they could grant your every wish." It hadn't been the first time nor the twentieth he had told me this, but I never got tired of it.

"It's your eyes that are the best. Like sea kelp floating on the blue waters where sea turtles like to roam."

We didn't always wax poetic, but sometimes we just needed to hear and tell each other how we felt. Like how to say *'I love you'* without saying *'I love you.'*

I wrapped a piece of his bright blond hair around my fingers. It was a wreck, sticking up everywhere. His hair had never been soft, always filled with sun and saltwater, but I loved that. If you researched images of typical surfers, you'd imagine Noah being on the top of the list. But he was so much deeper than his appearance, laid-back demeanor, or the way he talked. It was these moments I relished, filing away into my memories to be retrieved later.

Romance novels and fairy tales wrote about love like ours. We weren't supposed to be a reality. But here we were, proving the world wrong and that it was possible.

The knock on our door burst our little love bubble. We told them to come in, not wanting to crawl out of bed. Mat walked in, looking nervous as hell.

Apparently, it was Lucy all along he'd been crushing on. Noah had been right. He gave me a gleam in his eyes with a look that said, 'told you so,' making me smile.

Mat came to us, asking for help with kissing since he'd never kissed a girl before. Since there was no one else for help, he asked us. Instead of telling him, Noah showed him.

The poor guy had a little freak out when he was turned on by kissing Noah, but he'd been imagining Lucy the whole time. And Noah was great at calming Mat down.

When he left our room with a little more experience under his belt, Noah straddled me with a big grin on his face. "It's BJ time, Bae. On the beach tonight."

"You win, baby. You got it."

Noah and I walked out to the water's edge, holding hands later that night. We stood there looking out at the sparkling, inky water as the cold shallows lapped at our ankles. The full moon glowed down on us, so we weren't completely masked by darkness, but I didn't see anyone walking along the beach. Usually, it was easy to tell as they walked with the flashlights on their phones.

My stomach fluttered a little, worried about getting caught, but I wanted to do this for my little exhibitionist.

"Remove your shirt, No."

He grabbed the hem of his loose-fitting tank top and pulled it over his head, tossing it back onto the sand. His blond hair glowed in the moonlight like a halo. He looked ethereal. My angel. My exhibitionist angel. I choked back a laugh at the thought.

My hands trailed along his smooth, warm skin and went down, down, down as I dropped to my knees. The cold water covered my calves, and smaller waves smacked my ass, sending chills through my body.

I cupped him, feeling his hard length begging for attention. Then I untied his boardshorts, pulling them down around his ankles.

With another glance around the beach, I said, "Turn around, baby. Hands on your knees."

Noah didn't question it, doing as I ordered. Once he bent over, I spread his cheeks and devoured his ass.

"Fuck... this is so... hot, Bae."

While he had his back turned, and it was too dark to see, I knew his dick would be weeping in desperation. I couldn't wait to lick up his earthy sweetness. And he was right. This *was* hot.

"Zay... need your mouth on me... please."

I turned him around and smiled at his slack face, completely blissed out.

Just wait, baby. You won't be able to stand when I'm done with you.

I grabbed his cock at the base and brought his tip to my mouth. I swirled my tongue over his swollen, leaking tip, savoring Noah's flavor but wishing I could inhale his scent, but it was too breezy for that. The trade winds had been picking up as we got closer to fall.

His hands fisted in my hair, drawing his cock deep into my mouth, and I let him. If he wanted to control things, that was fine by me. This was his show, after all.

He moved his hands down to the sides of my face and used my mouth to fuck in. I gripped his ass, spread his cheeks, and grazed my fingers over his tight pucker as he thrust in and out of my mouth. He went so deep sometimes I gagged, bringing tears to my eyes, but I didn't stop him. Noah understood my limits already. We knew everything about each other.

I looked up at him, breathing through my nose to take him down my throat. His mouth was open, and while I couldn't hear him over the wind and waves, he was probably groaning, panting, and whimpering.

The beach and any worries of getting caught soon vanished as I got solely lost in Noah's pleasure.

"Stroke yourself," he ordered. Rarely did Noah force himself during sex, but when he did, it hit all my hot buttons.

I slid my hand into my shorts, feeling cold wetness from leaking pre-come and salt water, and grabbed my cock. I pushed my shorts down more, exposing my dick, and stroked. The blowjob was sloppy, and I drooled as he used me. And I burned for him.

Suddenly Noah threw his head back as his cock swelled, then hot spurts shot down my throat. I drank him down as I stroked myself faster and faster, but I didn't get to come.

When he was empty, he eased me back and pulled me to stand as he dropped to his knees to finish me off. As soon as his mouth hit my tip, I was done since I was already close. I cried out as he sucked me dry.

Noah stood up, and we wrapped our arms around each other with our shorts at our ankles, holding on for dear life as our hearts threatened to explode out of our chests. We probably looked ridiculous, but I couldn't give two fucks.

"We're *so* doing that again," he said, making me laugh.

CHAPTER TWENTY-TWO

Noah

WE WERE BACK AT THE NEW AND IMPROVED OHANA SURFING CLUB. Back in our small beds. While I loved what Anders did with the place and our rooms, I missed sharing a bed with Zay. And despite loud protests from Mateo and Levi, Zay and I shoved our beds together. Screw it. I refused to sleep alone anymore.

"Zay Bae?" I had to keep my voice low while Mateo and Levi slept.

"Yeah, baby."

"Are we going to get married one day?"

I looked at him and absorbed his sweet, soft smile, staring right at me in the dim light. "That's a given. I plan on spending the rest of my life with you, baby."

I nestled tightly into his side and pressed my nose in his neck to inhale all that I loved about Zay. "Good."

With a smile on my face, sleep found me surrounded by warmth and my happily ever after.

I wasn't sure what woke me up besides the empty space on the bed next to me. I ran my hand on the still-warm spot where Zay had slept. When I sat up, I rubbed my eyes until they adjusted to the sudden light.

"Get up. Everyone." Zay's loud voice had a sudden panic to it, making me instantly awake.

"What's going on?" Levi said, stretching.

"Where's Mat?" I asked, looking around the room and seeing his empty bed.

"On his way to hell. Fuck! I should've done a better job to stop him."

I grabbed Zay by the shoulders to calm his pacing. "Talk to me. What's goin' on"

"Mat woke up and headed to the bathroom, which woke me up. I didn't think anything of it and tried to go back to sleep, but he grabbed his phone and keys after getting dressed. Something seemed off about him... you both noticed, right? Lately, he's been... more withdrawn than normal. But when I asked him where he was going, he took off after telling me to do what I've always done... ignore his pain."

Zay sat on the bed and ran a hand through his hair. I sat behind him while rubbing his shoulders. "I should've done a better job. Kel told me Mat would eventually open up and not to pressure him. Look where that fucking got us. He's going to do something really bad. I feel it in my bones."

"This isn't your fault, Bae."

"I'm calling Kel," Levi said and quickly dialed his number.

An hour later, Kel and Anders entered the surf shop looking tired but alert. Zay explained everything that happened tonight.

Levi stayed behind to keep an eye on the shop in case Mateo

returned. The rest of us piled into Anders's SUV and drove off in search of Mateo. Fuck, he could've been anywhere.

My stomach twisted with worry for him. Zay had been right; Mateo hadn't been doing well lately, especially after he and Lucy broke up. We tried not to push him because he was already touchy about his past.

We'd been driving for hours as I lay on Zay's lap while he played with my hair, trying not to doze off, but I was exhausted. We all were. It wasn't exactly a big island, but the early morning darkness hid everything in shadow.

"There!" Kel yelled out, startling me awake. The sun barely peeked over the mountains, but the sky grew lighter and lighter as it rose. I sat up and looked around, thinking I'd see Mateo.

Then I noticed it. His beat-up pickup.

We parked behind it, climbed out of the SUV, and rushed to his truck, but there was no Mateo.

"Fuck!" Zay hissed.

Kel rested a hand on Zay's shoulder. "Calm down. We'll find him. There's a semi-private beach over there. He might be there."

We all ran through the small alley between houses and emerged to a beautiful beach. He wasn't hard to spot lying down on the white sand with no one else around.

Oh, god... was he dead? I didn't know why my mind went to the dramatic. He could've just been asleep, but something deep in my mind told me something was wrong with him. My eyes blurred with more tears as we ran to him.

When we reached him, drug paraphernalia scattered all over the sand, and a syringe hung limply out of his arm. His normally tan skin was as pale as the moon heading off for the day.

There was some movement of his head, so we knew he hadn't died. But that turned Kel from worried to fucking pissed, and all I could do was be useless and cry. Poor Mateo. He must've been really hurting to fall back into drugs again.

We all lifted and carried him to the SUV and laid him down in the backseat, where he rested his head on my lap and his legs on Zay. He sobbed, and the sound was guttural and visceral, hitting my very soul and making me cry harder for this poor boy.

My bae looked pissed, but if I knew him, and I did, he was more pissed at himself, believing he should've done more. I ran my fingers through Mateo's silky hair as we drove off to the hospital and to the unknown of what was going to happen to him.

It had been nearly a month since Mateo had been gone. He'd been in rehab for detoxing and therapy. We all met at the facility earlier that day with our found family. Kel was there with Levi, Moni, and Rumi. We all cried as we listened to his horror story of when he was a kid.

God, if Zay and I thought we had it bad, it was nothing compared to Mateo's life. His father murdered his mother out of jealous rage and nearly killed Mateo. Then he lived with his grandmother, who also died, only for him to live in the streets with a group of homeless people. One of them got Mateo hooked on heroin when he was only fourteen years old.

He'd been doing so well until Jon started dying, and Kel spent so much time with Anders and his newfound relationship, then Kel vanished entirely for three weeks as he grieved. Mateo slowly crumbled under the weight of his pain. Then Lucy came along, and the strain of their relationship had him breaking away even more until he was nothing left but a pile of rubble. Apparently, the cause of their breakup was his refusal to talk about his past.

I adored Lu Lu, but I didn't appreciate her pushing Mateo into a corner like that.

I was curled up next to Zay late at night after we got home. Levi was out with friends, so we had the room to ourselves, allowing us to have sex openly. It was hot and steamy as we let out our pain, missing the way we used to make love before the boys moved into our room.

I was still sweaty and catching my breath, resting my head on Zay's chest as his heart hammered into my ear. He drew lazy strokes across my arm and shoulder, making me sleepy.

"Maybe it's time I talked to Mom," I said.

"What do you mean?"

"After everything that happened to Mat, I... I feel like time's wastin' away with my Mom. What if something happened to her, and I never told her how I felt? I mean all of it, Bae. My anger, love, frustration."

Zay rolled over to face me and combed my hair away from my face. "If that's what you want."

"Do you... ever think you'd find your parents and tell them how you felt about them abandoning you? Like how angry you were? How alone?"

His face grew hard for a moment, flashing various emotions, and showing their actions still stung, but I knew him and understood that he'd mostly moved on. Then again, this wasn't something we talked about much.

"No. I never want to see them again. Fuck them."

I nodded. "They never deserved you, boo. It's their loss."

"Do you want me to go to your mom's with you?"

Normally, I'd say no, but this time, if I was going to talk to her openly and honestly, I finally wanted to tell her about Zay. To show her what healthy love really looked like.

"Yes, please."

He smiled and kissed my nose. "You're braver than me."

"I'm not... nothin' brave about me."

He scoffed. "You're the bravest person I know, baby."

The next morning, I woke up with another headache, and worse than normal, like someone stuck an icepick in my brain. It was probably from the stress over what I had to do. After washing down four Advil, I got ready for my meeting with Mom. She wasn't scheduled to work, and Zay and I had the day off. Hopefully, she wouldn't be so trashed or hungover that she wouldn't listen. It was a big ask, but it wouldn't stop me from trying.

We pulled up to the apartment complex and jumped out of the truck. My hands shook a little, and they were all clammy. Zay took one of them and threaded our fingers together, not giving a shit if I was sweating all over him.

"I'm not going to leave your side for a second, okay?"

I gave him a weak smile and nodded. "Okay."

We stepped inside the apartment, using my key, and found Mom sitting on the ancient sofa, watching a show on the battered TV, smoking some weed. At least she was up. Her blond hair was piled high in a hair clip, and she wore a tight T-shirt and some booty shorts.

"Noah," she said, craning her head to see who had walked in.

"Mom."

"Who's that?"

"This is Zay... my boyfriend."

Her eyes narrowed as she looked back and forth between us. "Since when have you been gay?"

"I'm not... it doesn't matter. It's just a stupid label, Mom. We just love each other and have for almost five years."

She couldn't hide the hurt in her eyes when she looked away, taking another drag off of her blunt. "I see. And you couldn't be bothered to tell me until now."

I took a deep breath because I was done putting on fake smiles and pretending everything was okay. With a tug of my hand that was still holding onto Zay, I led us into the living room. Zay and I sat on the sofa next to her. His hand pulled from mine and wrapped around my waist with the pressure of his fingers on my skin, reminding me he wasn't leaving my side.

I took the blunt from her fingers, put it in the ashtray, and held her hand. She looked at me with furrowed brows hiding an emotion I didn't recognize.

"No, I didn't bother telling you. You don't really care." I let the last sentence hang in the air between us, making it harder to breathe, especially through the stagnant air of the apartment. My heart rate jumped as I took the plunge. "You've never cared... maybe you used to when I was little, but you don't now."

Her silence was more disappointing than her biting words when she was hungover. I didn't know what to expect, but maybe I held onto a hope that she still loved me in there somewhere. With another deep breath, I pushed on.

My eyes watered. "I'm not comin' back. I can't take care of you anymore and watch you destroy yourself slowly every single day. I... love you, but I hate you, too. You've worn me to nothin'... all raw, and... All you care about is gettin' drunk and expecting me to take up the slack. I won't pay the bills anymore, make your meals, shop for you..."

The tears slid down my face, and Mom refused to face me, pulling her hand out of mine.

"I refuse to watch you die. Your life is in your hands now, and it's no longer my responsibility. I'm so, so fuckin' tired after being an adult since I was a young teen. It so wasn't fair, but I took care of you anyway because I loved you."

When she still said nothing, I wrapped it up. "I have a life now. A happy one. Zay is the love of my life, and he's made me whole again. Stronger." Fat tears rolled down my face, and I took a shuddered breath, staring at the ceiling when he tightened his grip on me.

"We've made *each other* whole," he said, speaking for the first time.

I nodded and choked back a sob.

"You're my Mom. You taught me how to surf. Somewhere somethin' happened, I'm not sure. I... just can't do this anymore. But I wanted you to know how I felt. Things I never told you before. You can be so mean sometimes, and I'm angry with you... so angry. Frustrated that you... it doesn't matter. Nothin's gonna change."

I sighed, wiped away my tears, and stood. There would be no resolutions, and I didn't expect there to be. Only that tiny sliver of hope that Mom would see what she'd done and miraculously get better. So stupid.

We walked to the door, and when my hand touched the knob, she called out my name. I turned to her with that stupid, microscopic shard of hope, daring to get made whole, but there was nothing. It would only be a shard that stabbed me in the heart. She didn't turn to look at me, stop me, or talk to me. Nothing. Just like our relationship was now.

"Goodbye, Mom."

Zay took me home, and I sobbed into him the rest of the day, letting out years of pain and frustration.

I wasn't sure I'd even feel remotely okay were it not for my Zay refusing to let me go as I let everything out.

My Zay Bae.

My anchor in this storm, we weathered out together.

CHAPTER TWENTY-THREE

Noah

January rolled along, and everything was fucking pumpin'. We were all living the good life. Kel got engaged to Anders, and the resort was going to be wrapped up before surfing competitions began in the fall, giving tons of jobs to the locals as the tourists flooded in. Mateo got better. Happy even. And he and Lucy got back together. And I slowly healed from severing ties with my mom.

It had been super hard not to rush over there to take care of her as I'd been doing for years. Not to mention all the guilt of not going to her. But Zay sat by my side every step of the way through all my tears and anguish. I grieved her even though she wasn't dead.

Even the waves today were pumpin'. The winter water was cold, and the trade winds grew fierce, making the swells huge, but they made amazingly perfect barrels.

After a few rides, Zay, Mateo, and I sat on our boards to catch our breaths. God, I fucking loved to see Mateo smile. Like, really smile. Not that fake shit he was prone to do if he even bothered.

"Dude, you looked awesome out there," I said to Mateo. "You... look so good too. I'm so happy for you and Lucy."

He held out his fist, and I bumped it. "Totally. I *feel* fucking good. It's taken a while, but thanks to Lucy, I'm... not feeling like a total loser anymore. And... thanks to you all, my family."

"Please. As if you were ever a loser, but if you ever feel that way again, you also have us to talk to," Zay said.

"I will," he promised.

Zay pulled me into a deep kiss. "One more ride?"

"One more," I agreed.

We waited for the next wave, then paddled hard and fast to catch it. Mateo went off in the other direction, catching air a couple of times while Zay and I rode the barrel together. When we finished, we dropped to our boards and paddled to shore.

I shook the water out of my hair and glanced up at a man watching us. As we got closer, my heart stopped. I'd recognize that smile anywhere despite not seeing my old best friend since middle school.

Malo Peleke.

God, he fucking grew into a man. Well, so was I, but he was huge. So tall and broad, thick with muscles. He was a full-blooded Hawaiian with long, thick, wavy black hair, dark eyes, and skin.

"Holy shit, bro! Malo?"

"Wassup, brah."

I rushed at him and pulled him into a hug so tight I lifted him off his feet. Barely. He weighed like a ton.

"Dude, get off. You're like wet and cold," he groused, but we were both laughing.

"It's so fuckin' good to see. I've missed you, bro."

"And I've missed you."

Soon Zay walked up to us with curiosity on his face, if not a little jealousy. As if my boo had anything to worry about.

I took Zay's hand, pulling him close. "Malo, this is my boyfriend, Zay. Zay, this is Malo. You remember me talking about him, right?"

"Hey, Malo," he said, shaking his hand.

"'Sup, Zay."

Then Mateo offered his hand. "I'm Mateo, their foster bro."

Through my excitement, I finally noticed that his smile never reached his eyes. His mouth was crooked with straight white teeth, but those eyes had some sadness to them. I was going to have to catch up with my bro and see what was going on with him.

"Malo," he said to Mateo.

"Malo is totally like an old friend. We went to elementary and middle school together. Bruh, you're like a man now."

He snorted a laugh. "And you're a man, too. That's how it works, brah. You're not that scraggly little blonde boy I used to know."

"You moved back then?" I asked.

"Yeah… I've come to see if your boss has any openings."

I doubled over with laughter. I'd never see Kel as my boss. "Duuude, Kel's like our bro. Our foster bro, or father, or whatever, man. He's fam."

"I'm off to see Lucy." Mateo said his goodbyes and left us.

"Kel's not around today, but come by tomorrow and see if he or Anders has anything for you. Oh, Anders is Kel's bae. Anders has a fancy resort going up, but that won't be ready until the early fall. But the surf shop's gotta cafe now. Maybe there."

"Yeah, anything, dude."

Zay curled an arm around me and pulled me close. Malo eyed his movements, and when I looked at Zay, he was eyeing Malo, too, like some kind of eye standoff.

"No. Nope. Zay is my bae, and Malo is my BFF. We're gonna get along. Understand?" I could practically feel the jealousy radiate from Zay. He wasn't prone to jealousy, so I wasn't sure what was happening.

They both looked at me and relaxed.

"Anyway, I'm sure Kel will have something for you. We need to catch up, dude. Why do you need money? Isn't your dad like super rich?"

Malo's dad remarried when we were in seventh grade after his mom died years ago. His dad had a string of restaurants called Peleke Hawaiian Grill and took the business to the mainland in California somewhere. So they all packed up and moved before freshman year of high school started. I'd missed him ever since, unable to talk to him since I hadn't had a phone at the time and had no way to reach him either.

"Yeah, they're still doing well."

Malo looked off at the ocean with a frown. "It's a long story, man."

"Why don't we go to Nui Nalu Cafe… the new addition at the surf shop," Zay suggested. "We've got pretty good burgers and shit. Let us get cleaned up, and we can meet you there so you and No can catch up."

"Sounds good, man."

An hour later, we all sat down at a table and ordered some food and drinks.

"Talk to me, brah… what's goin' on?" I asked with my mouth full of burger, eager to find out what happened to my best childhood bro.

"Dude… such a long story, but I'll try to shorten it. So, ah… it's good you're like into dudes… makes it easier. I'm, ah, gay. So, there's that."

"Please don't tell me your parents disowned you," Zay said, tightening his grip on my hand.

"Naw, man, the rents were cool. Sort of… until they weren't. Dude, it's my step bro. It started as some homophobic shit, bullying. This happened a while back. He's, uh, a year older. Then… ugh, this is hard. About two years ago, he started touchin' me and shit when I came out. It started small; then he'd walk into a room I was in and patted my ass. You don't need the details. It ended up with him comin' into my room and touchin' me. I kept telling him to stop and that I'd tell our parents, but… ugh, I wanted to punch that smirk off his face at the time. He told me he'd tell them I made the moves on him and molested him.

They wouldn't believe me 'cause I was gay and shit. He's not out. I mean, I don't know if he's gay or just an ass."

"Fuckin' bastard. You're a big dude. I'm sure you made him stop."

"Yeah… finally, I got the balls. I threatened to beat him down. He did stop, but not before he went through with his threat. My parents didn't believe me, man. Dad fucking sucked it up to his *'other'* son and his wife, and of course, she chose her son over me. So, yeah, instead of fighting and convincing them, I just fuckin' left, man. Why bother, ya know? They should've trusted me, but apparently, they weren't as accepting of me as I thought, especially for believin' I'd do that to my own step bro. So… yeah, I got nowhere to go. I heard Ohana Surfing Club helps out those in need, so…"

It would be a tight fit in our room, but I was sure Kel would allow him to stay and work.

"Anyway, here I am. So… Noah, what's goin' on with you? How's your ma? Still hittin' the hot sauce?"

"Yeah… I, ah, dumped her. Sort of. I took care of her for years, but this past fall, I said enough. So, I haven't seen her since. I've been living here since I was fifteen, man."

"Nice. I mean, not about your mom, but that you found this place, and you found a good dude."

I looked at Zay and beamed at him. "He's the best."

He smiled and gave me a kiss on my cheek.

"Hey, boys. What's going on?"

We all looked up to see Keo standing there. Kel's brother had been helping at the cafe whenever possible since we were short-staffed. Hard to believe with all the kids coming around to live and work, but we were all tapped out as the business grew.

Keo had his own remodeling business he had just started, and he needed the extra funds, too, so he did his best around here.

We've all kind of gotten used to Keo being around, though it took us a while to warm up to him since he had returned to Kel's life after like forever.

He looked a lot like Kel with those pale brown hazel eyes, but his hair wasn't as dark and had more of their dad's features. He was tall like Kel, too. Maybe taller. But you could tell they were bros.

"Sup, Keo," I said. "I'm catchin' up with old bro from when I was little. He's back and lookin' for work. Malo, this is Keo Quinn. Keo, this is Malo Peleke."

The two men shook hands, but Malo didn't smile back, and his dark eyes were a little zoned out. "Uh, hi."

What was wrong with him? I looked at Zay, who shrugged, noticing it too.

"Job, eh? We need someone around here, for sure. I can talk to Kel. Peleke... Peleke," Keo said, tasting a new flavor on his tongue. "That sounds familiar. You wouldn't happen to be related to Kimo Peleke?"

"Ah... he's my dad."

"Seriously? I'm surprised you're not working for him."

"It's, ah... long story."

Keo nodded. "Text me so I can have your number to make it easy to reach you after I've talked to my brother."

Malo's eyes were wide, staring at Keo like a fool, not saying anything, so I kicked him under the table. "Oh, right. Ah, thanks, man."

Keo recited his number, and Malo plugged it in and texted him back.

"Great! Looking forward to working with you," Keo said, patting Malo's shoulder and walking off.

"Yeah... same."

"Dude, what the fuck was that?" I asked.

"What?"

Zay and I snorted a laugh. "Seriously?"

His eyes dropped to his half-eaten burger, and he shrugged. "It's nothin', man."

"Are you crushing on him, bro?" I asked, unable to hide my broad smile.

Malo huffed and looked back to find Keo talking to a customer, saying nothing.

"He's like old enough to be your dad."

Malo looked back at me wide-eyed in surprise. "No way. He looks no older than like mid-thirties at most."

"Try forty-two," Zay said.

"No way... fucking hot," he said again, shrugging, and playing it off but glanced back at Keo again as he worked.

I let it go because Keo was straight anyway, despite Malo's sudden hard crush.

We spent another hour catching up and exchanging numbers. I couldn't explain how happy I was to have him back in my life and to renew our old friendship.

Zay and I showered together after we got back. "He has a crush on you... or at least he used to," he said while soaping me up.

I snorted a laugh. "No, he doesn't."

"Well, he's crushing on Keo for sure, but yeah, there was more to his looks than just a boyhood friendship."

I remembered Zay being jealous earlier, and he wasn't one to get wrapped up in overreactions. I turned to face him and wrapped my arms around his neck to pull him into a kiss.

"Well, it doesn't matter if he is or isn't. You're mine, and I'm yours. Forever and ever."

He smiled and gave me a deep kiss. "And don't you forget it."

"Pfft, as if."

CHAPTER TWENTY-FOUR

Zayden

My eyes blinked open to the darkness, and the clock on the table flashed just after two in the morning. Noah shifted in the bed and snuggled deeper into me. Before I went back to sleep, Malo began snoring. That was what probably woke me up. Dammit. He sounded like a fucking freight train in a hurricane, and even the pouring rain pounding on the roof couldn't drown him out. I hadn't been sleeping as well as I should have because of it. Apparently, the rest of the dudes didn't seem bothered at all, but I grew annoyed with the restless nights.

Five boys in one room while the two girls had all that space. Our room was crowded and loud, and smelled like body odor and farts half the time. It was fucking time Noah and I got our own place. We'd been saving our money and had created a nice little nest egg. Regardless, life wouldn't be cheap, but we had to move soon. I was so fucking over this.

I gently untangled myself from Noah and headed to the kitchen to get a drink of water. Maybe take some Advil PM. No, I'd struggle to wake up in the morning. I guess I'd grab my pillow and a blanket to go sleep on the sofa here. Ugh, but I hated not being tangled in Noah's warm body.

That's when I heard it. A banging sound that was hard to tell over the rain except for the rhythm. I headed back to our room and tossed on some shorts, and padded downstairs barefoot to listen again. There it was. More pounding coming from the front door.

Who the fuck would be out this late in this weather?

I rubbed my face but didn't rush to the door. It could be anyone, like some drugged-out crazy dude. I reached for a kayak paddle sitting in a bin to use as a weapon if I needed to. After waiting for a beat, there was no more knocking. I almost headed back upstairs, but something drew me to the door to check just in case, like fingers gripping my neck and making my hairs stand on end. With a deep breath, I held the paddle aloft and quickly unlocked the door.

Outside was inky and wet, yet no one was there. I craned my head to look around the building when my foot caught on something under the awning. Not something. A large basket. A flash of lightning showed it wasn't only a basket but belonged to a... baby. Like one of those baby bed things. Whatever they called them, not like I was an expert.

Fuck me.

I squatted in front of the basket and pulled back a few blankets to find... Sure enough, there was a sleeping infant inside. Did people still do that? Just drop off babies at places and hope for the best?

I looked around one more time and didn't see anyone, but the darkness cast everything in shadow. With little choice, I picked up the basket, brought it inside, set it on the counter, and then I turned on the downstairs lights. My eyes blinked and burned at the brightness, trying to adjust.

Removing the blankets entirely, I lifted the sleeping infant and held it in my arms. The little human didn't stir at all, making me suddenly worried. It was alive, right? I pressed my fingers to its throat, seeking a pulse, and found one. I breathed a sigh and gently swayed the baby as if I'd been doing it all my life. How did it sleep through that storm?

I had no idea if it was a girl or a boy, but the baby was beautiful with short black hair, a button nose, rosy cheeks, and cupid bow red lips, pretty much like all infants. The baby was heavy and didn't seem sick, so I assumed someone had been taking care of it.

"What's goin' on, boo?" Noah asked while yawning, rubbing his eyes, and plopping heavily down the stairs.

"We've just received a delivery."

He was more awake now and wide-eyed when he saw the infant in my arms.

"No way, dude. Someone just dropped an infant off?"

"Yeah. No one was there when I opened the door, but someone had knocked. They must've run off."

Noah reached for the baby and held it in his arms. "Check the basket. Is there any note or anything?"

I pulled back the blankets more, and sure enough, there was an envelope with a note which I read out loud.

I'm so tired. I tried. I really did. They say you take in children. Please take care of her.

"That's it, dude? Nothin' else?"

"Nothing. What the fuck, No? They left the baby with nothing. No food. No diapers. What the hell?"

He looked at me, then sadly at the baby. "We'll figure it out, Bae."

"Shit," I breathed and ran upstairs to grab my phone. Then I came back down and called Kel.

"This better be good, Zay," he grumbled, half asleep.

"We have a situation. Someone's dropped off a baby with literally fucking nothing other than a note and a prayer asking us to take care of her. She has no food, no diapers… Not one fucking thing."

"Oh, god," he said, suddenly alert. I heard him trying to wake up Anders, who complained about a lack of sleep. But I didn't need to hear that it was because they were fucking all night. Ugh.

"Shit, okay. Anders and I will hit the twenty-four-hour grocery store and pick up some things. We'll be there as quickly as we can. Then I guess I'll have to call social services. Fuck me. I've become best pals over there with the social workers."

We hung up, and all my anxiety suddenly melted away as Noah smiled and cooed at the baby girl. His finger trailed gently along the slope of her face, swaying from side to side in gentle movements as if he was made to hold babies.

"She's so cute, Bae. We should call her Storm because we found her in a storm."

I smiled at the name. It was pretty cute, but we were getting ahead of ourselves.

"Kel and Anders are grabbing some things, but social services are probably going to take her and find her a proper home. A surf shop isn't a place for a baby."

He looked up, wide-eyed and angry all of a sudden, which was not like him. "The hell they are. They can't put her into the system. Kel will foster her. I just know it. If not... you and I can."

I walked over to him and put my hands on his shoulder. "Baby, we aren't even married, and we don't have a home of our own. We're not equipped to raise a baby, No."

His eyes watered, making me want to give him the world. Give him anything he ever wanted. "I don't care. She's staying with us. She's one of us now."

I didn't argue with him. There was no point. It all depended on what Kel and Anders chose to do.

By the time Kel and Anders showed up, carrying a shit ton of bags, the baby was crying, waking everyone else up. The girls tried to soothe the baby while Malo, Levi, and Mateo covered their ears and stifled yawns.

Anders strode right over and took the baby from Moni. He was the only one here who had any experience after raising two girls.

"Hey, baby girl," he said over her wailing. "She looks to be about three months or so if I recall correctly, but a pediatrician will confirm it."

Anders rocked her and cooed, then we all headed upstairs.

"Kel, please make her a bottle, as I had explained in the car. Noah, please grab the wipes and diapers out of the bag. Zay, there's a pacifier buried in another bag there somewhere. Tomorrow, we can go out and grab her a few things to wear when the other stores open. That should tide her over until we get her to social services."

"No!" Noah shouted.

Everyone stared at him, shocked into silence since it wasn't like Noah to yell.

I quickly reached him and kissed his head. "Babe, just get her things, and let's take care of her for now. We can talk about this later with Kel. Let's make her happy first, okay?"

He quickly nodded but didn't seem happy at all, with a deep frown on his face. "Okay."

In the morning, I woke up on the couch upstairs to Noah taking a picture of me with his phone. "So stinkin' adorable, Zay Bae."

I glanced down at my chest to the baby girl sleeping on her tummy. It probably hadn't been the best idea to do that. She could've fallen, but I was exhausted and passed out after we got her settled. Anders had shown me how to burp her, and soon after, she finally fell asleep. But it wasn't as if we had a proper crib or anything.

Noah took her from me so I could get up. I headed to the bathroom to take a piss and brush my teeth. When I came back to the kitchen area, Noah was at the table, feeding the baby again, with Kel and Anders sitting across from him. Noah had tears in his eyes as he watched the infant eat. Shit. He got instantly attached to her. She was so cute, and while I knew nothing about babies, I understood enough that they were a lot of work.

"Noah, social services is here. We need to hand her over," Kel said gently.

"No. She's ours. She's one of us."

"We don't have a choice. I will do what I can to foster her, okay?

But they may not allow it. We don't have the space for a baby, and we just can't keep her at the surf shop. She needs a real home."

"This is a real home," he said. "You've given all of us more real homes than we ever had before."

I waved Kel over without Noah seeing me. He strode my way, and we stepped out.

"Talk to him, Zay."

"I'll try. Look, is there anything we can do? Noah's already fucking attached to her. What if I get a place? I've been meaning to move out. It's... crowded, and I can't sleep these days."

"I don't blame you."

Anders soon came out and grabbed Kel's hand. "So, what's the story?"

"Zay is thinking about getting a place of his own with Noah so they can foster her."

"I realize Noah and I are young, but you've taught us well how to care about others and stuff. She'll be a lot of work; I understand that, but... Noah and I can do this if we get a place of our own. Besides, Noah has always been good about taking care of others."

"Why don't you just move in with me, Kel? You're always over at my house, anyway. It's a drive, but you rarely stay at your house anymore. You can rent the place to Noah and Zay? It's paid off already, so..." Anders said, shrugging.

"Actually, that's not a bad idea."

Could I actually have a house of my own? Well, I'd be renting. It wouldn't be mine, but fuck, to live in a house with Noah without the rest of the guys would be amazing.

"Yes, we can take care of her over there," I said.

Anders grew concerned, giving me that 'dad' look full of understanding but with a hint of patronization. "Zay, a baby is a lot of work."

"I understand that. But people do it every day. We'd learn."

Kel nodded, looking at Anders. "They may not foster her to two young men who aren't even married. I know they technically could with other children. There's no requirement that says they can't, but with an infant, it'll be trickier."

"Then I'll marry him," I blurted. "Tomorrow if I have to. He... seems to need her. And she needs us. Noah's right. She came to us, so she's one of us now."

Noah and I already planned to get married, eventually. We could just go to the justice of the peace and do it.

Anders looked at Kel. "I'm sure they'll allow us to take her until the boys get settled."

I was so grateful to this man. A man I couldn't stand when I first met him. Now, he'd been our champion for a long time, and I trusted him.

"Are you sure about this?" Kel asked.

"I think Zay and Noah can do it. They're both responsible and smart, and they've had a healthy and loving relationship for years."

Kel looked at me and rested a hand on my shoulder. "Are you ready for this, Zay? You wouldn't only have a husband but a baby. All at once."

I swallowed hard and nodded. Our lives were going to be drastically different from here on out, but I was ready for it.

The following night, our found family watched Storm as I walked Noah out onto the beach. He had no idea what to expect, or so I hoped. We held each other's hands as we slowly walked through the shallows of the surf.

Fuck, my heart was pounding in my chest, and I released his hand because mine was getting clammy. It wasn't that he'd reject me. Probably not. But this was a massive commitment. This would change our entire lives. This was always in the cards for us, but not so soon while we were still so young.

Let's do this.

Suddenly I dropped to a knee and took Noah's hand. His face was confused in the moonlight for a moment before it dawned on him what I was doing.

"Bae..." he breathed.

"I know this is really soon. Earlier than we had planned. But why not now? We love each other more than anything. We've been together for years, and it's been an amazing ride, No. I never once dreamed I'd find my soulmate until you. You are everything I'm not, and I'm everything you're not. You are the sun, and I'm the moon. Days, weeks, months, and years cannot exist without one or the other."

Noah sniffed, his eyes glistened with tears in the pale moonlight, saying nothing.

"I also want to do this to help us foster then adopt Storm. Us being married will make the process easier. It's not as romantic, but regardless, I love you so fucking much. More than life itself. I cannot exist without you. Will you marry me?"

He covered his mouth and stifled a sob. "Yes," he croaked. "Hell, yes, boo."

All my tension washed away with his words. I pulled out the ring I bought at the last minute from my pocket. It wasn't fancy or anything, but I paid for it with my own money, and I picked it out. I didn't have a lot of time either since we had to get the ball rolling. Once the ring was on his finger, he lifted his hand to look at it and touched it.

"I love it."

"It's nothing special."

"The fuck it isn't. It's from you. That's all that matters."

He helped me stand, grabbed my face and pulled me into a deep kiss.

"Best day of my life," he said.

I quirked a smile. "Wait until our wedding."

Noah and I stood on the beach barefoot, wearing linen shorts and white Hawaiian shirts, holding hands and facing each other. The officiant talked about love and taking care of each other, but the words were drowned out as I stared into Noah's wet, green depths. I wiped away a tear and smiled at my future husband. So weird. It was something I'd have to get used to, but it was also something I'd always wanted with him. My husband, Noah. It had a nice ring to it.

We didn't make vows or do anything special. Our vows and special words we always told ourselves in private, even if we loved PDA. I had previously planned to take him to the Justice of the Peace, but Kel and Anders insisted we do something small on the beach behind the surf shop. All of our friends and found family were there to celebrate with us. I even invited Duncan, and though I hadn't seen him since graduation, we'd kept in touch.

All our plans took longer than we would've liked. Noah and I moved into Kel's old house once he grabbed all that he needed, leaving us the furniture to save us money. He also didn't charge us nearly enough rent, but I didn't argue.

Because of Kel's great track record of taking care of kids and fostering them, social services allowed him and Anders to take care of baby Storm. We all agreed she'd be named Storm since she came to us nameless. Storm Beckett once Noah and I were married. We'd foster her, but if we did a good job, hopefully, they'd let us adopt her. Noah wouldn't accept anything less. I'd never seen him this determined before, and I loved him for it.

The wedding was short but perfect. It was so us. We didn't need anything wild or big.

Turned out we didn't have to get married to foster Storm, but it helped our case, especially if we wanted to adopt her. With a house, marriage, and steady income, we had a greater chance.

"I love you," I mouthed to him.

He smiled, sniffed, and mouthed the words back.

Once we said our 'I do's,' I pulled Noah into a deep kiss filled with the sounds of cheers from our friends and family, the crashing waves, and the cool breeze.

"You're my everything, Noah Ellis."

He held me tight and stifled a sob. "You're my everything, too, Zayden Beckett."

Absolutely fucking perfect.

The stout woman from the county social services stopped by a few weeks later when we finally got the house in order to assess it and talk to us. There would be a few visits before we could be licensed and bring Storm into our lives.

Kel and Anders helped us set up the spare bedroom for Storm with a crib, changing table, and more, along with baby-proofing the place. Noah even gave up weed. I didn't know how he did it since he'd been smoking for as long as I'd known him, probably longer, but he was willing to give it all up for that little baby.

We were both fucking nervous. Honestly, being a parent was a little scary. Noah and I didn't prepare for this or even talk about it. It had only been an abstract idea. A *'what if'* down the road when we got older. We were still so young, and while marriage was in our future, it wasn't supposed to have been so soon.

My husband—shit, I still needed to get used to the word—was determined to do everything right by Storm. She wasn't living with us yet, but we tried to visit her as much as possible. To get her used to us as parents.

The social worker strolled through the house with a clipboard, some documents, and a pen. She opened cabinets and checked for safety and what we could offer the baby. There were more qualified couples than us out there dying for a baby, so I was sure Kel's reputation in the community helped our cause.

After her inspection, we sat down at the kitchen table, holding hands as she asked us a slew of questions. We'd done our background checks and came back sparkling clean, of course. Noah and I had never been in legal trouble other than that time when I stole from Kel and Jon so long ago, which had only been a misdemeanor, and I'd been a minor.

When she left, Noah and I breathed a collective sigh. That was long and stressful, though it wasn't over yet, it was a start.

Then finally, two weeks later, we sat on the sofa at home with Storm cradled in Noah's arms. I rested my head on his shoulder as he gently touched her perfect porcelain skin with a finger.

"I don't know why, Zay."

"Why what, baby?"

"Why I've been so drawn to Stormy. As soon as she arrived, I just needed her in our lives. She's so fragile and sweet and beautiful. How could anyone abandon such a precious thing?"

Our parents had abandoned both Noah and me, so it wasn't a surprise that he'd want someone to protect and love. And Noah had a lot of love to give. He'd always given himself to others selflessly.

As for me, I was sort of terrified at being a parent, but I'd do my best, and I had love to give, too.

I tucked his overgrown blond hair behind his ears. "Because you have a beautiful soul. You love everyone."

"I... I hope we made the right decision. That we don't mess her up."

I had a feeling that was every parent's fear.

"Storm is in good hands, baby, and we have a big, found family to help us."

Noah brightened with that and nodded. "You're right. We aren't alone."

"And we're in this together."

He nodded again and smiled back at me. "Together."

CHAPTER TWENTY-FIVE

Zayden

THE DAY HAD BEEN LONG AT WORK. I'D TAKEN ON EXTRA LESSONS while my husband stayed home with the baby. When she got older, we could bring her to the shop and let her hang out with us. There'd always be someone around to hold her and play with her.

Calling Noah, my husband, still felt so weird yet so amazing.

I rubbed a hand through my stiff salty hair when I got home, desperately needing a shower. I was hungry too. If Noah was too tired, I'd make dinner for us. Hell, we'd both been fucking tired. I understood that having a baby would be exhausting, so it was a good thing we were still young and healthy.

As soon as I walked in the door, Storm was crying. I smiled, wondering how Noah handled things on his own today. He was probably stressed out, but he had so much patience for her. And so fucking cute when he tried to sing her old classic rock songs, always off-key, but Storm didn't care. She'd stare at him wide-eyed and entranced.

I walked into her room to find her on her back screaming. Her monitor was on, but where was Noah? I lifted Storm into my arms and made her a bottle. While I fed her, I looked around for Noah. Did he go somewhere? No. He'd never leave the baby behind.

"No? Where are you?"

Still no answer. Did he fall asleep? God, probably from sheer exhaustion. I related. Though I strongly doubted he'd do that, and even if he did, he'd hear her crying.

When I walked into the bedroom, there was no Noah there either.

What the hell?

"Noah?"

By that point, hairs stood up on my neck. Something happened. I couldn't point my finger on it, but the house felt... off. My heart picked up speed as I raced to the bathroom to see if maybe he was taking a shower.

I calmed down when I heard the water on the other side of the door. Thank fuck. Storm probably just woke up recently while he was showering.

I knocked on the door to tell him I was home. "No? I'm home. I've got Storm."

But he didn't answer.

I put Storm's bottle down and cradled her with one arm while I freed up a hand to open the door.

When I did, my entire world bottomed out.

Noah lay face down on the floor with his body contorted like he fell into a heap.

"Baby?"

I dropped to my knees, careful with the Storm, and placed shaking fingers on his throat. A pulse. Thank fuck.

I pulled out my phone from my pocket and struggled to call 9-11 with my increasing panic. Once the ambulance was on its way, I did everything I could to not freak the fuck out. I needed to stay calm for not only Noah but the baby. After I called emergency services, I called Kel and told him everything. He said he'd let everyone know.

Once I had a towel under his head, I waited for help as the tears spilled. I combed my fingers through his still-damp hair. He only had a towel wrapped around him, and I wanted to get him dressed, but I didn't want to move him.

"You're going to be okay, baby."

I choked back a sob, lifted Storm against my chest, and patted her back. It was like she realized something was wrong and didn't fuss.

All those fears from the last time he nearly drowned crashed over me. I struggled for breath, desperate to stay calm for the baby, but I couldn't. Noah was my everything.

In the distance, I heard the siren.

"They're almost here, baby."

I rushed out of our room and put Storm in her crib, where she started to cry again, but I needed two hands to make sure I had all I needed for her and Noah when we got to the hospital. Once I filled her diaper bag, I rushed out and filled a duffel bag full of clothes and necessities for Noah.

After I dropped everything by the front door, I rushed to grab the baby. By the time she was in my arms, EMS was pounding at the front door.

I let them in and led them to where Noah was. They checked his vitals and then eased him onto a gurney, covering him with a sheet. I followed them out as they loaded him into the ambulance. Once he was in and secure, they started the IV and closed the doors, leaving me standing on the street holding Storm as the tears spilled. I tried not to let the grip of fear that I'd lose him own me.

There was no way to ride with them this time. Not with a baby. After wiping my face dry, I rushed back inside, grabbed the two bags, and tossed them into the back. Then I got Storm in her baby carrier and secured her in the back seat of the truck.

God, I wanted to speed to the hospital, but I had to be careful. How different it was to be a parent. Where I'd normally be reckless when it came to a hurt Noah, my impulsivity vanished because I had to protect the baby, too.

We sat in the same waiting room as last time when Noah hit his head. Kel and Anders arrived earlier, always the support and anchor, keeping me from losing it. They were two men we could always count on and lean on. They were better than any of our birth parents. Then again, it was why we all ended up at Ohana Surfing Club. Because we couldn't rely on our parents, those who were supposed to take care of us and love us unconditionally but didn't.

Storm had strong legs. I held her by her armpits and bounced her on my thighs. She kept pushing up and kicking while she ate her fist with a massive smile. God, she was so fucking cute, which helped keep me sane. Her eyes, which matched her name, were wide and glimmered with health and happiness.

If I didn't have her to keep me distracted, I'd be fucking losing it. I had to stay strong for her and me.

"He's going to be okay," Kel said for the thousandth time, and I wondered if he kept saying it more for his benefit than mine.

"I don't understand what's going on. He seemed fine this morning."

"You said you found him on the bathroom floor. Do you think he slipped?" Anders asked.

"Maybe. I don't know. It looked that way."

Finally, a doctor came out and approached us. He didn't look sad, so I hoped he had good news.

"Hi, I'm Dr. Jackson, the neurologist on duty. Are you family?"

"I'm his husband, Zay," I said. "Please... is... is he okay?"

"He's fine and resting right now. We did a battery of tests on Mr. Ellis, from bloodwork to giving him an MRI. It looks like he's suffered a seizure that caused him to fall. He hit his head as he went down, which was probably why he was unresponsive when you found him.

Has he been having problems at home? Cognitive impairment? Sleep problems? Headaches? Behavioral changes?"

I shook my head. "No, not that I'm aware… he's been a little more sensitive than normal, but he's always been pretty empathetic."

"I looked back at his health records and read he had a severe concussion a while back. It's possible to have lingering effects from it. We believe he had a seizure caused by his old concussion."

"Oh, god…" My eyes welled with tears as I tried to listen, shifting the baby on my other hip.

"We've sedated Mr. Ellis, elevated his head in bed, and boosted his salt levels to reduce the edema which happened when he hit his head. It's not in the same spot as his last concussion, but he's definitely got a new one. We've also got him on a diuretic to reduce fluid levels and prevent hematomas, an anti-seizure drug, and pain meds. We'll monitor him in the ICU. He, fortunately, didn't need surgery."

I nodded. "How long will he be… sedated?"

"We'll keep him like that for several days, afterward, we'll run another MRI and do some blood work. But he'll probably have to be on anti-seizure medicine for the rest of his life."

My poor Noah. "What does that mean? Will… he be able to do stuff like surf or… care for our daughter?"

He gave me a nod and a small smile. "He'll be able to do all those things just fine as long as there's no severe impairment to the brain, but as far as I can tell, I don't foresee any permanent damage that would keep him from activities and having a regular life."

The pressure in my chest finally lessened. He'd be okay, right? Right. *My Noah will be just fine. He'll wake up and be his old self.*

"I'll have a staff member bring you all the information you'll need for his future care and how to live with someone who has seizures. You can see him now."

"Hand us Storm. We'll take care of her while you spend time with Noah."

"Thanks, Kel. For… everything. You too, Anders."

Kel smiled softly. "Go be with your husband."

I hugged them both and followed the doctor to Noah's room.

He was sleeping as expected. God, it was his concussion all over again, except this time, he didn't wake up with a smile. Wires covered him, crisscrossing all over his body, but at least he could breathe on his own.

After I pressed several kisses to his face and sleeping lips, I pulled up a chair and sat next to him by his bed, grabbing his hand and stroking it with my thumb.

"I love you, baby. You're going to be fine."

God, I wanted to crawl in bed with him and hold him close, but I was afraid I'd injure him more. He wasn't supposed to move.

"Storm's okay. She wasn't happy when I came home, but if you get some food into her, then she's as happy as a clam. She kicked me a lot, too, as we waited for you." I blew out a laugh. "Like she was as impatient as me to get to you."

I yawned since it was really late and rested my head on his leg, still holding his hand, and shut my eyes. Just a little nap.

CHAPTER TWENTY-SIX

Zayden

It had been three days since Noah's seizure and fall. I'd been staying over at the hospital as much as possible, but I had to take care of Storm, and go grocery shopping because we needed more formula, diapers… fucking everything.

Honestly, it was nice to get out of the hospital for a bit and pick up the house. Storm slept in her crib as I did days-old dishes, did some laundry, and cleaned the bathroom. By the time I wrapped that up, the baby was awake.

I loved that she rarely cried. Sure she screamed when hungry, but she'd been a pretty happy kiddo with lots of smiles. When I walked in, I found her on her back, looking up, smiling, and eating her hand.

"Well, how did you end up on your back?"

Noah and I did a lot of reading about babies and their milestones, or how to pretty much keep them from dying because that shit was always on my brain. She was five months old, and she finally rolled over.

"Aren't you a big girl now? We're going to have to tell your daddy when he wakes up."

I lifted her out of bed and held her against my chest, and pressed my nose into her to inhale her baby scent. How did babies always smell so good? Like the contaminants of the world couldn't reach them.

I set her on the changing table and cleaned her up before I fed her.

"Bawabwaba," she babbled.

"Oh? Is that so? Please tell me he did *not* say that. What a jerk. Spill the tea, girl."

She squealed and tried to reach her toes to munch on, but I had to finish with her diaper.

Once I had her in my arms and dressed in a onesie with yellow bunnies, we headed to the kitchen to feed the bottomless pit.

We got in bed after she ate her weight's worth of formula, and I put her in the middle of the bed between me and a pillow. I lay on my side, using my arm as a pillow as I watched her eyes grow heavier and heavier. I smiled and gently touched the soft skin on her arm.

"Your daddy will be home soon. Then we can be a family again."

We weren't her dad's yet, but if everything went well, hopefully, we'd be able to adopt her. Then flashes of Noah dying on me hit me like a Mack truck, and I shut those thoughts right down. Despite the doctor's reassurances, I couldn't stop the worry that he'd have a seizure and something worse would happen than a fall. A life without Noah wasn't a life at all.

Soon, I drifted off myself. I was exhausted and figured it was a good time to nap before we headed to the store.

"Let's see... you need more formula. Jeez, this sh... stuff is expensive. Did the cost go up again? Why do babies cost so much?"

Storm watched me as I chatted with her, tossing the formula in the cart. Good thing people didn't assume I was crazy, right? People talk all the time with their babies, right?

"Now for the diapers, baby wipes... you're good on powder."

I pulled down a set of colorful plastic keys and dangled them in front of her. "Do you like these?"

She babbled and tried to reach for them, but I had to clean them first before she shoved them in her mouth. In they went with the rest of the baby stuff.

I picked up some deli meat, cheese, and bread for sandwiches. And a few things to pre-make some meals and freeze them so I didn't have to cook all the time while Noah stayed in the hospital.

"Oh, what a cutie she is," said some woman smiling at the baby.

"Thanks."

"Is she yours?"

No, I fucking stole her. I had to cut the woman some slack. I know I looked young to have a baby despite being twenty-one.

"Yes."

"What's her name?"

"Storm."

"How unique. Where'd you come up with that name?"

"I didn't. My husband did. She was born during a storm." Not quite the truth, but she didn't need to know how she came to be with us.

"Oh... I see. Well... have fun."

I rolled my eyes as she stammered her way out of there. People were so weird about gay couples sometimes. I didn't give a fuck what they thought. It might have mattered when I was younger, thanks to my parents, but no more. Being married to Noah, and loving him, was the best thing to ever happen to me. I was proud of him and proud to be his partner.

"Zayden?"

I turned around to the woman's voice that sounded strangely familiar. Then recognition hit. How ironic to be thinking about my parents right when I stumbled into my mother after all these years.

She looked the same but a little bit older. Her hands were wrapping around themselves in nervousness, and her eyes were uncertain.

I couldn't think of anything to say like my tongue swelled or my brain short-circuited. There were days after they kicked me out, I thought about what I'd say to my parents if I ever ran into them, but I didn't care anymore. Shit, I barely hated them anymore, refusing to give them my worries, thoughts, and wonder. They didn't deserve to live rent-free in my brain.

And being with Noah proved how wrong they were. There was nothing wrong with me. I loved and was loved back. No amount of praying would ever change that.

"Zayden?"

My heart suddenly hammered, and the anger slammed into me despite my need to walk away. I stopped caring a long time ago. Why her? Why now? No. I couldn't deal. I had Noah to worry about. A baby. No time for hateful mothers.

But I still couldn't fucking find the words to tell her to fuck off or even leave.

She took a step closer, looking at my face, and scanning it for signs of the boy I used to be.

"It *is* you. You're… a man now. So… handsome."

My eyes watered along with hers, but mine spilled from pure hatred. I thought those feelings were long gone.

"Handsome? That's it? I haven't seen you for fu… fudging six years…"

I took a shuddered breath and closed my eyes before I started yelling. Not in front of Storm. My emotions were already full of live wires, with Noah being injured and me being so tired from caring for a baby with little sleep.

Her eyes lasered right to Storm, and I moved in front of her like a shield to guard her from my Mom like she would ruin her too somehow.

"I... looked for you," she finally said, unfazed by my anger or pretended to be.

I scoffed. "Yeah, right."

"So many years... you look so good. I was afraid..." She took a deep breath. "Afraid you had died when I never found you. It was my fault. I should never have let your dad talk me into kicking you out. I'd been so weak."

My lip trembled, and I looked away, not wanting her to see. She deserved nothing, not even my angry tears.

"I wanted to go to the police, but they arrested your father when they learned we kicked you out. He called me to bail him out, but... I refused. I had already left him to look for you by then. But there was no trace."

Her eyes watered, and I wanted, no, I needed to get the fuck away from her, but my legs stayed glued to the floor.

"You refused. You refused because you didn't want to get arrested for child abandonment, too."

"Yes... because I had to find you."

"Well, clearly, I didn't die," I said with as much venom in my voice as I could muster. "No thanks to you and... him."

"I'm so glad you are okay and healthy, and—"

She took a shuddered breath, trying to hold back her tears as much as I was. But one stupid traitorous tear rolled down my face, so I wiped it quickly away, refusing to let it show the world my hurt.

"I lived on the streets for a year," I hissed. "In a tiny shack, starving, but I did my best to survive."

"Oh, god..."

"Fuck your god!"

I turned away, unable to face her any longer. I was going to fucking lose it.

Storm must have sensed my upset because she started crying. I pulled her out of her carrier and held her close, desperately trying not to cry. I had no idea what to do. Storm needed things at the store, but I desperately needed to get out of there.

A hand on my shoulder made me flinch, and it was quickly removed. "Please talk to me. I finally found you. I can't let you go again. Please. Let me help you shop, and then go somewhere to talk. Just talk. Once. If... you never want to see me again, then I won't stop you. I won't beg. Knowing you're alive and healthy... it's almost enough. It has to be."

I choked back a sob as all that pain from my youth that I thought was long gone came flooding back deep into my soul. It fucking hurt so much. On top of nearly losing Noah fucking again, I was crumbling from the inside out.

With a deep breath, I turned to face her. Maybe she did want to talk. Maybe she did look for me. At the end of the day, I was married to a man. She'd never forgive that, and I told her as much.

"You don't want to talk to me. I'm married now. To a man. How about that? See, I've committed a sin too great. A sin for loving and marrying a man." I wiped my face as I stared her down, itching to get her to show her true, hateful self.

She nodded. "That changes nothing. I know you're expecting it to, but I've had a lot of time to think over the past six years without my son. My only son. My only child."

"Yeah, I bet... *he* wouldn't be too happy." I refused to call him my dad.

She shook her head. "No, he wouldn't. Please, we can talk about this somewhere else. Somewhere you can relax and feed the baby. I'll tell you everything."

"I have to finish shopping. You can... come back to my house. It's close. But you only get thirty minutes. My husband is in the hospital, and I need to be with him."

"Yes, anything."

I held Storm as my mom pushed the cart for me, not bothering with her own groceries. What was she doing here? She never shopped at this little grocery store but usually at the bigger chains. I didn't bother asking. It wasn't important.

I tossed things in the cart in silence as she pushed it down each aisle. Once I finished, I put Storm back in her carrier and checked out.

Back at home, my mom helped me carry the bags inside. I left everything where it sat to feed the baby, who was crying now. My mom looked around the place as I prepared the bottle.

"What a pretty little house you have here."

"We're renting it from a… friend."

My mom returned to the kitchen and sat down with me as I began to feed Storm.

"So, out with it," I said.

Her fingers fidgeted on the table as she watched me feed the baby with longing.

"You were only gone a couple of days, and I couldn't take it anymore. It was wrong. So wrong. You were too young. We should've tried harder with you. To… understand more. Your dad and I fought and fought. It never ended. He refused to go find you. I should… never have told him about you. What a mistake. I finally left him. I had to get a job, and I stayed with a friend of mine. We finally divorced."

I looked at her finally as she wiped the tears from her face.

"Seeing you that day… kissing that boy… I was just so shocked. And afraid. And… angry. I thought all we taught you was the right way." She scoffed at herself and took a shuddered breath. "How wrong I was. How ignorant. When I left your father, I started attending a different church. A more accepting church. There are even gay couples there. I got to know them, and I talked about you. I didn't have the guts to tell them what I allowed to happen to you. Who's the sinner now? I hurt you, abandoned you, and lied to people."

She put her hands to her face and cried.

I stood and headed to the bathroom and came back with a box of tissues.

She looked up at me in surprise and then thanked me after blowing her nose.

I wasn't sure how I felt about her story. And I wasn't sure I'd ever forgive her. But I wasn't as angry as I was earlier.

"Did you… really look for me?" My question came out as a mere whisper and filled me with more hope than I wanted and more than she deserved.

"I did for a couple of years. I… eventually gave up and grieved the loss of you. You were only a boy. And it was my fault for telling your father and letting you go when he... *we* kicked you out. How did you survive?"

I ended up spilling everything from living in the shack, teaching surfing lessons where I could, to trying to keep up with my studies which had been going well until my board broke, then I stole for the first time. I told her how Kel and Jon took me into their home and loved me, and protected me.

My mom really cried by then. "I'm so, so happy someone took care of you and doing what I failed at."

I didn't dispute her words or reassure her with lies.

"And you're married? So young and with a baby."

By now, Storm had fallen asleep in my arms. I held her as I dug my phone out of my back pocket, opened it, and scrolled until I found a photo of Noah. I slid the phone to her, and she picked it up to look at it. "He looks very sweet."

"He's the best. Kel and Jon may have saved my life, but Noah saved my soul. And no, not like that. I was so angry and bitter. But Noah... he's my everything. My brick. He's kind, loving, and empathetic. His heart is so big. Big enough to take in this angry boy and show him that not all was lost. That I could have happiness and love. And that it was okay to love a man."

I wiped my eyes of stray tears, but I didn't give in to the sobs again. I explained to her how and why we got married so young. Storm, the little sleeping baby in my arms, needed us.

"Can... I hold her?"

I was afraid to. I didn't quite trust my mom despite her words, pressing the baby closer to my chest. That would take time—a long time—if I accepted her back into my life. But I didn't think she'd hurt Storm, so I eased the baby into my mom's arms.

"What a beautiful girl you are." Then she looked back at me. "Your... husband is in the hospital? Is he going to be okay?"

That she didn't freak out about my marriage to a man was a step in the right direction. Maybe mom was salvageable. But at the end of the day, she abandoned me, and I didn't think that was forgivable.

"I don't know. He had a seizure." I didn't bother going into the details. "Anyway, I need to go now. He needs me."

"Oh, of course."

She handed back Storm, and I stood to get us ready to go.

"Can... I see you again. Please."

"I need some time. I'm not saying no, but... there's a lot of built-up resentment. Give me some time."

She nodded and tried to hold back the tears. "Of course. Anything."

I sighed and rolled my eyes at myself for my weakness. "Wait." I rummaged through our junk drawer and pulled out a piece of paper and a pen, jotting down my phone number. "You can... call me once in a while."

She pressed the piece of paper to her chest as if it was a lifeline to keep her heart pumping. "Thank you for this."

When she left, I put the baby down in her crib so I could get all the groceries put away, then I looked back at my phone sitting on the table. Would he hate me? No. He never hated, but he might get upset. Yet if there was hope for my mom, what about Noah's mom? The only hope for her was if she got her shit together. We had no idea how she had been doing after Noah left her that day. He even changed his phone number so she couldn't reach him. But we had hers.

After he left, maybe it was the wake-up call to his mom. The same wake-up call that happened to mine.

Maybe.

If she sounded trashed, I'd just hang up. But if there was a chance...

I quickly dialed and would deal with Noah's wrath later. Maybe if she knew how sick he was, she'd finally stop being an ass.

"Hello?"

She sounded sober. That was a start.

"Nora?"

"Yes?"

"This is Zayden, Noah's husband."

CHAPTER TWENTY-SEVEN

Noah

My eyes burned when I blinked them open to the dim lighting. They felt dry and scratchy, like someone rubbed them with sandpaper. My head fucking hurt too. Everything was a blur as I smacked my dry lips.

A shadow blocked out the light, and someone touched my lips with a straw. I took several pulls from it, sucking up the needed water. The coolness cleansed me, washing away the dust in my brain.

When my body shifted, the pain shot straight to my head.

"Easy, baby. Don't move too much."

"Zay?" My voice was raspy and hoarse from misuse.

"Yeah, it's me. Let me get the nurse and tell her you're finally awake."

His lips pressed to my forehead, and I tried to reach for him, but he'd already slipped out of the room. I whimpered for his warmth and touch.

By the time he came back in, my vision had cleared some. He sat in the chair next to my bed and held my hand, kissing my knuckles.

"Where's Stormy?"

"She's with Levi and Mat. They're taking her for a walk in her stroller outside the hospital. Do you… remember what happened, baby? Why you're here?"

I shook my head. "I don't know why I'm in the hospital. The last thing I remember is getting out of the shower and feeling super weird. Like my brain was fighting something while being in some weird freefall. I'd been having really bad headaches…"

Zay's hand stiffened in mine, and I turned my face away from him, not wanting to see his disappointment at my lies and secrets. "For how long, No?"

When I didn't answer, he asked again. "How. Long."

"Since my concussion."

He stood up abruptly and paced. "That was like nine months ago!"

"Please don't yell, Bae… it hurts."

"Dammit, No. Why didn't you say anything?" He was still pissed, but at least his voice came down to a yelling whisper and a level I could handle.

God, even shrugging hurt. "I was so tired of people fussing over me. I spent a month being smothered with nothing to do. And besides, I thought it was kinda normal. Like I hit my head, yeah? Of course, I'm gonna get headaches."

"I recall specifically what the doctor said. That if you get headaches, you had to go see him."

"I know…"

"Fuck, No."

"I'm sorry, Zay Bae."

He breathed out a sigh and sat on the edge of the bed, holding my hand again. "Okay, we'll worry about this later. Then what happened?"

"Everything was like weird and hard to explain. I didn't hurt or anything, but I got like really panicky, and I knew something was wrong but not what. My brain was totally fighting whatever it was, as if I was losing control, and my mind said no way, brah. I remember falling and falling, then nothing. Next thing I remember, I'm wakin' up just now."

Zay leaned over and kissed my mouth. "I've been so fucking worried about you."

"How long—"

Just then, a couple of nurses and the doctor walked. "Hello, Noah. I'm Dr. Jackson."

"Hey."

The nurses fussed over me with my IVs, taking my blood, while the doctor shined a light in my eyes that sent an ice pick of pain into my brain. "We'll get some pain meds for you in a second. I've been keeping you pretty sedated so your brain could heal. We took scans this morning, and since the swelling has gone down, I slowly pulled you out of sedation."

"How long did you put me out?"

"Five days."

"Will... will I be okay?"

I swallowed hard and tried to reach for my water, but Zay grabbed it and fed me the straw.

"Yes, you'll be fine. Unfortunately, you suffered another concussion when you fell from your seizure."

A wave of depression slammed into me. Not again. No, I didn't want to be cooped up anymore. The tears welled, and my lip quivered. Thoughts of being a prisoner in my own house filled me with anxiety. "I don't wanna be stuck inside for another month again." I sounded like a baby, but I didn't care. There wasn't anything to do. Not even sex with my bae.

The doctor looked sympathetic, but I knew he wouldn't give in. "Noah, I know it's rough to take it easy. That it's boring, but you need to take special care of that brain of yours. The last concussion was severe enough that you've had a seizure. Have you been having regular headaches?"

I nodded.

"You're going to have to take seizure medicine, but once you've recovered from your concussion, you can go back to your regular life."

"Can I still surf and stuff? It's like my life."

"Yes, exercise is good for your brain. You can live as you've always lived, but now you have to take some meds to prevent future seizures. And no more hiding your headaches. We'll monitor you for a couple more days; then you can go home."

"Okay. Thanks."

When the doctor and nurses left, I opened up like a burst dam. Zay crawled into the bed with me, careful of my wires, and held me as I cried. I hated being cooped up with nothing to do. Mostly it was the not surfing and not having sex part that killed me the most.

"Ugh, I can't even cry without pain."

"The meds will kick in soon, baby. I'm so sorry. But don't ever hide your pain again. Please. I'd fucking lose it if I lost you. You're everything to me, No. Everything. I love you so much."

"I love you."

He grabbed my hand and started playing with the simple gold band around my ring finger. "A lot has happened in the past five days, too."

"What happened?" I asked, unable to hide my yawn.

He kissed my forehead. "Get some sleep first; then we can talk."

"Ugh, this isn't fair." I whined.

"At least we're sharing the tub, naked together."

Zay was bathing me while we took a bath together. I hated it and loved it. I always loved bathing with Zay, but I couldn't do anything with it. No sex. So fucking unfair.

We'd sent Stormy off to hang out at the surf shop, so Zay and I could spend some time alone, not that it was anything earth-shattering.

He huffed a laugh on my neck and kissed it. "You're the worst patient ever."

"Yeah, well, try having a messed up brain and see how you like it."

"Is this our first fight, No?"

Was that what he thought? "No, I'm not fighting. Please, I'm not trying to. I'm just… pouting."

He kissed my shoulder. "Relax, baby. I'm only teasing you. Are you sure you're not upset more because your mom is coming over later?"

That was a big fat yes. Zay told me he called Mom, and they talked for a while. He said she sounded good. Almost normal. So he talked me into giving her another chance. If he could talk to his mom, I could talk to mine, I guess.

I nodded as he scrubbed my back and then rinsed it. "I don't want to have hope, Zay. Hope hurts sometimes."

He pulled me against his chest as we laid back and stretched our legs in the warm water. "I get it. You know my mom and me. What she did, hurt like shit. What your mom did also hurt like shit. But I think… they're trying. Hopefully, they realize we're worth it. You and I are worthy of love. Do you know who taught me that?"

I shrugged. "Kel?"

"He helped but no. That was you. You showed me all the ways to love someone and that they are worthy of being loved. Even an angry boy who refused to talk to you at first and wasn't so nice. Your mom will see that, too, as long as she stays sober long enough."

"But what if she's lying?"

"Then we don't have to see her again. I understand a lot of what you're feeling is because of this." Zay gently pointed at my head. "It can affect your moods sometimes because the Noah I know doesn't get depressed. He lives life to the fullest. Yes, you get sad like we all do. But you bounce back quickly with a smile on your face, even on your roughest days. You thrive on happiness and love because you're surrounded by it. This, too, will pass."

"Promise?" Was it fair of me to ask?

"I can't promise you that life won't deal us a shitty hand of cards sometimes. But I can promise that I will always be here by your side when it does. Just like now."

Later that afternoon, Stormy came back to us. I lay in bed, resting on my side, watching her take her nap. She was so sweet and beautiful, with plump rosy cheeks and fuzzy black hair. I dragged a finger across the soft skin on her forehead and chipmunk cheeks.

"Zay and I will do our best with you, Stormy Wormy. We'll make sure to keep you happy all the time, show you how to surf, make sand castles, and I'll never make you eat peas because gross. But you'll have to eat your carrots and broccoli so you can grow big and strong."

There was a short knock on the door. "Your mom's here, baby. Want me to send her back here or home? The choice is yours."

Here we go.

My stomach turned from uncertainty and a little fear. I wasn't mad at Zay for trying to fix us. Especially after what happened to his mom, but I had gotten used to the idea that I'd never see my mom again. Now here she was.

"Nah, you can send her back."

He leaned over and kissed me. "Okay. I'll take Storm to her crib."

I nodded and sat up in bed, pulling the covers over my legs.

A minute later, Mom knocked on the bedroom door and came in. I looked up at her, and she seemed... different. She had cut her hair to her shoulders. Her eyes weren't all bloodshot, and she looked alert.

"Hi, No."

"Hey."

God, this was awkward as hell already.

"Can I sit?"

I nodded and waved to the edge of the bed, picking at my cuticles as my stomach continued to turn. The doctors said to stay away from stress, and while I was afraid of what she'd say, I needed to know if I should hold on to hope or finally let go. Maybe I was stupid to feel that way after everything, but she was still my mom.

"I have a boyfriend," she blurted.

"Cool." I didn't care. She always had dudes. He would only be another dude in a long line of dudes.

"I mean… it's real this time. He seems to like me."

"Uh, huh." Why did she always make shit to be about her?

She stood up and wrapped her arms around her as she looked around the bedroom. "This is a nice place you have here. I'm… proud of you."

Yeah right.

"I'm sorry, Mom, but do you got a point to all this?" It wasn't like me to be rude, but I just couldn't with her. I listened, but there was nothing to listen to.

"Uh, right… yes. I came here to see how you were. I heard you got really hurt, and I wanted to come to the hospital, but… Zay said no. It's… I understand. But I also wanted to tell you that I… I've been sober for four months."

That's when I looked up at her and really scanned her body and face. She did look good, I had to admit. Better than before. More color to her face and less gaunt. She'd never even bothered trying to quit before. Why now? Did her boyfriend talk her into it? Was he able to do what I couldn't? Her own son? I should be happy, but I only felt worse and even more unloved. Why wasn't I good enough?

"When you left… I heard you. *Really* heard you. You've been in my life for so long, taking care of me, that I… took you for granted that you'd be there to lift me up and you'd always be around. But when you left, I had a feeling I'd never see you again. Once I got over my anger toward you, then came the self-blame…"

She wiped her face and looked away from me. Like if she looked at me, she'd crumble. "I've been a fucking horrible mom. I get that. It took months of being clean, group therapy, and… god, I'm so sorry, Noah." Then she turned to me with a wet face and trembling lips.

My stupid eyes watered, too.

"I'd been in self-loathing for so long that I drowned out my pain in drink, then took everything out on you. It was never your fault. Believe it or not, I do love you. You were never a burden despite my hateful words."

I choked back a sob and curled into the bed away from her. Words that I'd always wanted to hear, she finally said, and I wasn't sure how I felt about it. I understood alcoholism enough to know that this wasn't necessarily a permanent thing. She could easily slip back.

The bed dipped, and she placed a hand on my back which made me cry more. The gentle, loving touch I'd always craved was there, but it made me flinch, so she removed her hand.

"I am trying so hard, No. I've tried to reach you, but your phone's been off or something. To tell you how sorry I am and to please not give up on me. It's unfair of me to ask... I know."

I turned to face her and wiped my face with my hand. "Are you here because you want me and love me? Or is this part of your program to heal yourself? Because I need healing, too. I can't take it if you fall again. I can't take care of you anymore. It hurt so much, and you were so... mean."

Her face morphed into guilt, but she nodded. "I can't tell you how sorry I am... about everything. To answer your question, I came here for you. Yes, this is part of my program, but I chose to do this program for you. Because of you. Your leaving was a big wake-up call for me. I don't think I would've done it had you not left. I got so damned weak and dependent on you. Please, No. Please give me another chance to be a good mom or at least a better one. One more. I'll never ask you again if I fail.

She tentatively reached for me as if she was afraid I'd bite, but her hand landed in my hair, stroking gently. "I... hope I didn't ruin you." Then she covered her face and cried, making me cry more. God, I was so sick of crying and feeling pain.

Fuck it. I sat up and pulled her into a hug as we cried into each other. How weird for her not to reek of sweat and alcohol. She smelled clean and like flowers. We sat like that for a long time when we finally separated.

"So... you're married now?"

"Yes."

"And have a baby?"

"We're fostering her."

She nodded again. "I'm so proud of you, No. I realized I've never told you that. You're so strong. So much stronger than I ever was. And you have so much love to give. I'm not sure where you got that from because it wasn't from me."

We sat in silence for a while, not knowing what else to say.

"Does this mean... you forgive me?" she finally asked.

I shook my head. "No, Mom. But it means I'll try."

She nodded with disappointment on her face, but I just couldn't give her anything more than that. "Okay. I'll... take what I can get."

She leaned over and kissed my head. "Get better, No. Can I call you?"

"Sure."

"Okay... bye."

"Bye."

Then she was gone. Like Zay and his mom, I'd give her a chance. A chance to trust her once more. But repairing our relationship would take a lot more work, and I wasn't sure how much I wanted to invest in it.

CHAPTER TWENTY-EIGHT

Zayden

Two months without his taste. Without his intimate touch. Without his cock. He needed more rest than the last time, but the doctor finally cleared Noah to have sex and surf and work.

Kel was kind enough to keep paying him and gave me a lot of time off to care for my husband while taking care of Storm. If I had to work on top of that, I would have been too stressed. How did other parents do it? Sometimes I felt like a failure, but Kel kept reassuring me that I was doing just fine.

My brothers and sisters all joined in to babysit Storm overnight, so Noah and I finally had some alone time. I was fucking starved for him. But if I thought I had it bad, Noah had been nagging and begging for a month to make love. He grew downright grumpy about it, and I didn't blame him one bit. It was making me irritable too. It was the longest we'd ever gone without sex, but we didn't have a choice. So we suffered.

We weren't used to going so long without it. By nature, our relationship revolved around sex, closeness, and touching, but things needed to slow down, not only from his injury but from taking care of a baby.

I wasn't about to squander our time by rushing into it for a quickie despite Noah's demands. Instead, we shared a bath while I washed his entire body, hair included. Then he washed me. Just touching his soapy skin made us both hard. That was how desperate for each other we were. I fucking ached for him, but it would make it all the sweeter when we finally came together.

When we finished, I helped him out of the tub and dried him off, taking my time. I could see the impatience on his face, but Noah also loved being cared for as much as I loved taking care of him. It was during these tender moments that made our relationship that much better and stronger. The closeness of it revealed the amount of love we shared for each other.

"What do you want, baby?" I asked, on my knees, drying his feet with his hard cock flopping as if seeking out my mouth. "Specifically."

"To come," he whined, combined with a moan, making him sound almost like a caricature from a cartoon.

I couldn't stop my broad grin, trying not to laugh as I stood. "Yes, I'm aware, sweetie… I said specifically. What do you want me to do to help you come?" I cupped his face and pulled him into a deep kiss as we stood on the bathmat. "Do you want me to suck you dry?"

He closed his eyes and groaned. "Yes, please."

Kisses to his nose and each of his cheeks. "Or would you like me to fuck you stupid?"

He vigorously nodded. "Definitely."

I kissed each of his eyes. "Or you can ride me."

"That sounds super nice."

My mouth trailed kisses down his throat. "How about me licking your rim until you're completely blissed out."

His eyes rolled up into his head as if I was rimming him already, and he groaned. "Ugh... Yes, that's... fuck yeah."

I nipped his earlobe and licked it. "What about you fucking me and using my body any way you want?"

His body melted into mine, like letting go of all his pent-up frustration and pain for the past two months. "All the above, please."

The laugh bubbled out though I tried to contain it. I wasn't laughing at him but at how fucking cute he was, which made me stinking happy.

I took his hand and led him to the backyard. While we had privacy, it had a view of the mountains behind us, giving Noah just enough exhibitionism that he always craved to make him happy.

"Put your hands on the table and bend over for me, baby."

Once he was in position, I stood behind him, fell gently to my knees on the concrete patio, and pried his cheeks apart. His tight pucker fluttered for me as if begging to be consumed. I had a feeling Noah would want me inside him first, so this would help get him ready since it'd been far too long.

He did a cry and moan combination as soon as my tongue swirled around his rim. He rested his head on the table, pushing his ass further into my mouth as I ate him out.

God, I missed all his little noises and grunts. I loved turning my guy into mush with my tongue alone.

His hole opened more and more for me as he relaxed, and soon he was open enough for me to tongue fuck him.

"Mmm, fuck... God... Zay... more."

As I buried my face between his cheeks, I reached for his dick and swiped a thumb over his leaking and swollen cockhead. There was enough pre-come to use as lube so I could stroke him while I ate him for lunch.

"I don't want to come yet," he breathed.

"You're coming; then we'll recuperate. When we're ready, you're going to ride me, baby. We have all day for this."

Noah was so tightly wound and turned on that it only took a few more strokes to have him spurting all over my hand and the ground. His cock swelled and burned in my hand as I stroked him until he was empty, leaving his body in shudders as he chased his orgasm.

He cried out and nearly dropped to his knees if I hadn't been holding him up. I stood and turned him around to face me, then pressed my lips to his and treated his mouth as I'd treated his hole. Our tongues danced, and our mouths sucked and nipped.

When we pulled away, his eyes dropped half-closed, and he parted his swollen lips as if seeking more.

"Feel better, baby?" I asked.

His Adam's apple bobbed as he swallowed and shook his head. "No. More."

"Having trouble with words, No?"

He slowly nodded. "Yep."

I smiled and took his hand to lead him to our bedroom. We could fool around until he was ready for me to be inside of him.

We curled up in the bed, facing each other and making out. Just kissing and touching. I loved sex with Noah, but this slow intimacy and kissing him became one of my favorites. He had a special kiss for every mood. Every moment. He gave me one of those satiated kisses, slow and languid. His hands stroked my waist and hip while my hand feathered through his hair.

"I miss this so much, Bae."

"You and me both."

"I love being married to you. I love being your husband. It's probably snobby or something, but we're like a perfect couple."

"Why do you think I married you?" I bopped his nose and kissed him again. "As soon as I got my head out of my ass and you first kissed me so long ago, I knew you were the one. No man would ever do it for me. You and me, forever and ever."

Noah's smile was sweetly adorable as he nuzzled into me. We held onto each other with tangled limbs for a while until Noah was ready for me. My cock ached something awful, and he tried to relieve me, but I wanted to wait until I had him wrapped around me.

"I need more. I'm ready," he said after we snuggled and made out for thirty minutes.

"You sure?"

"I don't think you understand the desperation my nuts are in, boo."

I snorted a laugh. "Oh, I've got a pretty good idea."

"Oof," I let out when Noah climbed on top of me to reach for the lube in the drawer.

He opened the cap and poured some into his hands. First, he slathered up my very red and angry dick. Then he fingered himself though he didn't need much prepping at this point. Not after the tongue job I gave him.

When he straddled me, I gripped his thighs as he glided my cock into his tight and warm embrace. We both took a deep breath, him from the pressure and me to keep from fucking blowing already. I hadn't even rubbed one off, so Noah wasn't so alone while recovering.

My eyes rolled into my head when I fully seated him.

"Fuck... I'm gonna fucking explode, dude."

"No... not yet, Zay Bae."

"I'm... trying."

I took several slow and steady breaths to calm my dick the fuck down. Noah wrapped around me so tightly, and I had already been close just from fooling around. And god, the fucking heat.

Noah leaned down and pressed his lips to mine with one of his languid kisses. One that told me I was his forever, yet meant to calm me down and focus on his mouth and tongue.

"Ready?" he asked, hovering over my face.

"Yeah. Move, baby. Let's do this, and after, we can rest again so you can fill me in later."

"I like the way you think, Bae."

While we loved Storm as if she were our own daughter, it was nice to have alone time with my husband. We didn't have to rush things and could enjoy each other in all ways.

Noah leaned over me and rolled his hips, and used my cock to find his sweet spot. To watch his eyes roll and his mouth part as his breathing picked up set me on fire, making my heart beat a little faster as I surged with more love.

"So beautiful," I whispered.

His eyes slid shut, and he smiled. "So are you... God, you feel so good filling me again."

Noah maintained a slow and steady pace, making it obvious that he didn't want this to end yet. That was fine by me, but my nuts had other plans as they tightened and tightened. That sweet pressure built, and my eyes shuttered close.

"Nope, no comin' yet, Bae."

"Noah..." I didn't mean to sound so whiny.

He snorted a laugh, rested his body on top of mine, and kissed my nose... *not* moving. Dammit!

"Just a little longer."

I wrapped my arms around his back, covered in a sheen of sweat, trailing my finger gently up and down around the muscle indentions. His breath steadied as it ghosted the skin on my throat.

"Please move, baby."

"But you feel so good inside me."

"Think about how good it will feel when we finally get to come. We can do more... I'm begging you. My balls are gonna explode."

He sat up with a crooked smile. "Fine, but only because I love you."

I rolled my eyes and laughed. "You're too fucking kind."

"You know it."

Noah wasted no time, giving in to my demands as he pounded up and down on me hard and fast. And I thrust up into him each time he slammed home on my cock.

"Yes..." I breathed.

My sweet release was coming.

And release I did. I exploded almost out of nowhere as if my release was right there, waiting. I arched my back into him and threw back my head as my body froze. It would've been better had Noah come first, but my nuts weren't polite at all, filling him, spurt after never-ending spurt.

Before I could pass out, I quickly grabbed his cock and used his leaking pre-come as lube and stroked hard and fast.

Soon his hot release shot out, hitting my stomach and chest. His body shuddered on me, and he squeezed the hell out of my softening cock, stirring it back to life already.

With a heavy sigh and groan, Noah bent down and ran his tongue across my chest, and lapped up his come.

"Holy shit... so hot, baby."

Then he kissed me so we could share in his earthy release.

I finally slipped out of him, and he whimpered at the loss but fell onto the bed. I gathered him in my arms, covered in stickiness and sweat.

Once we caught our breaths, we hauled our carcasses out of bed and back into the shower to rinse off. We stayed naked because who was going to see anyway and made our way into the kitchen, where I made us a couple of sandwiches to rebuild our strength.

Noah straddled my lap and fed me half of a sandwich, and I took a bite, slowly chewing as we stared at each other like love-sick puppies. Still, even after all these years.

Honestly, I never dreamed of loving someone like this. I imagined having someone in my life, marrying them, making love to them... but not to this extent. It was like our romance was written in a book. Life hadn't been easy for either of us, but it made all that pain and suffering worth it if it brought us together like this.

There must've been something on my face, or maybe Noah felt it too. He put down his sandwich, grasped my face, and pressed his forehead to mine. Then warm tears hit my face and chest. My ever-sensitive and empathetic Noah and I wouldn't have it any other way.

"This, right here... you and me... there are no words. How did I get so lucky, Bae?"

"We got lucky. Together."

After he calmed down, we finished our food and headed back to our room for more love-making for the rest of the night until we had to pick up Storm.

CHAPTER TWENTY-NINE

Noah

ALL OF US KIDS PUT THE FINISHING TOUCH OF GREEN PAINT IN THE girls' bedroom at the surf shop. Kids? Shit, we were all adults. Mateo and Levi still lived here because Mateo was waiting until Lucy finished college so they could get a place together, while Levi waited until he graduated himself.

Moni and Rumi would start college next year, but soon the surf shop would have a new addition. The police had picked up a thirteen-year-old girl off the streets, and since Kel had been known to take in troubled teens, social services had called him first.

He and Anders met her once she got settled. No one learned about what happened to her, who her parents were, or anything. We didn't know how long she was staying here because the police had a missing child report out in case anyone claimed her. If not, Kel and Anders would officially take her in permanently. The only thing we knew was her age and that her name was Tallulah, but she liked to be called Tally.

Once we finished with the painting, we put the furniture back and decorated the new girl's bed with cute throw pillows to make her feel at home.

By the next day, she walked in holding onto a large worn stuffed rabbit as if her life depended on it. Her blond hair looked like it'd been cleaned and cut recently, and her dark brown eyes were wide and watchful. She was a skinny thing with knobby knees and unusually tall for her age. Almost as tall as Moni, who stood at five feet, eight inches.

Moni tentatively put an arm around the girl to see how she reacted. When she didn't pull away, Moni showed her the room and where she'd be sleeping.

"It's about time we got another girl around here. There are way too many boys," Moni said, winking.

I approached the girl with my baby in my arms. "Hey, I'm Noah, and this squirmy little thing is my daughter Stormy. She was lost like you. Like we all were. You're in a good place here, Tally."

Stormy reached for the girl and tugged on the rabbit's ear, trying to eat it.

Tally hid behind her rabbit, hiding her smile. "She's... cute."

"Stormy's the best. Wanna hold her?"

Tally hid behind a shy smile and shook her head. "I don't wanna hurt her."

"Nah, you won't. You can just sit on your new bed and hold her tight in your arms."

"Okay."

The girl sat down and put down her rabbit while I eased the baby into her arms. Tally didn't say anything or touch Stormy other than hold her, but she had a small smile on her face.

Yeah, Tally would be just fine. Just like we all were, thanks to this loving found family.

I floated on my board wearing a wetsuit since the waters got cold again by mid-October. I watched Zay take the air, like fucking high, trying to reach the sun or something. He spun before he came down, only to do it again. He'd been practicing to be ready for some upcoming local surfing events. While he was good enough to go pro, he still refused. Honestly, I didn't blame him. Going pro meant traveling and being away from home and family. Then there was the hefty price tag unless you could find a sponsor.

As for me, I'd missed surfing for the longest time while I'd been in recovery months back, but after my second head injury, I didn't jump back on the board as quickly. Two concussions would do that. I was afraid of another injury, so it took more time to hit the water and surf again.

The doctors kept me on the anti-seizure meds, and I hadn't had a problem since that first time, but that fear it would happen again always lingered in the back of my mind. But with the encouragement of my family, I finally got back on and surfed like I'd never stopped. The fears didn't completely go away, but I felt whole again.

I shaded my eyes to the glaring sun with my hand and waved to the group of people—my family—babysitting Stormy. She'd been crawling all over the place, getting into trouble, and trying to get into everything she could get her little hands on.

Social services periodically visited us to see how she'd been doing, which was fantastic; thank you very much. She grew to be a super happy baby, and we had an amazing support system. We were never left struggling, so Zay and I never felt out of our depth.

Kel and Anders were soon going to have their lawyers draw up adoption papers for us now that I'd turned twenty-one and Zay recently turned twenty-two. The lawyers said we had a really good chance since we'd taken such good care of her, and we'd been given raises, allowing us to save more money since the business was booming again.

And soon, the resort would be open to the public. We'd all gone on tour over there, and it was freakin' stunning. There was a massive pool that looked like it was a hidden oasis surrounded by rainforest. The place also had a gourmet restaurant, a nightclub, a smaller bar, and shopping. Instead of hotel-like rooms, there were bungalows of different sizes. Once completed, there would be events like authentic luaus.

It was definitely not for the rest of us plebs. None of us would be able to afford it, though Anders did say during the off-season he'd allow us to stay in one of the bungalows for free since we were all family. Zay and I never got a honeymoon, so we thought about doing that sometime next year. Shit, maybe we should fly somewhere. I'd never been on a plane before. I wouldn't have minded going somewhere cold with snow. Surf the snowy cliffs instead of water.

Then there was Ohana Surfing Club which had expanded its services, now offering whale-watching tours during the winter months, and during the rest of the season, there would be dolphin watching, snorkeling with the sea turtles, and deep-sea fishing. All of which were attached to the resort. Lu Lu, Mateo's Lucy, did most of the whale-watching tours now while she was in college, majoring in marine biology.

Zay and I still taught surfing lessons because we loved it too much, and there was nothing else I'd rather do. Teaching others our hobby had been a dream job. And we were booked all the way into next year.

Kel and Anders finally got married, too. What a perfect match they were, and I loved them both.

My mom and Zay's mom did pretty good, too. Each of us slowly healed. Zay and his mom still struggled. She wanted to see him more than he wanted to see her, but he was trying. We even let her babysit Stormy once. She was super polite to me despite being Zay's husband. If she disliked me for being a man and her son's lover, she didn't show it.

While Zay may have trusted his mom with Stormy, I didn't trust my mom at all with the baby. She had proven she could quit drinking with tons of work, and she still dated the same dude, so that was something. I'd even gone to some of her AA meetings to show her support.

We were healing, but who knew when and if she'd slip again? If she did, I didn't want it to be around the baby. I wanted to trust her, but too much had happened between us. Trust was earned. It was a hard lesson we both needed to learn. For her, she had to work hard for it. For me, I needed to stop over-trusting.

Zay paddled back to me with a big smile on his gorgeous mug. He looked more like a grown man now. He even sported a short beard which was super fucking sexy, except for the beard burn problem. My face always seemed to be red and sore these days, but I loved the prickly sensation when we kissed, which we were doing now.

"You surfing?" he asked.

"I wanted to watch you. Those were some epic moves, hubs. You're so ready, and you're gonna win. I know it."

His smile was broad, with white teeth against his still-tanned skin from the summer and dark beard. "Ah, are you psychic now, *hubs*?"

I winked. "Yep."

"Go surf. Shoo. Have fun."

With one more kiss, I paddled out and caught the next swell. I didn't spend too long doing my flips and spins, wanting to glide through the barrel. Only catching air twice before I paddled back to shore.

I propped my board in the sand and peeled down my wetsuit, laughing at Stormy trying to reach me, but Moni held her back to keep her crawling in the sand.

"Dada!" she squealed.

God, I never got tired of her calling me that. I loved being a daddy, even as young as I was.

"Give me a minute, Stormy Wormy."

Once I dried my upper body off, I reached down to lift her into my arms. She gave me a big smile with four little teeth and squealed again. Her little fat fingers took a strand of my wet hair and twirled it, and shoved her thumb in her mouth as we walked closer to the shore to watch *'Papa.'*

I stared at her gray, stormy eyes, watching her other daddy surf.

"Your Papa's rad, right? He's epic, and we'll teach you to be as good as he is."

Zay jumped off his board and walked toward us. The closer he got, the more Stormy jumped and kicked her legs in my arms with excitement. When he reached us, he kissed her cheek and then kissed me on the mouth.

"Alright, I promised Tally I'd teach her some more surfing today." With two more kisses, he ran off.

Zay and Tally had become super close. Probably because the two had both lived on the streets, alone, cold, and afraid. Once Tally warmed up to us, she explained she'd been living with her dad alone until he started hanging out with a group of people along with some new girlfriend of his. She'd woken up one morning to find everyone gone. They'd fucking abandoned her.

She'd been on the streets, barely surviving for a few weeks before the police picked her up. No one could find her dad, so she stayed at the surf shop. Sort of. She practically lived with Zay and me, loving to babysit Stormy. Though Zay became more and more of a father figure to her. Slowly, Tally became part of our little family more than an Ohana Surf Club foster kid and soon moved in with us.

I carried Stormy to the water's edge and set her down while she held onto my fingers with tight fists. Her feet danced and pirouetted like a little ballerina. Pretty soon, she'd be walking, and then we'd have to baby-proof the house even more.

I squatted next to Stormy and pointed in the distance. "Look, it's Papa and Tal. She's getting so good at surfing. That's gonna be you one day."

After a little while, Zay and Tally came out of the water and set their boards down in the sand. He tossed his long wet bangs back from his face and smiled, looking sexy as fuck.

Tally was headed toward the towels when he grabbed her hand and dragged her toward Stormy and me. When he reached us, he pulled all three of us into a tight group hug.

"What an amazing little family we are," he said.

I smiled and nuzzled his neck. "We have the best family."

The End

ABOUT THE AUTHOR

Thank you for reading *Double Up*.

Courtney W. Dixon loves to write steamy romance, but in each story, she gives her characters challenges and struggles. She writes m/f and m/m stories within one series to add a variety to her characters. And she writes her characters as having flaws, imperfections, and who don't always do the right thing. Humans are never perfect, and make a lot of mistakes in their lives. In the end, she tries to help them grow to be better as they achieve their HEAs.

You can find Courtney working in Central Texas with her husband, two boys, and two crazy dogs, none of whom know how to knock on a door while she's working.

She's an independent author. As such, she needs you to help her grow and thrive. She is always appreciative of feedback from you, the reader. Good or bad, if you have the time, please leave a review. Ratings are good too, but reviews say so much more. This helps her learn what you like to make her books more enjoyable.

You can also send feedback via email at courtneywdixonauthor@gmail.com

Connect with me:
www.courtneywdixon.com

Courtney's Corrupt Readers Facebook Group
Courtney's Corrupt Readers | Facebook

Goodreads

Bookbub

Twitter

Amazon

Subscribe to My Newsletter